JABLONSKI AND THE EROTOMANIAC

Also by Perry Lafferty

Birdies Sing and Everything
How to Lose Your Fear of Flying
The Downing of Flight Six Heavy
Jablonski of L. A.

JABLONSKI AND THE EROTOMANIAC

by Perry Lafferty

DONALD I. FINE, INC.
New York

Copyright © 1992 by Perry Lafferty

All rights reserved, including the right of reproduction in whole or in part in any form. Published in the United States of America by Donald I. Fine, Inc. and in Canada by General Publishing Company Limited.

Library of Congress Cataloging-in-Publication Data

Lafferty, Perry Francis.
Jablonski and the erotomaniac / by Perry Lafferty.
    p.   cm.
ISBN 1-55611-323-4
I. Title.
PS3562.A278J29   1992
813'.54—dc20   91-55608
CIP

Manufactured in the United States of America

10 9 8 7 6 5 4 3 2 1

Designed by Irving Perkins Associates

This novel is a work of fiction. Names, characters, places and incidents are either the product of the author's imagination or are used fictitiously. Any resemblance to actual events, locales, organizations or persons, living or dead, is entirely coincidental and beyond the intent of either the author or publisher.

For
Norman Corwin

JABLONSKI AND THE EROTOMANIAC

CHAPTER ONE

AFTER sliding out of his vehicle, he closed the door carefully by leaning his full weight against it. In the stillness of the night, he winced at the sound of the two sharp clicks that resulted. He straightened up and looked around the deserted area. Except for a few splashes of luminescence created by floodlights planted on the lawns of the three expensive homes that occupied the immediate vicinity, there was nothing but blackness. Off in the distance the anguished barking of a small dog made a staccato counterpoint to the wail of a siren.

For a moment, he felt like Norman Bates in Hitchcock's *Psycho*. Of course there were important differences: for one thing, his plans didn't include stabbing anyone in the shower; also, he wasn't crazy. But then, he thought to himself, had the great director been around to put it on film, the scenario that was about to unfold would surely have been as suspenseful and dramatic as Janet Leigh's gory demise.

The dwelling he sought nested in a *cul-de-sac* off Laurel Canyon, high in the hills overlooking the San Fernando Valley. The two residences that adjoined it were at a comfortable distance, several hundred feet away. After a short walk, he approached an entrance set into a six-foot-high wall. Imbedded in the top of the barrier were shards of glass.

It was shortly after midnight when he threw a piece of poisoned meat into the back yard, silencing the big Doberman pinscher forever. With safe access assured, he slipped into a pair of surgical gloves, turned the knob on the heavy oak door and crept into the garden that lay behind the handsome Spanish-style abode. Kneeling next to a metal box attached to the side of the house, he removed a Boy Scout knife from his pocket and unfolded its largest blade. Quickly he severed a thick wire, rendering the telephone and the alarm systems ineffective.

Because of the strong Santa Ana winds blowing in off the northern desert, the night was crystal clear. From his vantage point the lights on the valley floor below pulsated unevenly across the enormous expanse of flatland that connected Los Angeles, to the east, with the Pacific Ocean. On this particular evening, because of the absence of smog, he realized it was possible to see all the way to Pasadena, a city normally hidden under a miasma of dark brown pollutants. Before he slipped on the black ski mask, he inhaled the smell of the orange blossoms.

It was sad, he thought, that things had come to this, but there was no other way out. At least no way he could conjure up. He hoped he wouldn't vomit or lose his nerve when it came time to immobilize her. *But she had to be taught a lesson.* He would not be ignored, relegated to some nether world.

He looked down at the body of the huge dog. Its coat glowed faintly in the pallid moonlight and the dark, empty, wide-open eyes seemed to plead for help. Gingerly he stepped over the corpse and tiptoed around to the far side of the house, skirting the kidney-shaped swimming pool as he went.

The sliding doors to the bedroom were open and the chiffon curtains swayed restlessly under the urging of the warm winds. Hugging the stucco walls, he painstakingly made his way along the patio until he reached the entrance. Holding his breath, he forced himself to lean around and look into the room. As his eyes adjusted to the greater darkness of the sleeping quarters, the faint contours of the young woman's body slowly became visible. She was nude, lying on the top sheet on her side. She was turned away from him. Warily he drew back the billowing white folds that obstructed the entrance and stepped inside. Before moving to the bed he listened intently for any alien sounds.

When will she turn over? he asked himself. In order for me to get at her, she must be on her back.

Seconds, minutes, went by. She didn't stir. He began to fixate on her round, white breast as it moved in synchronization with her slow, shallow breathing. After what seemed an eternity, she began to stir.

Instantly, he reached into the handkerchief pocket of his jacket and produced a test tube an inch in diameter, six inches in length. A cork protruded from the top. He turned toward the patio and held up the object so that it was profiled against the moonlight outside. With exquisite care he worked the cork out of the receptacle and returned the plug to his pocket.

The woman moaned softly in her sleep. When he pivoted around to look at her again she had arranged herself in the perfect position: face up, arms at her sides. For a moment he felt dizzy. Then, in one swoop, he grabbed her by the hair with his left hand, brought up his right leg and jammed it down across her mid-section, pinning her arms to the bed. As she came awake, he sloshed the acid onto her face.

For a moment the shock of the assault blocked the waves of pain that flooded over her. Then she began to claw at her damaged eyes. This move caused some of the deadly liquid to get onto her hands, further increasing her agony. She writhed on the bed, her screams growing more and more shrill as the chemicals ate deeper and deeper into her skin.

Satisfied that she could never again bedevil him, he turned and rushed out onto the patio, tripping over the end of a chaise longue in the process. During the attack a few drops of the fluid had been absorbed by the glove on his left hand, causing him to feel a slight burning sensation. He tore off the offending article and stuffed it into the jacket pocket that held the empty vial.

Cautiously, he cracked open the oak gate. Before stepping outside, he took care to push in the button on the knob so that no one could gain entrance without a key. With panic building in him, he ran toward his car. As he drove away, the woman's distant screams followed at him.

In one of the adjacent residences a sleeping couple lay entwined on a king-sized bed. The purr of the central air-conditioning unit diluted the agonized moans of the victim, so almost five minutes went by before the woman shook her husband awake.

"Listen," she commanded.

"Wha . . . ?"

"Doesn't that sound like someone in trouble?"

Then, abruptly, the sounds ceased.

"It's nothing," the man said, turning over.

"It's *something*. I know it is."

"Don't interfere, Mavis." He burrowed deep into his pillow.

At five-thirty the next morning the local patrol discovered the nude woman, blind and mutilated, whimpering as she lay crumpled on the street in front of her house.

CHAPTER TWO

It was another relentlessly beautiful California day, almost three weeks after the attack on Mikki O'Reilly. Jackson Jablonski, rumpled and on the wrong side of fifty, sat alone in his compact, neatly furnished office on San Vicente Boulevard in West Los Angeles. The last month had not gone as he had anticipated. Not even close. As a result, he was prodigiously pissed off.

A year earlier, overcome with disgust at the clearly immoral way his former employer, the Federal Bureau of Investigation, had instructed him to handle a particularly dicey situation involving The National Interest, he had resigned his post in Washington, D.C. and journeyed to California, accompanied by his wife of twenty-five years. At the time neither of them had planned on relocating permanently but, while in the process of selling the beach cottage bequeathed to Daphne Jablonski by her late brother, the lure of the western life-style had proved potent.

To facilitate the move, the Jablonskis utilized the considerable sum that resulted from the real estate sale as the down payment on an old Tudor residence with separate guest quarters that sat on the south edge of Brentwood. They rented their abode in the nation's capital to a young congressman and applied the monthly remuneration received therefrom to the mortgage payments on the California dwelling. Fiscally, it was a perfect setup.

But, after six months spent puttering around the house, playing golf, and going deep sea fishing, certain emotional bacteria began to infect Jablonski's psyche. The results of this invasion were irregular bouts of boredom and spells of feeling unworthy and ineffectual. More and more frequently it became necessary to reduce the pressures he endured. So, since there was no one around except his wife to serve as a punching bag, voices began being raised in the Jablonski household on a regular basis.

One night at dinner, after dousing his dish of peach cobbler with freshly whipped cream, Jablonski announced, "Fifty-five is too young for a man to retire."

Upon hearing this long hoped-for observation, Daphne found herself light-headed with relief. Although stout of heart, she unconsciously responded by undergoing a series of premature ventricular contractions (of absolutely no medical moment) so prolonged that her husband's almost covetous consumption of his dessert was momentarily arrested.

He looked up. "What's the matter with you?"

"Absolutely nothing. I take it you've *finally* decided to become gainfully employed. Now, perhaps, you won't have time to eat so much."

"Who said anything about going to work? I merely suggested that I am too young to wander about aimlessly. Also, may I point out that eating is one of the few genuine pleasures still left to me."

"That may be. I find it unfortunate, however, that watching you blimp up provides *me* with no great satisfaction." She studied her husband. "You weighed two-ten when we moved out here. Now what are you, two-twenty? Two-twenty-five?" She clucked unhappily.

"Someone who's five feet nine should weigh no more than a hundred and fifty. At the *most*."

Jablonski put down his spoon. "Now, my love," he said, ever so gently, "just because you're female and top me by three inches in your stocking feet, is scant reason for you to feel insecure."

Daphne cut to the punch line. "It's a shame, considering how much you eat, that some of the calories didn't turn to height."

Jablonski polished off the remains of the cobbler. "I'm going to let that one go by. Instead, for the three hundred and eighty-seventh time, I must point out to you that private investigators rank right below meter maids on the ladder of law enforcement."

"But that's what you're *qualified* for, Jack."

"Be that as it may. Case closed."

A week following this encounter, a neighbor across the way called the police to report that his three-year-old son was missing.

The authorities followed the usual investigative procedures for cases of this type. One team of detectives telephoned the parents of the toddler's friends while a dozen officers fanned out and thoroughly searched the neighborhood. After the group came up empty-handed, the lieutenant in charge decided that there was a strong probability that the boy had been abducted.

Jablonski, having earlier been drawn toward the excitement, explained to the officer in charge that, since he had been working in his front yard for several hours prior to the incident and would certainly have noticed any strangers who might have been lurking around, kidnapping was highly unlikely.

The lieutenant thanked Jablonski for advancing his theory but suggested that someone could have come in through the back alley. Considering that the area behind the child's residence had been blocked for the entire day by a crew installing a cable television line, Jablonski didn't buy this either. He decided to take matters into his own hands.

When the police had finally departed the scene, he introduced himself to the distraught parents and volunteered his services. Grateful that this stranger, a former FBI man at that, felt there was some other explanation for what was looming as a terrible tragedy, the man and woman eagerly agreed to cooperate in any way they could.

After endless questions aimed at trying to pinpoint whether anything out of the ordinary had taken place in or around the house during the hours before the boy disappeared, Jablonski, in passing, picked up on the fact that the bottle containing the mother's sleeping pills was missing from the bedside table where she kept it.

"But even if Teddy had gotten his hands on it, it has a child-proof cap," she said. *"I can hardly get it off."*

Instantly Jablonski recalled the prodigious feats his grandson had performed at the age of three. Opening up a prescription bottle would be extremely difficult for a toddler but, he knew from experience, not impossible.

"I think there's a good chance your son is somewhere in the immediate vicinity," he told the parents. "Sound asleep. Full of pills. That's why he never heard anyone call him."

The mother went crazy. "Oh, my God, he may be dead!"

Jablonski said urgently, "We know he's not at a friend's. Now think: where else might he have gone?"

A protracted silence followed that grew more ominous with each passing moment.

Then the father shouted, "The tree house!" He ran toward the backyard and climbed up into the yoke of a big elm that held a small, homemade shack. "He's here!"

Jablonski ordered the woman to call the paramedics.

Gently the father lowered the unconscious boy into Jablonski's arms. The child's breathing was exceedingly shallow.

"Thank God, he's still alive," the ex-agent said fervently. "To save time, let's get him out front so we can meet the van."

It was only moments later when the red-and-white vehicle, siren screaming, skidded around the corner and pulled to a stop. In radio consultation with a doctor, the paramedics were directed to rush the boy to Santa Monica Hospital so that his stomach could be pumped out.

The episode had a happy ending.

"Maybe a higher power is trying to tell you something," Daphne observed, after Jablonski had related the details of the occurrence.

"What's that supposed to mean?"

"You saved the child's life."

"It wasn't a hundred percent certain the kid was a goner."

"For God's sake, Jack!" Daphne exploded, "You did a noble deed!"

In spite of his remonstrance, his wife's fervently stated opinion caused Jablonski to revise his previously held evaluation of private investigators. After considerable hemming and hawing, he decided to offer his talents for hire.

During the course of the next three months, while locating office space, having it suitably decorated, getting the necessary authorizations from the state, ordering an ad in the Yellow Pages, and hiring a secretary, he became so distracted he lost almost twenty-five pounds.

"Since you're so busy," Daphne observed, "this would be a good time to give up smoking."

Jablonski, a pack and a half a day man, responded, "Wrong, my love. There *is* no good time to give up the wondrous weed."

But his mate wouldn't be denied. "You're on the way to becoming handsome again, Jack. It would be super if your clothes didn't always reek of tobacco. Not to mention your breath."

"Reek is a pretty strong word."

"My first choice was stink."

"I think I'm being nagged."

It had been at least five years since his wife had mentioned anything positive about his physical appearance. In response to what he felt was an important compliment, Jablonski started cutting back on his nicotine intake. At the end of two months he found that he was able to shed his addiction and, much to his amazement, keep his weight in check.

"Tell you the truth, Daph, I didn't think it was possible."

"People can do what they *want* to do, Jack." She leaned down and gave him a peck on the cheek. "Now, keep up the good work. You've still got at least twenty-five pounds to go."

"I'll never make it," Jablonski sighed.

"Now don't be negative."

"That's not negative, it's realistic."

Having thus turned over several pages in the Book of Life, a slimmer and sweeter-smelling Jablonski set out for his new office.

In the dozen weeks that ensued after opening shop, he turned aside several pleas from distressed wives who wanted their presumably wayward husbands shadowed, two inquiries regarding missing persons, one in which the man in question had last been seen in Argentina, and the second involving a seventy-five-year-old former bodybuilder who disappeared one afternoon from an aerobics studio near

Disneyland, and finally, an offer to become a bodyguard for a rock star.

"Maybe you shouldn't be so picky, Jack," Daphne cautioned.

"At this stage in life, I don't have to take on anything that doesn't appeal to me."

"That's true. But if you keep turning cases down, the word will get around and *nobody* will show up."

"Be that as it may."

"I can't imagine what your new secretary is thinking. She must be going crazy from boredom and frustration."

"That makes two of us."

Then, one morning, shortly after this exchange took place, Shirley Bernstein-Mandlebaum, pert, cute, and a born mover and shaker if there ever was one, cupped the phone with her hand and turned toward the inner sanctum where Jablonski was doodling on the envelope containing the month's phone bill.

She called out, "Do you remember that newscaster who got the acid thrown in her face a couple of weeks ago?"

"What about her?"

"She's on line one. Says she interviewed you last year, the time you landed a plane at LAX." Shirley cocked her head. "I didn't know you were a pilot."

"I'm not. What's she want?"

"She wants you to come to her house." Behind her back, the secretary crossed her fingers. "I think you should speak to her."

"I speak to everybody."

For all the good it does, Shirley thought.

"Does she have a name?" the detective inquired, somewhat sourly.

"Mikki O'Reilly. I have a hunch you'll feel a lot better if you talk to her."

"Is that a professional opinion?" Jablonski asked grumpily.

"It is."

"I didn't know you were licensed to practice medicine in California." The fact that Shirley had a B.A. in psychology from Columbia University was one of the reasons he had hired the young woman. Of late, her persistence was getting on his nerves.

Shirley pushed a little harder. "I got the impression Miss O'Reilly's not gonna go away."

Jablonski sighed deeply. "What line's she on?"

"I told you: one."

He lifted the receiver. "Jack Jablonski."

The lilting voice that, five nights a week, enchanted half the Southland, as the Los Angeles Chamber of Commerce liked to call the area, sounded strained. It said, "I don't know if you remember me."

"There were a lot of reporters that day at the airport. And I was pretty shaken up. What can I do for you?"

"I'm getting tired of waiting for the police to nail the son of a bitch who wrecked my life."

"No progress?"

"So far, not very much."

"The L.A. cops are among the best, Miss O'Reilly."

"They may be, but they're slower than a goddamn arms negotiation. I want someone working directly for *me*. Personalized. If I don't get some action, I'll fucking bust."

Shirley appeared in the doorway and stared hopefully at her boss. Jablonski replied, "I'm flattered you think I might be able to help."

Mikki continued, "Anyone who performed the way you did that day at LAX is brave and smart. I like that."

"Your request for help may be premature. If I recall correctly, the incident is fairly recent."

Shirley's face fell.

"Incident?" Mikki snapped. "I'm lying up here in my house blind as a bat with half my cheeks eaten away and you call it an incident!" The fear in the young woman's voice was palpable.

Jablonski was quiet for a moment. "Forgive me, Miss O'Reilly. Of course, I'll try to help you."

Shirley smiled and retreated to her desk in the outer office.

Mikki continued, "The day of our interview at the airport, you insisted that the only thing you could think about up there in the wild, blue yonder was what your wife was cooking for dinner."

"That was a joke."

"How about coming up for lunch today? I've got a great lady in the kitchen."

"I think that could be arranged."

"Would twelve-thirty be acceptable?"

"Perfect." The young woman gave him directions. "I feel better already."

"Very well then. See you shortly, Miss O'Reilly."

"Mikki."

"Mikki. But don't expect too much. The trail may be cold by now."

He hung up the phone and pushed his big upholstered chair away from the desk. After brushing off a speck of dust from the lapel of his overly loose polyester jacket, he hiked up his pants. He walked out to Shirley's desk. "You satisfied?" he inquired of his assistant.

"Ever since I signed on with you, all you've done is turn down business. You can't blame me for being a little bit upset."

"When I hired you, I expected that more rewarding opportunities would come my way."

Shirley ran her eyes up and down Jablonski's diminished frame. "Now that you've lost weight, that outfit doesn't work. Before lunch, why don't you drop by the men's store and pick up your new suit?"

"They said it wouldn't be ready until Saturday."

"I just checked. You can go over now."

Jablonski looked up at the wall clock. "I guess there's time."

"Also, you should get a shirt that fits."

"What goes with dark green?"

"Almost anything. Ask the salesman."

"The guy has a diamond in his nose."

"So what?"

"He makes me nervous." The detective removed his fedora from the hat rack near the door. "For thirty years something's been bugging me. Why is it always two weeks between the time you select a suit and the date when the alterations are finished?"

"Why not?"

Jablonski plopped the hat on his head. He pulled open the door and stepped out onto the walkway that paralleled the side of the building. "Be back when I'm back." He started down the narrow walk that led out to the main drag.

Shirley ran after him. "I'll walk you to your car."

"What?"

"You can't leave without telling me what happened in the plane."

"It's a long story."

"Bottom line it."

"I was up in a single engine Cessna and the guy who was flying it, a small-time drug dealer, tried to dump me into the ocean off Catalina

Island. I hit him so hard I broke his jaw and he passed out. I had to take over the controls and land the craft." Out on the boulevard Jablonski noted the summons that rested under the windshield wiper of his old Honda. "You didn't feed the meter," he said ominously.

"I goofed. How could you land a plane if you weren't a pilot?"

"I had a little help from a friend." He reached over and grabbed the ticket and stuffed it into his pocket. "Deduct eighteen beans from your paycheck."

"For what?"

"Inattention to detail."

"Let me quote you verbatim, Jack: 'Miz Bernstein-Mandlebaum, I need someone of intelligence to size up clients and to assist me in helping them with their problems.' At no time during my initial interview with you was any mention made of hourly trips to insure the parking place for that wreck you call an automobile." She paused for breath. "What friend?"

"What friend what?"

"The one who helped you land the plane."

"Did you ever hear the expression 'to talk somebody down'?"

"Sure."

"Okay, that's it." Jablonski slipped in behind the wheel and started the engine. "Now, may I leave?"

"Your friend talked you down? Where was he, in the back seat?"

"I told you it was a long story." He snapped on his left blinker and pulled out into the stream of traffic.

As she stepped back into the office, the phone was ringing. "Jablonski Investigations."

"Missus, this is Piedad."

Piedad Santa Maria was the young Mexican-American who served the Mandlebaums as part-time baby-sitter and housekeeper. Although the suspense was considerable as to whether or not she would show up on any given day, due primarily to the temperament of her 1952 Chevrolet, whenever she appeared, the wait always turned out to be worth it.

"Saul wants to ask you a favor, Missus."

"Oh, good! Put him on the phone." Shirley was relieved Jablonski was out of the office because the frequency and the inconsequentiality of the calls that flowed from Saul to his mother had lately caused the detective unbridled annoyance.

Saul was two and a half and English was his second language. "Talk to your Mommy, Saul."

Shirley listened to a burst of gibberish.

"He wants to know if he can have another juice box," Piedad interpreted.

"You know the rules. One in the morning. One in the afternoon."

"Mommy says no, Saul." Upon hearing this news the toddler started screaming. "I think you hurt his feelings, Missus."

"Give him my apologies and take him out to the sandpile."

"He's already been. He ate a rock."

"What?!"

"S'okay. I got it out of his mouth."

Shirley groaned. "I'll be home early, Piedad. Try and hold things together."

"Sure, Missus. Have a nice day."

After hanging up, Shirley flopped down on the anteroom's little sofa and ran her hand through her long, brunette hair. For the hundredth time since taking the job with Jablonski, she considered the advisability of both parents going to work five days a week. Her husband Rob, a clinical psychiatrist who taught at UCLA, was hardly in a high paying bracket, and the extra money that she brought in helped them enjoy a decent life-style.

Both Shirley and her husband were confirmed New Yorkers. They had met when she was a student in one of Rob's classes at City College of New York. They always vowed never to desert the Big Apple, but the position that was offered to Dr. Mandlebaum in Los Angeles was too attractive to pass up.

Once she had decided to go job hunting, she took a refresher course to polish the secretarial skills acquired while working her way through college. Becoming involved with a private investigator was the farthest thought from her mind but, after a series of uninspired interviews at various overly-structured institutions, she began to look around for something less inhibiting. When she spotted Jablonski's ad in the Help Wanted columns of the L.A. *Times,* she called for an appointment. After a somewhat cursory interview he had hired her and she reported for work the following week.

Almost immediately she found herself feeling more like a sentry than a secretary. Until today, when the unexpected breakthrough took place.

The phone rang again.

"Good morning, Shirley," the deep-ish voice began. "This is Daphne Jablonski."

"Good morning to you," Shirley chirped happily. "Your husband isn't here."

"Do you know when he'll be back?"

"You won't believe this, Mrs. Jablonski. A few minutes ago Jack took a case."

"Well, thank goodness! And just in time, too."

"Pardon?"

"I would have hated to leave town with him still down in the dumps." Daphne sounded somewhat agitated. "I just had a telephone call from our daughter in Atlantic City."

"I hope nothing's wrong."

"On the contrary. Did Jack ever mention that our Susie was pregnant?"

"No, he didn't."

"Well, she is. *Very* pregnant in fact. The doctor handling her case has become convinced that the baby's due any day now."

"How exciting for all of you!"

"That's why I'm calling. Susie wants me to get on a plane first thing so I can be with her when she delivers. Will you book me on an early flight in the morning?"

"I'd be glad to."

Before the young woman could inquire whether her caller preferred first class or coach, Daphne said, "Because of my long legs I'm much more comfortable up front. Much as I hate to spend the extra money."

Although the two had never met face to face, Shirley had assumed Jablonski's wife to be shorter than he was. True, the photograph in the silver frame on her boss's desk did not indicate this. It was merely a head shot of a woman with a prominent nose, straight hair that had been curled up in a bun on the back of her head, and an intense expression.

"Being nearly six feet tall has its disadvantages, you know, Shirley."

"I expect it does. Do you have a preference among the airlines?"

"I think they all should be grounded. Poisonous food and undependable departure times. Not to mention lost baggage. I yearn for the old days, don't you?"

Since Shirley had just passed her twenty-fifth birthday she was without Daphne's frame of reference. "I guess traveling used to be a lot better."

"Not only better. It was an *adventure*. People would dress up. The stewardesses treated you like kings and queens during the whole flight. Why, the very idea of traveling at speeds of five hundred miles an hour six miles up in the sky was thrilling beyond words."

"After what goes on today, that's hard to believe. I'll pick up your tickets and send them home with your husband."

"I'm so happy for Jack."

"So am I. Now, finally, I can find out what kind of a detective he is."

"He's a very good one. I can promise you that. Way better than most. Get him to tell you about what happened last year when we first moved out. He solved the most puzzling case involving an absolutely beautiful dead girl in a small plane."

"I'll certainly do that, Mrs. Jablonski."

"Now, if you'll forgive me, I must start thinking about what to pack. The weather back east is so changeable this time of year."

"Pack everything. That's what I always do."

"Thank you for the suggestion, Shirley. That certainly solves a lot of problems. Now be sure and take care of Jack while I'm away."

"Oh, I will. Don't worry." After hanging up the phone, Shirley redialed and booked her boss's wife on an eight o'clock flight the following morning.

CHAPTER THREE

JABLONSKI squared his shoulders and adjusted the jacket of his new suit. Within seconds of the time he knocked, a frenetic, spiffily dressed man, four inches shorter than he was, answered the front door to Mikki Reilly's house.

"Veck's the name. Alvin Veck. I'm Mikki's agent." The pixie stuck out a tiny, well-manicured hand on which an enormous pinky ring rested. "Come on in."

The foyer of the residence was circled with dozens of plants, most of them members of the cactus family. A huge painting of a bullfight hung on the wall facing the entrance and, on the right, an arch opened into the dining room. The heavy, carved table stretched for eight feet and, in its center, bore a huge wicker basket from which a profusion of vegetables flowed. Six high-backed chairs upholstered in south-of-the-border earth tones stood mutely around the empty board.

"Through here," Veck said, indicating the double doors on the side opposite from those that led to the dining room. "She's out back by the pool."

As Jablonski followed the agent, he noted the grand piano, covered by an elaborate silk shawl edged with fringe, and the high, glassed-in cabinet crammed full of ceramic reproductions of horses. Several dozen pillows, carefully arranged along the back of the large U-shaped sofa, dared the observer to put so much as a dent in them. In spite of all the care that had gone into designing it, the room was cold, a too perfect example of the decorator's art.

Indicating the opulence, Jablonski commented, "The TV news business must be good."

"Would you believe Mikki makes four hundred thou per?" Veck shook his head in frustration. *"Now,* what's going to happen?"

To you, or to her, Jablonski wondered. Ten percent of four hundred thousand dollars could buy a lot of Kitty Litter.

As the agent reached to open the screen door, a voice inquired, "Is he here?"

"That he is, beautiful one."

"Come on out, Mr. Jablonski," Mikki called.

The young woman sat rigidly on a metal chaise longue near the side of a pool. Her face was marked with patches of ugly scabs. Bandages over her eyes were held tightly in place by gauze wrappings. Only her full, sensual lips had somehow been spared. One side of the short terry cloth robe she was wearing had fallen open, revealing several angry abrasions along her right leg.

"Get Mr. Jablonski a chair, Al."

After the detective was seated he suggested, "First names are more friendly. Mine's Jack."

"Fine by me." Mikki turned in Veck's direction. "Let's get the money stuff over with. You want to discuss it, Al, or should I?"

"Allow me, sweetheart, that's what you pay me for." The agent paced as he talked. "As you must know, Jack, the Los Angeles Police will probably crack this case sooner or later. It's the later part that bothers Mikki."

"So she told me."

"What do you usually charge for involving yourself in something like this?"

"Hadn't thought much about it. Are you thinking exclusive or nonexclusive?"

Mikki interposed, "Full-time, Jack. Around the clock. How about twenty thousand? Ten now and ten when you nail the creep."

Veck exploded. "Mikki, for Christ's sake! That's way out of line."

"Your agent is right," Jablonski agreed. "Let's do it by the day. Five hundred plus expenses."

"You're not reading me, Jack. The state I'm in, I need your undivided attention. Nights, weekends, holidays. The works. I want to be able to call you anytime. I have to know you're there. I'm a fucking wreck and I can't even cry with these goddamn bandages on."

"Okay, seven-fifty, day and night."

She wouldn't let up. "Plus expenses."

"Fine."

"Make up a contract, Al," she directed.

"That won't be necessary," Jablonski reassured her.

"When does the clock start ticking?" Veck asked.

"If Mikki's ready, so am I."

For the first time since the interview had begun, Veck sat down next to his client. "You don't need me for this, sweetheart. Now that you're all set, I've got to get to my lunch date. I'll drop in again on my way home tonight."

"Thanks."

Veck picked up the young woman's hand and kissed it on the palm. "Chin up." He nodded to the detective and disappeared into the house.

"We'll eat in a few minutes, Jack. Hilda will serve us out here on trays. Crab cakes."

Jablonski smacked his lips. "Back in Washington I used to eat crab cakes at least twice a week."

"I hope you won't be disappointed." For a long moment she didn't say anything. When she finally spoke her voice was husky. "You don't know how lucky you are."

"Sorry?"

"For the past ten years you haven't had people telling you you're a knockout every other minute."

"How true," Jablonski said wryly.

"Beautiful, gorgeous, exciting, desirable, perfect. I've heard them all. Endlessly, and from just about everybody. It started when I was a teenager, even before I won the Miss Napa Valley contest. And the compliments never stopped until this horrible thing happened."

"Your face is your fortune."

"It has been so far. Maybe I had a little talent too. Who the fuck knows?"

A substantial matron, dressed in a gray uniform, approached. She was carrying a tray table.

Hearing the tinkle of dishes, Mikki called out, "Hilda?"

"Luncheon is served."

"Take care of our guest first. If I remember rightly, he's nice and plump and we want to keep him that way."

"Not quite so plump anymore, Mikki."

The woman placed her burden in front of Jablonski and started back to the kitchen.

"Don't wait for me," the young woman instructed. "Tell me about the crab cakes."

The detective arranged his napkin and leaned over his plate and sniffed. "The little darlings smell too good to eat."

"Force yourself."

Jablonski cut himself a generous portion and popped it into his mouth. He chewed ecstatically and at length. "Nirvana."

"That good?"

"I trust you have seconds."

Hilda, overhearing the exchange as she approached a second time, set down a tray next to the chaise longue. "Plenty more."

Jablonski promised, "At the appropriate moment I'll send up a flare."

Hilda urged, "Try the salad too. The endive's fresh as can be." She unfolded Mikki's napkin and placed it on her employer's lap. "You want me to feed you?"

"No, thanks. Just show me where everything is." Once the woman had finished her orientation she moved away toward the house. Mikki continued, "You want to wait until we've finished eating before I go on?"

Jablonski replied, "No need."

"How much do you know about what happened?"

"Just what's been in the newspapers and on TV. Mostly about the notes he wrote you."

"My station's been downplaying the whole business. The management doesn't want to let the audience know what bad shape I'm really in."

Jablonski took a bite of salad. "What do the doctors say about your recovery?"

"The son of a bitch hit me right in the eyes with sulfuric acid. At some point I'll have corneal transplants. Maybe I'll see again, maybe I won't." Her voice began to quiver. "But even with the best plastic surgery in the world, I'm never going to look like I did before the guy worked me over."

"I'm sure you'll look good enough," Jablonski said reassuringly.

"If you're an anchorwoman on TV, good enough isn't good

enough." She slammed her fork down on the plate. "I want the bastard put away for the rest of his miserable life."

"As he should be," Jablonski said gently. "I don't mean to sound negative, but these things can take time."

"Every waking minute of every day I sit here helpless, driving myself crazy waiting for someone to tell me they've uncovered something." She started to lose it. "Jack, if you pitch in real hard, isn't there at least a *chance* you can beat the cops to the punch?"

"There's a chance."

Mikki took a moment to get herself under control. "I'm so goddamn lonely."

"I can imagine."

"Can you?"

He wiped his lips. "Maybe not. Who does one have to know around here in order to get replenished?"

Mikki located a small silver bell on the top of her tray and jingled it. "Coming up."

After Jablonski had consumed a second helping of crab cakes, he sat back in his chair and, with great satisfaction, announced, "No dinner tonight."

The older woman approached with a pot of coffee and proceeded to pour each of them a cup. "Hilda," Mikki said, "ask Belle to bring out the file of letters the guy wrote to me." She turned to the detective. "Belle's my aunt, Jack. Came down from Modesto couple years ago to help out with the mail, calls. Stuff like that. Never went back."

"When did you receive the first of these communications?"

"February. Nine months ago."

"And the most recent one?"

"Yesterday."

At this news Jablonski straightened up in his chair. "What'd it say?"

"I'd rather you read it for yourself."

"Have you shown it to the police?"

"First thing."

A tall, bony-looking woman wearing sneakers and a T-shirt labeled ME, SURFER, called out from the doorway to the patio. "I'll have the stuff to you in a minute, Mick. I'm making copies."

Jablonski remarked, "I take it that's Belle."

"Sweet, darling Auntie Ding Dong."

The detective smiled. "Your tormentor write you a lot?"
"Enough. There are fourteen notes."
"You ever have personal contact with him?"
"A while back I was pulling out of the parking lot at the station when this big, bald-headed ape came over and tried to stick some kind of a package into my car. I freaked and rolled up the window. In the confusion he left a palm print on the glass. The cops said it matched up with impressions on some of the letters. He got away in a pickup truck."
"And nobody made the license plates."
"Right. The only witness said he thought they were out-of-state."
"And the handprint hasn't led anywhere?"
"Not so far. There was no record at the FBI." She sighed deeply. "Anyone who's on television regularly is a celebrity and celebrities get pawed over wherever they go. Autographs, requests for money. I even had a ten-year-old boy pinch me on the behind one time."
Belle came rushing across the patio. "Here," she said, thrusting a manila envelope at the detective. "You're Mr. Jablonski. I'm the one who tracked you down for Mikki."
"Nice to meet you, Miss . . . ?"
"*Mrs.* Boudinot."
"Mrs. Boudinot." He indicated the package. "May I keep these?"
"Sure. As long as you like. They're numbered in sequence and I noted the date each one was received."
"I'm obliged."
Belle moved Mikki's tray away from the chaise. "It's time for you to take your nap."
The young woman turned to Jablonski. "There's a lot more you should know about this business, but I think maybe I better rest now."
The detective said, "Before I go, it would be helpful if you could review what happened the night of the attack."
"Mr. Jablonski," Belle said warningly.
"It's all right," Mikki reassured her aunt. "There's not much to tell. Of course, I couldn't see anything. After he ran away, I stumbled into the bathroom and tried to wash away the pain, but I couldn't. I finally located the phone, but the line was dead. The dog didn't come when I called him. At that point, I totally panicked. Being blind and nearly out of my mind with agony, I stumbled around until I finally

located the front door. I went outside and tried to call for help. I must have tripped on the front steps and banged my head. The patrol found me in the morning."

Jablonski stood up. "If it's okay, while you're having your nap, I'd like to look over the premises."

"Sure."

"I'll be in touch in a day or two."

Mikki held out her hands. "You won't mind a call in the middle of the night? Sometimes that's a pretty scary time for me."

Jablonski squeezed the young woman's outstretched fingers. "The crab cakes were scrumptious. My taste buds are in your debt."

"Anytime, Jack."

He dictated his home phone number to Belle.

Her aunt helped Mikki out of the chaise and led her slowly across the patio.

Jablonski turned away and began to study the back yard. Suddenly he felt very glad that damaged, frightened, beautiful Mikki O'Reilly was his first customer.

CHAPTER FOUR

IN a cramped and darkened living room in a tiny bungalow on the easternmost edge of Westchester, a southern suburb of Los Angeles, Clem Barren was slouched down on the ramshackle and faded sofa that faced an ancient television set. He was sucking on the barrel of a .38 Smith and Wesson as he watched a composite videotape he had made of dozens of Mikki O'Reilly's past appearances on the Channel Ten Evening News.

In six of the clips she wore a black sweater with a deep V-neck lined in some sort of white fur; in four of the others she was dressed in a pale green cashmere sweater with a yellowish, gauzy scarf that fell over her right shoulder. But in his favorite, the one that had just come up on the screen, she was wearing a skin-tight red leather jacket and huge white hoop earrings.

As she had every night since he began watching her last spring, she always talked directly to him.

Sweat covered his big, shiny bald head and ran down along the deep, leathery crevices in his face and the sides of his thick neck. He tightened his grip on the handle of the pistol and squeezed his eyes shut. He sat frozen until he heard the tape snap to a stop. Then, slowly, he removed the weapon from his mouth and leaned over and retched. When the spasm had passed, he reached for the remote unit that controlled the VCR and punched the rewind button. For nearly a minute the roar of static from the set intermingled with the rattling sounds emitted by the ancient refrigerator in the kitchenette.

Once the tape was again ready for viewing, he placed his huge index finger on the start button and pushed. Seconds later, Mikki O'Reilly's image again flashed onto the screen, her cornflower blue eyes drilling deep into his soul.

She loved him too much.

And now she was ugly.

He didn't know if he could stand to go on living.

CHAPTER FIVE

JABLONSKI'S recently rented office was housed in a medium-sized, chalk white, modern edifice. Principal ingress to the establishment was through the main entrance facing the street. Along the west side of the structure, several additional businesses were scattered. On the corner, adjacent, was a self-service filling station that carried a lesser known brand of gasoline, as well as cigarettes, soft drinks and seldom-purchased hot dogs that rotated endlessly on electric spits.

The surface of the building that ran perpendicular to the boulevard was bordered by a walkway approximately fifty feet in length. This area was entered through a wrought iron gate that connected two square, matching brick columns, six feet in height. Assorted plaques had been attached to each post identifying the tenants who occupied the ground floor space along the sidewalk.

San Vicente Boulevard is divided in half by an island. Across the way from Jablonski's building stood a mini-mall, housing a boutique, a tiny art gallery that featured pencil sketches, a deli, a One Hour Photo Service, and Bootons Jewelers. Several first-rate restaurants existed in uneasy proximity to a Pioneer Chicken outlet.

It was mid-afternoon when the detective slid the Honda into a parking spot half a block from his office. On the day before Thanksgiving, Jablonski wasn't surprised to note the large number of ladies crowded into the corner beauty parlor getting spruced up for the holiday. Briefly he wondered what it felt like to be marooned inside a hair dryer.

As he passed the small, dark quarters that, according to the gold lettering affixed to the glass of the open door, housed Marla May Willowbrook, Psychic, he was accosted by his neighbor.

"I'm glad your recent depression has dissipated somewhat, Mr. Jablonski."

"I beg your pardon, Madame?" This was the first time since the old woman moved in several months earlier that he had exchanged more than a nod with her.

"As you can imagine, dear sir, I am very sympathetic to any vibrations, particularly negative ones, that emanate from my fellow man."

"You have been tuned to my wavelength?" the detective asked, attempting to smother a smile.

"I see you are not a believer." She stepped outside and peered long and hard at her fellow tenant. "In any event, I am relieved that whatever has been giving you grief and torment for the past few weeks has gone away. Not only for your sake, but for mine as well."

Jablonski found the remark intriguing. "I don't follow you."

"Frankly, you have been interfering with my clients."

"I have?"

"Depressed, cynical resonances tend to confuse my thoughts when I am giving a reading. It took me quite awhile to identify the source of the extra-sensory static."

"Me?"

"You. Your discomfort has been an irritant of uncommon proportions ever since I came here. If your distress hadn't suddenly dissipated, it would have been necessary for me to find a more suitable haven to pursue my craft."

A harassed-looking matron wearing a sable coat approached. Marla May nodded to her and commented, "Right on time, Mrs. Harrington." The detective stepped back, allowing the patron to enter. "Good afternoon, Mr. Jablonski," the psychic said, starting to close the door. "Think positive."

As he entered his office, Shirley looked up from her desk and began applauding. Jablonski demanded, "What's that for?"

"The suit looks great!"

"How about the tie? The guy tried to unload a yellow job with tiny green four-leaf clovers on it, but I fought him off."

"You want an honest opinion?"

"Go ahead. Break my heart."

"Purple never was my favorite color."

Jablonski tossed his fedora onto the hatrack. "One out of two ain't bad." After loosening his tie, he started for the inner office. "What about the crone next door?"

Shirley picked up an envelope from her desk and followed her boss inside. "Marla May Willowbrook?"

"The same."

"She's a darling. We've become sort of friendly in the past few months."

"Aha!"

Shirley added, "Marla May reminds me of Auntie Mame."

"I didn't get that impression." Jablonski collapsed in his big upholstered chair. "You've been gossiping with her behind my back."

"I have *not*!"

"How else could the woman be so familiar with my mood of the past weeks?"

"She's a mind reader."

"For God's sake, you ought to know better. You're a psych major."

Shirley pulled up one of the chairs that stood in front of the desk and sat down. "Jack, haven't you heard of ESP?"

"I have. I've also heard of dowsing and I don't believe in that either." He removed a sheaf of papers from his inside coat pocket. "Anybody call?"

"Your wife."

"And?"

"She wanted to tell you she's leaving tomorrow morning for Atlantic City. Apparently the arrival of your new grandchild is imminent."

"I don't understand. Only day before yesterday the doctor said Susie's baby wasn't due for another two weeks."

"Maybe Susie got a second opinion."

"But tomorrow's *Thanksgiving*!" Jablonski complained.

"So what? They'll have turkey in first class."

"That's not what I meant. I was thinking about having to eat dinner by myself."

Shirley shrugged. "I'd ask you to come to our house but I know you're allergic to Saul."

"I'm not allergic," Jablonski explained. "It's just that little kids drive me nuts."

Shirley leaned across the desk and gave him the envelope she was carrying. "These are your wife's tickets."

The detective looked at the trip itinerary that the travel agent had prepared. "Eight A.M. The plane's leaving at eight A.M.?"

"Providing no little red lights show up in the cockpit."

"That means we'll have to hit the deck at six bells. That's the middle of the goddamn night." Jablonski took a deep breath. "I better settle myself down or Marla May'll be back on my case." He tossed the tickets to one side and examined the notes Aunt Belle had given him.

"What're those?" Shirley demanded.

"All in good time."

"You make a deal with Mikki O'Reilly?"

"I sure did." He outlined the terms.

"Wow! When do we start?"

"We've started." He pawed through the missives.

"Any first impressions you want to share with me?"

"Someone who was familiar with the young lady done her in."

"How do you know?"

"I don't *know*. I deduce. Since, as a matter of course, it would be somewhat unusual to carry around a piece of poisoned meat in one's back pocket, we can assume that Miss O'Reilly's assailant was aware she had a big, fierce dog who needed eliminating. It would also seem he knew the spot outside the house where the telephone lines terminated, and that he either had a key to the door leading into the backyard, or came prepared to pick the lock. Most important, he had a good reason to be mad as hell at her."

"You keep saying 'he'."

Jablonski tapped the pile in front of him. "Once you've read these little beauties, it seems pretty obvious her attacker was male." He identified the first one Mikki had received and handed it over. "Take a look."

The message had been typed on a letter-quality printer, using standard computer paper. Shirley read it aloud. " 'You're not only the most beautiful, you're the best weather girl they ever had. It's true. Please send your picture.' " She shrugged. "Not very threatening."

Jablonski countered, "That's what fascinates me. None of them are. Except the one she received the day of the assault." Jablonski took back the note. "Call the Valley Division and see who's on Mikki O'Reilly's case."

"Okay." Shirley stood up.

"One other thing. Find out how much it would cost to coat the wall that separates this office from our neighbor the soothsayer."

"Coat it with what?"

"Lead. The metal, I believe, stops X-rays. It certainly should be able to contain my innermost feelings."

Shirley smiled. "It's nice you're feeling so chipper."

Five minutes later, while his secretary was busy on line one, the second line rang. Not wanting Shirley to be distracted from her task, Jablonski picked up the call. "Jack Jablonski."

Piedad Santa Maria was highly agitated. "Is the Missus there?"

"Missus who?"

"Hurry! Saul is in the bathroom!"

"Saul?"

Shirley cut in on the line. "What about Saul?"

"Saul's locked himself in the bathroom, Missus, and he won't come out!"

Jablonski hung up in disgust.

Moments later his secretary came charging in. "I've got to rescue my baby. I hope you don't mind if I leave now. Someone named Baxter has the O'Reilly case. Happy Thanksgiving! See you Monday." She turned and rushed out.

Jablonski called 911 and informed the operator of the possible emergency at the Mandlebaum house in Encino, then dialed the Valley Division. After two rings a male voice answered. The officer informed him that Sergeant Baxter was off-duty until seven-thirty in the morning.

CHAPTER SIX

THE disfigurement and subsequent immobilization of Mikki O'Reilly was of considerable concern to many of her associates at Channel Ten News, not the least of whom was Will Waterbury, the chief anchorman of the nightly strip. Waterbury had started in the newscasting business more than a quarter of a century earlier and, during his previous dozen years with the TV station, had successfully positioned himself as the central figure in all matters relating to the gathering and dissemination of stories used on the nightly telecast. Although his successful usurpation of the news director's functions put Waterbury in a position of power, it also exposed him to certain dangers.

When, just over twelve months ago, the program's ratings dipped for the first time within memory, the station's ever-vigilant management dispensed with the then-current news director's services and hired Arnold Tolkin, a young black hotshot from Philadelphia, to take over. Tolkin, ambitious and tough, was not easily pushed around.

One of the newcomer's first decisions was to remove Mikki O'Reilly as the weather girl and send her out into the field as a segment reporter.

When Waterbury questioned the wisdom of such an assignment (Mikki was hugely popular with the viewers), Tolkin explained that he wanted to develop credibility for Mikki as a newswoman. "If she turns out like I think she will, maybe we'll move Bettina Rawls out and let Mikki sit next to you."

"I don't think that's wise," Waterbury said tersely. "Bettina's an experienced reporter and she's nearly my age. Mikki looks like my granddaughter."

"So what?"

"News is a serious business, Arnold. Kewpie dolls are fine and dandy when it comes to weather. But not in the sub-anchor spot."

"Trust me," Tolkin reassured the anchorman. "Mikki's a comer."

And Tolkin had been right. Several months after Mikki had been brought back into the studio, the ratings began to edge up. Not long thereafter, Channel Ten's evening news was tied for first place with its chief competitor.

Then, suddenly, Mikki was out of the game.

Waterbury hoped, now that the show had regained its previous momentum and he was on his own once again, that the ratings would hold steady. He didn't want to think about what would happen to him if audience interest began to erode.

CHAPTER SEVEN

Snoopy, the Jablonski's nine-month-old black cocker spaniel, started to have a fit the instant she spotted her master park the Honda in the driveway. She was relegated to the fenced-in area that lay between the main house and the modest guest cottage some twenty feet behind it.

Daphne had purchased the dog several months earlier when it became obvious that her husband was getting bored with his retirement.

Her hope was, by devoting himself to training the animal, Jablonski would shed some of his testiness.

Although Snoopy had helped him while away many hours, it turned out that training a puppy wasn't one of Jablonski's many talents. Because of the dog's resistance to being housebroken, it had become necessary for the couple to bar her from the house whenever they both were absent. This served to cut down on the accident rate, but the decision was not without a downside.

As a result of her banishments, the dog turned to digging a seemingly endless series of holes in various parts of the backyard, leveling a bed of calla lilies in the process.

Jablonski opened the gate and knelt down and cuddled the squirming bundle. "Easy, girl," he said, trying to dodge the barrage of kisses. In her excitement the puppy lost control and spotted Jablonski's new suit. Thank God I picked dark green, the detective thought, disengaging himself from the adoring attention of his pet. He stood up and patted the soiled area with his handkerchief. "If you will calm down, you may come inside," he informed his friend. Snoopy responded by jumping up and placing her mud-stained paws on his left kneecap. "Okay, that does it. Wait right here while I go get a towel." While he was cleaning up the puppy, the phone began to ring. He hurried back into the kitchen with Snoopy in trail. He wiped off his hands before answering.

"Yes?"

"Daddy, I'm so glad you're home! I tried the office but no one was there." It was Susie, his daughter, calling from Atlantic City, New Jersey.

"How're you feeling, Sooz? I hear tell you're due to deliver any day now."

"That's what my obee says, although Dean doesn't agree with him." Susie's husband, Dean Philbrook, was also an obstetrician but, as is customary in these situations, he had relegated his wife's care to a colleague. "No need for you to worry about me. I'm doing great. How are *you* feeling, Daddy?"

"Fine, sweetheart. I'm okay."

"How okay? Real okay or sort of okay?"

"Believe it or not, I took a case today."

"That's great! I'm so glad. Really! Dean's at the hospital and Billy and I are calling to wish you Happy Thanksgiving. I was afraid to wait until tomorrow because I might be in labor. I hope you don't mind if I borrow Mom for a week or two."

"I wish I could be there, too. Where is my grandson?"

"Right here."

There was a moment of off-stage dialogue before the seven-year-old took over from his mother.

"What case are you on, Grandpa?"

"It's pretty gruesome, Billy."

"That's *great*! Somebody get stabbed?"

"Worse. A pretty lady had acid thrown into her face."

"Oh, boy! And you're gonna catch the guy?"

"That's the general idea."

"Show him no mercy, Grandpa."

"Don't worry. I won't."

"Here's Mom. Happy Thanksgiving."

Billy was gone before Jablonski could respond.

"How's Snoopy doing, Daddy?"

"She's a real pal." Jablonski looked around at the puppy, who was making a puddle in the middle of the floor. "Wait a minute!" he exclaimed. He dropped the phone, scooped up the animal and tossed her out into the backyard. "Bad dog!" he called after her.

"Daddy, are you there?" his daughter was saying when he picked up the phone.

His response was somewhat bleak. "Yeah, I'm here."

"What's the matter all of a sudden?"

He sighed deeply. "Tell me something: when do puppies get control of their bodily functions?"

"Is that all?" Susie laughed.

"It ain't funny. A few minutes ago she peed on my new suit."

"I have an idea. Just don't pick her up until you're sure she's trained."

"Easy to say, Sooz. I can't keep my hands off her, she's so goddamn adorable."

"Patience, Daddy. Oh, I meant to ask you about your weight. You still taking it off?"

"Let's just say I'm holding my own."

Daphne appeared in the doorway. "Is that Susie?"

Jablonski nodded. "Your mother just showed up. You want to talk to her?"

"We already talked four times today. Remind Mom we'll pick her up in the baggage area. Love you, Daddy."

After finishing dinner and the dishes, Daphne announced, "I think I'll go to bed now. I have to get up at five."

"Five! What the hell for? We don't have to leave for the airport until six-fifteen."

"I want to wash my hair. It needs time to dry."

"You could wash it now."

"I'm afraid a shower would key me up."

Jablonski rolled his eyes.

"Now, please don't whistle in the bathroom before you come to bed."

"I hope you don't mind if I use my electric toothbrush."

"Of course not. Whirring doesn't bother me. Only whistling."

As soon as his wife had retired, Jablonski retrieved the sheaf of papers Mikki's aunt had given him and flopped down on the sofa in the living room. After ascertaining that the notes were in chronological order, he sat up and spread them out on the cocktail table in front of him.

He reviewed the first one, dated February 11 of this year: *"Your not only the most beautiful, your the best weather girl they ever had. Its true. Please send your picture."* Noting that the sender was unidentified, he reasoned that a self-addressed envelope must have been included and that no record had been made of it. He picked up a pad and pencil from a side table and jotted down a reminder to ask if the envelopes containing the subsequent epistles had been preserved.

It was impossible to determine anything of a personal nature about the author except that he possessed only a limited education, or was *pretending* that he did.

The second note was dated two weeks later, February 25: *"Id been hoping for a color picture. Your lips look soft."* The guy's pushy, no question about that, Jablonski thought to himself. Even in bulk, eight by ten color glossies are expensive. He compared the first two missives. So far our hero thinks that Mikki's beautiful and has soft lips. You'd think the man was falling in love. But wait.

Number three, dated March 14, read: *"I know how you feel about me. You shouldnt dress so sexy. I dont like my girls to advertise. I have big muscles. Do you like big muscles? Im going to come to the station. Maybe Ill get your autograph. Ill give you mine. Ha ha."* What a switch. Now the ape figures Mikki is under *his* spell.

Wrestlers have big muscles. So do weight lifters. Jablonski wondered if the cops had tried staking out some of the body-building establishments in an effort to spot a big, bald-headed man who drove a pickup truck with out-of-state plates. Probably not. Too many joints spread out over too wide an area. He re-read the note. Sex rears its ugly head for the first time. And the guy is possessive: *". . . You shouldnt dress so sexy. I dont like my girls to advertise."* My girls. How many girls? Who? *"Maybe Ill get your autograph. Ill give you mine. Ha ha!"* When it comes to jokes, Romeo needs a new writer.

Number four was dated April 4: *"Why did they take you off the weather? You must be lonely. When are you coming back?"* Jablonski wondered what this meant and made a note to ask Mikki.

May 5: *"I was there when you were at the big fire yesterday. I couldnt get close because the police kept everybody back. I could see you were looking around trying to find me. Dont worry. We'll be together soon."* What fire? Jablonski wondered when the writer began stalking Mikki.

The sixth epistle was the most intriguing so far. Dated May 17, it stated: *"I hope you understand why I had to come and stay in your apartment. You are my first real love and I know I am yours. I rubbed your clothes all over my body so you can feel me nearer to you."* Jablonski didn't need a note to remind him to ask Mikki the details on this one. It seemed obvious, by now, that the guy has decided he has found a soul-mate.

May 24: *"You shouldnt have run away. People who love each other shouldnt hide from each other. Anyway whats the point? I can always find you."* Jablonski mused that this was the first letter that might be interpreted as being slightly threatening.

Number eight, May 30, had a plaintive tone: *"I watch every night hoping that we can be together. How long are they going to keep sending you away?"* Away to where?

Number nine, three days later, was the longest of the batch: *"When you were with that homeless man last night I got tears in my eyes. You are so kind. I dont deserve someone as good as you. Ill try and be someone you can be proud of. Im starting to think about how we can be together always."* Sounds as if he's following Mikki regularly by now, Jablonski determined.

The next one was dated July 20 and had ominous overtones: *"I know where you live now. Why did you try to fool me? I get angry when you try and fool me. You mustnt be afraid. Our love for each other will take us through anything."*

August 1: *"More and more I feel the magic coming out of your eyes. I love your love."* No question about it: Baldy is three bricks short of a full load.

Then, a month later: *"I know you want me to come and get you. I cant stand waiting much longer. I will be worthy of your love."*

Then nothing for nine weeks. November 7: *"Soon I must help you understand what is right. It's important. Maybe I'll put my mark on you. Then you'll be mine forever."* Jablonski recalled that the attack took place a day later.

Finally, on November 13: *"Now that your ugly I must give you up. Goodbye. I am sorry."*

Jablonski dropped the last letter on the cocktail table and leaned back. He closed his eyes. Some weird stuff here, he thought to himself. Not only does the guy love Mikki, he's decided that Mikki loves *him*. He threatens to mark her and he does. Then he dumps her because she's ugly. As he reviewed the notes he felt himself becoming drowsy. Just as he dropped off to sleep, Snoopy jumped up into his lap and made herself comfortable.

CHAPTER EIGHT

About an hour later Jablonski was jarred awake by the ringing of the telephone. After he'd opened his eyes, it took him a few seconds to acclimate himself. When he stood up he reacted to the sharp pain in his back, the result of the unorthodox position he had inadvertently adopted on the sofa during his nap.

Being careful not to step on the dog, he limped across the living room and picked up the phone. "Hello?"

"Jack?"

It was a female, but the voice wasn't immediately identifiable. "Mikki?"

"Yes. I hope I'm not disturbing you."

"Not at all. I'm right here at my post. At your service." He reached over to the wall switch and snapped on some more lights. The wall clock read nine forty-five. "How you doin'?"

"Like I told you. I get lonely a lot."

"Holiday weekends are rough."

"Holiday week *nights* are worse. Especially around ten."

"Hmmm?"

"That's when my show starts."

"I forgot. TV news people work Monday through Friday nights no matter what."

"Present company excepted."

Jablonski decided he should change the subject. "I was planning to call you tomorrow. I have a few questions about those notes you received."

"I thought you might."

"You want to talk now?"

"Love to."

"To begin with, did you save any of the envelopes?"

"All of them, except the first. Starting with number two, the one where the creep wrote that my lips were soft, my agent told me to hang onto everything from then on."

"What did the writer mean, I think it was in number four, when he said something about you being taken off the weather?"

"Maybe I should give you a chronology. At the time the letters began arriving, I was the weather girl on the show. That was back in February. Not too long after that the new news director made me a segment reporter. After my promotion, I wasn't on every night anymore."

"What's a segment reporter?"

"Someone who's assigned to cover stories in the field. You show up on tape once or twice a broadcast, or not at all. Depends. Sometimes, when something's fast-breaking, segment reporters report live from location."

"That would account for his remark about seeing you at the fire."

"Yeah."

"He must have staked out the TV station and then followed you from there to the scene."

"It's goddamn spooky, isn't it? Sometime in July, I don't remember exactly when, the news director moved the sub-anchor on the ten o'clock news. She's an elder lovely named Bettina Rawls. Betty ended up in the co-anchor job on the *afternoon* show. That's when they brought me in from the field to replace her. And that's where I've been until the attack."

"How's a sub-anchor different from a co-anchor?"

"A co-anchor is on the same level with the anchor. At our joint, *no one* is Will Waterbury's equal."

"He's the main man."

"Believe me."

Jablonski switched gears. "Is there anything you did on the telecasts, as a matter of course, that this psychopath might have been able to interpret as being directed solely at him?"

"I've wondered about that too." She paused. "At the end of every show I always said, 'Goodnight to you. Until tomorrow.' But it's a stretch to see how that could get anybody's attention."

"Maybe not, Mikki. Consider. When someone turns on the news, the reporters and the anchor people appear to be looking directly at the viewer."

"Because we concentrate on the camera lens when we talk."

"A normal person understands there's no real eye contact being made."

Mikki inhaled sharply. "You're saying a cuckoo might think he's being singled out and everything being said is aimed right at *him*? Jesus! That's so off the wall." She interrupted herself. "Wait a minute. Something else I did might have helped to push him over the edge. I told you the letters started when I was the weather girl, but I didn't mention my gimmick."

"Enlighten me."

"I decided to punch up my act with a little flesh."

"Flesh?"

"You know, so I would stand out from the competition. From time to time I'd dress to match the day's weather. Once, when it was pouring, I wore a sheer plastic raincoat over a bikini. Last Christmas Eve, after a snowstorm in the mountains, I wore an abbreviated Santa Claus outfit, red hotpants and calf-length black boots and a cap with a white tassel. Whenever dry, warm Santa Ana winds blew, I'd show up in a bathing suit. It didn't take too long before the rating was up almost a point."

"Is that a lot?"

"On a local news show it can be the difference between being number one and number two."

"Sorry I didn't watch you regularly. When we first arrived out here, my wife and I got hooked on Channel Three."

"Old Herb Feldon and Jill Carlino with the dimple in her chin?"

"The very same."

"We beat their ass by two points the last week I was working." Mikki stifled a yawn.

Jablonski carried the phone over and sat down on the sofa. "I've saved the most interesting question for last."

"About when he stayed in my apartment."

"Exactly."

"One night, some months ago, when I was still doing segments, Will Waterbury announced on the air that I was being sent out of town to Mexico City for four days. I'd been assigned to do a series of reports on the drug situation. After the trip, when I got back to my place, I noticed a lot of little things that were kind of strange. You know, stuff wasn't where it was supposed to be. The dishwasher was empty. When I left, it was a quarter full. The louvres in the blinds were slanted the wrong way. There were fresh flowers in the vase on the kitchen table. I contacted the lady who comes in once a week to clean for me but she said she hadn't been around. At that point I went fucking nuts."

"Did you check with the super of the building?"

"Sure. Right away. He, and some of the neighbors, told me that a big, bald-headed guy had moved in while I was gone. They figured he was my new boyfriend."

"At this point you called in the *Federales*."

"Believe it!"

"Fingerprints?"

"The police said the apartment was lousy with them. Matched those on the notes."

"And, so far, the prints haven't turned up a suspect."

"It makes me damn mad. How is it possible for the cops to be so stupid?"

"There aren't many sources that maintain reliable fingerprint banks of any size. If the guy who went after you wasn't in the service, or if there's no record of his prints at the FBI, it'd be difficult to track him down."

"How about the DMV? In this state they fingerprint everybody who gets a driver's license."

"Since he was driving a truck with out-of-state plates, the police are probably in the process of contacting all the other DMVs. They may come up with something, but it'll take a lot of time." He could hear Mikki stifle another yawn. "I'm not sure that every state has the same fingerprint requirements that California does. Also, he may not even *have* a driver's license."

"Shit!"

Jablonski consulted the sheaf of papers on the coffee table. "After his visit to your place, according to the May twenty-fourth note, you fled your apartment. Where'd you go?"

"I moved in with my agent and his wife. Al hired a company that furnished bodyguards around the clock and we started looking for a secure house where I could live." She paused to gather her thoughts. "About a week after I was called back into the studio as sub-anchor, the real estate agency located the place I'm in now."

"And you bought a big dog and hoped for the best."

"Until the guy jumped me in the parking lot, I wasn't too worried, because I had the patrol meet me at the door each night when I came home after the show. They'd check the inside of the house. Then I'd put on the alarm and go to bed."

"Hell of a way to have to live."

"Tell me about it." Finally Mikki let go with a full-blown yawn. "Thanks for letting me talk to you. I feel better."

"I'll probably call you tomorrow. I'm going to have a lot more questions."

"Goodnight, Jack."

"Goodnight." He dropped the phone into its cradle and looked down at Snoopy. "Whadda you say, pal, shall we turn on the TV and see what Mr. Waterbury and company look like?" In response, the puppy grabbed hold of his pants leg and began pulling. "Enough!" he said forcefully. After disentangling her, he switched on the television set.

Moments after he clicked the channel selector to ten, the signature of the news program faded in. Directly following this, Will Waterbury appeared. He was an imposing presence in his late fifties, somewhat overweight, with a large double chin. His bushy eyebrows dominated his seamless face and his great mop of reddish-brown hair (dyed? Jablonski wondered) had been teased up into a soft pyramid that rode atop his head. Waterbury's resonant voice was edged with doom as he delivered the lead story about a young mother and her four children who had been burned to death earlier in a tenement fire in downtown Los Angeles.

As the program unfolded, the lesser lights in the cast of characters paraded across the screen, separated one from the other by various nerve-wracking explosions of color-saturated graphics. They included a Mexican-American man in his late twenties, with bulging eyes and a pencil-thin black moustache, who read a consumer feature on the procedure that should be followed if a loved one got a turkey bone stuck in his throat at Thanksgiving dinner; a small male of indeterminate Asian origin with the improbable name of Wee Snee, who was in charge of the weather segment; and the sports maven, a muscular black giant with an eighteen-inch neck, who seemed to have difficulty synchronizing his words with the film unfolding on the screen.

No question, Jablonski concluded, Channel Ten was an equal opportunity employer. But clearly, the show could have used a woman's touch.

He snapped off the set and looked around for the dog. Snoopy was lying next to the heating vent, flaked out. He, on the other hand, was wide awake. Goddamn nap, he mumbled. He tickled Snoopy's ear, then took her out into the backyard and waited until she gave her farewell performance of the evening.

After tucking the puppy into her basket, he slipped into his pajamas. Finally, he gave his troubled gums a massage with the electric toothbrush.

As he slid under the covers, Jablonski looked over at his wife. Daphne, eyes closed and not a hair out of place, had a beatific smile on her face. He adjusted the sheet around him, leaned over and shut off the bed lamp.

Moments later he drifted off into the twilight zone, a state where he did some of his best work. As the contents of Mikki's notes swirled around in his head, he waited for an insight to present itself.

But it was not to be. Shortly after midnight he finally fell into a deep sleep.

CHAPTER NINE

It was still dark on Thanksgiving morning when Snoopy began licking Jablonski on the ear. "For cris'sake, Snoop, lay off," he grumbled, as he tried to bury his head under the pillow. But the sound of his voice seemed to spur the puppy on to even greater expressions of affection. She dug under the barrier and stuck her cold nose onto the back of his neck. Jablonski sat up and peered at the inch-high illuminated numbers on the bedside clock. "It's only four-thirty," he complained. He pointed at the dog's basket. "Git!"

Having restored order, he wriggled himself into a comfortable position. It was at this point that he realized the shower was running. He groaned and forced his way back to the Land of Nod. The next thing he knew, Daphne was standing over him saying, "It's six o'clock, Jack. Rise and shine!"

"Aargh."

"I'm afraid you won't have time for breakfast." She bustled around, tossing things into her vanity case, then started for the kitchen. "I'll make us some coffee."

Knowing when he was defeated, Jablonski rolled out of bed and crossed to the window. In the gradually lifting darkness he could see that a clear, crisp day was coming. Before beginning the morning's ablutions, he removed the top of his pajamas, picked up two barbells, and embarked on his regular series of exercises. He was somewhat vain about his upper arm development, a residual of a youthful stint as a boxer in the armed forces. Without fail, for over a quarter of a century, he had meticulously pursued a maintenance course designed to preserve, as much as possible, the results of his earlier activity.

Snoopy, her head cocked first to one side then the other, watched this strange ritual unfold. When he had finished, Jablonski turned to the full-length mirror on the open closet door and observed his physique. His abdomen which, through the passing years, had responded to the demands of gravity, protruded somewhat but, he was pleased to note, not as much as when he was twenty-five pounds heavier. In one motion, he sucked in his stomach, made an L-shape at his sides with both arms, and balled up his fists. The resulting image, he decided, wouldn't give Arnold Schwarzenegger pause, but, on the other hand, it wouldn't clear a room either.

The traffic was almost non-existent and the couple arrived at the airport at five minutes to seven.

"Look what time it is," Jablonski grumbled. "I could have slept another half hour."

"You maybe. I always wake up early when I go on a trip. Besides, what if we'd had a flat tire?"

"Daph," Jablonski sighed, as he hefted his wife's bag out of the car trunk into the arms of a waiting skycap, "what the hell are you talking about?"

"If we'd left a half hour later and then encountered some sort of delay, I could have missed the plane."

"But we didn't and you haven't."

"Exactly my point."

While Jablonski tipped the skycap, Daphne leaned in the front window and gave Snoopy a pat on the head. "Be a good girl while I'm gone," she told the dog.

"You want me to park the car and come up to the gate with you?" the detective asked.

"Heavens, no! I'll be fine."

The couple embraced.

"Call me when you get in," Jablonski instructed his wife.

"I will."

"One more thing. Tell the pilot to be sure and put the wheels down before he comes in for a landing. I wouldn't want anything to happen to you."

"You know something, Jack? You're sweet."

"I love you too, Daph. Lots. Give Sooz and Dean a hug."

Daphne patted him on the stomach. "Remember: no noshing."

It was a half hour later when Jablonski and the puppy returned to Brentwood. The twosome got out of the car and made their way into the backyard. Without pause, Snoopy made a dive for one of the flower beds and, in moments, repeated her performance of the previous evening.

"Great going, girl!" Jablonski exclaimed.

The puppy started pulling him toward the gate, nearly choking herself in the process. "Hold it!" he ordered. He leaned down and loosened her collar several notches. "There. That should feel better. Now attempt to restrain yourself. Walk proud and smell the flowers."

Once on the street Snoopy not only smelled the flowers; she smelled everything. After fifteen minutes of sniffing, the two of them had progressed less than half a block. "At this rate I'll be eligible for social security before we get to the corner," Jablonski informed his companion. "Tomorrow I'm going to teach you how to heel. How would you like that?" Snoopy, spotting an itinerant butterfly, chased madly after the insect, wrapping the leash around Jablonski's legs in the process. After freeing himself, the detective decided that he'd had enough for one morning. Back in the house he skimmed the Los Angeles *Times* before deciding to call Sergeant Baxter, the officer in charge of the O'Reilly investigation.

"Just a second," the young policeman who answered at the Valley Division directed, "I'll see if she's in yet."

After an endless period of waiting, a crisp, somewhat masculine voice said, "This is Sergeant Baxter."

After identifying himself and stating the purpose of his call, he requested an appointment. "I'm wide-open today," he said, "if you have a few minutes."

"Come on over after lunch. Being Thanksgiving, it looks like it's going to be pretty quiet around here."

Expecting the resistance often put up by local law enforcement officials when they perceive their bailiwick is about to be invaded by an outsider, Jablonski managed to mumble, "You're very kind."

"What'd you say your name was?"

"Jablonski. Jack Jablonski."

"Okay, Jablonski. I'll see you around two-thirty."

Figuring that his meeting with Sergeant Baxter probably wouldn't last for more than a few minutes, the detective decided to take Snoopy along on the trip. After lunch he dressed in his new green suit and loaded the dog into the front passenger seat of the Honda. The temperature wasn't so high that he would worry about leaving her alone in a parked car for a short period, and he hoped the puppy might find the ride invigorating.

He drove north on Twenty-sixth Street and turned east on Sunset Boulevard where, after a couple of miles meandering through the high rent district, he joined the San Diego Freeway. He made it to the parking lot of the Valley Division in Van Nuys in twenty minutes flat.

"Now control yourself," he told the puppy, "and don't bark at any of the boys in blue lest you get chucked into the slammer."

As he walked away, Snoopy began to howl dolefully.

Sergeant Baxter was seated at her desk in the nearly deserted squadroom poring over some reports. Jablonski walked up next to her and removed his fedora. "Good afternoon."

The look she gave him was disconcertingly blank.

"Jablonski?" he said. "I telephoned this morning."

"Oh, yes," she answered summarily. She pointed to a chair. "Park it." After shuffling the documents into a manila folder, she leaned back. "So Mikki thinks the LAPD needs some help."

The detective couldn't tell whether the look on her face was quizzical or hostile. "Nothing could be farther from the truth," he assured her.

"Okay then, Jablonski, what *is* your function?"

"Mikki is, as you know, in a damaged state, both physically and emotionally. She called on me to furnish around-the-clock support to her during this difficult time. A luxury, I might point out, an officer in an overburdened police department such as yours can ill-afford to provide."

The sergeant smiled. "Eloquently put, Jablonski. I thought I'd heard them all."

"Pardon?"

"The reasons people in your profession give for their involvement in police business."

Jablonski studied her rather plain face. No makeup except for a touch of pale lipstick on her wide, full mouth. Close-cropped black hair. A tiny pearl earring in each earlobe. And a definite sparkle in her eyes.

Suddenly she asked, "What is it you want to know?"

"Beside fingerprints, what else did you discover in Mikki's apartment following its occupation by the uninvited caller?"

"The man apparently cut himself while shaving. He's type O."

"I'm curious. How did you determine that the blood belonged to the intruder?"

"Mikki insisted she didn't have any overnight visitors. Whenever she was with her boyfriend, it was always at his place. Seems he didn't like a single bed."

Jablonski made a mental note to ask his client about her love life.

Sergeant Baxter continued, "The lab boys scraped some dried urine off the edge of the toilet. The guy could be a borderline diabetic."

"That narrows the field."

"He apparently scribbled notes to Mikki while seated at the table in the dining nook. The writing instrument he used made impressions in the tablecloth. He's left-handed."

"Their contents?"

"It was nearly impossible to make them out. The few lines we could decipher were drivel. Either he destroyed his work when he finished or took it along with him when he left the apartment. Anything else?"

"Since I understand from Mikki that the Veterans Administration and the FBI were unable to come up with a fingerprint match, may I assume the police are querying the DMVs outside of California?"

"You may."

"One more thing. Did your technicians establish that all the letters Mikki received were printed on the same computer paper by the same printer?"

"The first five matched. The lab stopped making comparisons at that point."

Jablonski summarized. "So what we have is a big, bald-headed man who left his fingerprints all over Mikki's place, who owns a small pickup truck with out-of-state plates. He's left-handed, possibly diabetic, with type *O* blood."

"And we don't have the remotest idea who or where he is."

Jablonski retrieved his hat from the desk and pushed himself up out of the chair. "Thank you. I'd like to think we might work together on this."

She looked the detective up and down. "I'm all for that, Jablonski."

As he hurried across the parking lot Jablonski felt the least bit unsettled by the sergeant's final remark. Such an excess of cooperation seemed out of place. But what the hell, he told himself, every little bit helps.

The puppy was still whimpering as he approached the Honda. He opened the door and examined the interior of the car. Finding everything in order, he exclaimed, "Good girl! Suppose we take a walk around the block before I try to locate a place in the neighborhood to eat."

In response, Snoopy made a puddle on the back seat.

CHAPTER TEN

An ancient, emaciated waitress, burdened down with Jablonski's order, was approaching his booth in the small deli located a block from the Valley Division's headquarters when Sergeant Baxter pushed open the front door to the establishment. The old woman set down the plateful of turkey, mashed potatoes and cranberry sauce. "Anything else I can get you?" she asked.

"No, thanks. I'm not sure I can handle all this."

Business was slow. Beside the sergeant and himself, the only other customers were an older couple seated in the back. The police officer crossed to an area adjacent to the counter labeled "Takeout" and studied the items in the display case.

Nancy Baxter stood about five feet four and was wearing a large black leather bag over her left shoulder. Her trim figure was encased in a severely tailored gray suit with a skirt that ended an inch above the knees. Her stockings were skin tone and the black flats she wore were polished to a high sheen. She appeared to be in her mid-forties.

As Jablonski was savoring the first mouthful of his meal, he heard the sergeant ask for six slices of white meat of turkey, a small container of coleslaw, and a bran muffin, to go. The swarthy, sloppy-looking man behind the counter took an inordinate amount of time writing down her order and totaling it up before he finally devoted himself to assembling the various elements she had requested. Impatient at the delay, Baxter took a cookie from a basket on top of the display case and was about to bite into it when she spotted Jablonski. She nodded and strolled over to his table.

He made a futile attempt to rise, then said apologetically, "Pretty close quarters here."

"Don't get up."

He indicated the seat opposite him. "Care to join me?"

"Maybe for a minute." She slid into the booth.

He indicated the plate in front of him. "This is Thanksgiving dinner. I just put my wife on a plane for the east."

"Nothing wrong, I hope."

"On the contrary. Our daughter is about to give birth."

"Boy or girl?"

"The kids want to be surprised."

She nodded, then stared at Jablonski for a long moment. "If you don't mind my saying so, you remind me of a basset hound I had once. Name of Bonkers."

Jablonski waited.

"The dog had great soulful eyes like yours. And jowls. Although Bonkers' jowls were ever so much more pinchable."

"How can you be sure? You never pinched mine."

She broke the cookie in half and nipped off a piece. "Who knows, perhaps we'll get to that later."

Hello, Jablonski thought to himself. What do we have here? To cover his momentary confusion he said, "My daughter's married to an obstetrician."

"My ex-husband is a mortician or, as he prefers to be called, a funeral director."

"One brings them in and the other sees them out."

Sergeant Baxter smiled. "Not bad, Jablonski."

The counterman ambled over and set a paper bag with her purchases on the table. "I added fifty cents for the cookie," he informed her. She gave him a ten-dollar bill and he went off to make change.

Abruptly Baxter said, "I just thought of something. The left front headlight of the truck was burned out."

"Run that by me again."

"The truck the guy was driving the night he tried to shove something through the window of Mikki's car: its left front headlight was either burned out or smashed. The witness couldn't be sure." She shrugged. "On second thought, that probably isn't of much help."

"Not at the moment, perhaps," Jablonski replied, "but someday, who can tell."

The counterman returned with the sergeant's change. She gave him a dollar then turned back to the detective. "Do you think maybe Mikki's assailant will lay off her now?"

"Because of his comments in the final note?"

"Yeah. What a bastard! Imagine messing her up, then telling her she's out of the game because she's ugly."

"In answer to your question, I don't know whether Mikki's off the hook. This guy sounds pretty weird."

She picked up her package and began wiggling her way out of the booth. "Well, Happy Thanksgiving."

"Likewise."

As she stood up, Jablonski's attention was drawn to a tall, burly, black teenager who had just entered the deli. The youth moved toward the counterman who sat behind the cash register, his head buried in a copy of the *Enquirer.* The detective stiffened when he noticed that the boy's right hand was buried deep inside the coat pocket of his frayed jacket.

"What is it?" Baxter asked, sensing the abrupt change in Jablonski's attitude.

"Turn around real easy," he whispered. "I think maybe we got trouble."

Slowly, the sergeant pivoted in place. Before the kid said a word, he flipped open an ugly-looking switchblade and shoved the point under the counterman's chin. "Okay, Pablo, let's have the bucks."

"Right away, man! Right away!" The attendant dropped the newspaper and punched open the cash drawer.

When the intruder glanced over at the line of booths, Jablonski was momentarily unnerved by the wild look in his eyes. "He's higher than a kite," he murmured under his breath.

During the time it took the counterman to collect the money from the cubbyholes in the drawer of the register, the teenager stepped back and addressed the room. "Don' nobody move. I'll be through in jus' a minute and you can go on enjoyin' your turkey." He turned to his terrified victim and stuck out his left hand. "Forgit about the change. Lay the bills right here." Fumbling, the counterman attempted to comply.

During this transaction Baxter handed her package to Jablonski. "There's a pay phone outside the men's room," she said softly, her lips scarcely moving. "As soon as I get the kid's attention, see if you can sneak back and call for assistance." She opened her shoulder bag and removed a snub-nosed .38.

"Careful," Jablonski urged.

She assumed the firing position. "Police!" she said in a loud, forceful voice. "Drop your weapon and put your hands on your head!"

In response, the kid wheeled around and faced her. "A lady cop?" he said tauntingly, pocketing the money. "What do you think about that?" He sniggered. "Why don't you go ahead and shoot me? Get your pitcher on TV." He started toward her, tossing the knife back and forth from hand to hand. "Go ahead."

As Jablonski was about to attempt to distract the intruder by throwing the sugar container at him, Baxter dropped the pistol back into her purse. "Okay, no gun," she told the youth. "Now put the knife away and maybe things won't go so badly for you."

The kid's lip curled up in a sneer. "Is that so?" he snorted. "You want to know what *I* think? I think I'm going to stick me a lady cop."

Sergeant Baxter let the purse slide off her shoulder to the floor.

"You heard what she said," Jablonski interjected softly.

Without taking his eyes off the officer, the youth hissed, "Before I stick her, she's gonna help me get outta here, aren't you, baby?" With his right arm outstretched, he lunged.

Jablonski wasn't sure exactly what happened next but, before he could blink, the teenager was flat on his back on the floor. Baxter stomped her foot on his wrist, reached down and relieved him of the knife.

"Hand me my gun," she ordered Jablonski, "and go call for some backup."

As the detective hurried to the phone, the youth sat up groggily.

Baxter looked over at the counterman who, along with the waitress, was cowering behind the cash register. "You can come to the station and claim your dough after we book him."

A minute later Jablonski returned. Almost immediately a siren could be heard winding up in the next block. "The boys are on their way," he announced.

"There's a pair of cuffs in my bag. Would you do the honors?" While Jablonski was completing the chore, she read the kid his rights.

The front door opened and two burly uniformed policemen burst in, guns drawn. "You okay?" the first one asked her.

"Fine, Dick." She indicated the boy. "He's all yours, guys. He's been Mirandized. I'll be back in a little while to do the paperwork." As the patrolmen led the teenager away, she looked at Jablonski. "I have to sit down."

"I should think so." When she was settled, he asked, "Black belt?"

She nodded. "A druggie with a knife doesn't have a chance."

"So I observed."

"I could use a cup of strong coffee."

"A fine idea." He called over to the waitress and placed the order.

"Suddenly, I'm ravenous," Baxter said, opening the paper bag. "Do you mind if I eat part of my holiday feast?"

"Of course not."

She removed a thin packet of butcher paper and broke it open. "Help yourself," she said, indicating the pristine, white slices of meat.

Jablonski glanced down at the plate in front of him. The gravy that had been liberally splashed over his turkey and mashed potatoes had congealed. "As a matter of fact, I will." When the waitress brought the coffee, the detective handed her his dish.

"No good?" the woman asked.

"Cold."

The waitress turned to Baxter. "I only saw judo once. In the movies. You're some fancy stepper."

The sergeant smiled. "It can come in handy."

"If you ever decide to give private lessons, lemme know. Every night I walk to the bus I'm nervous."

"I'll do that."

After ordering a scoop of vanilla ice cream, Jablonski picked up the switchblade knife from the table and flipped it open. He slid his thumb across the blade. "Scary how quick a little piece of crack can change someone's personality." He closed up the weapon. "New subject. I read a story in the paper the other day about a guy named Ed Merriweather. Do you know if he's reliable?"

"Ummm." She downed the mouthful of turkey and wiped her lips. "Ed has probably the first, maybe the only, centralized clearing house for reports on obsessions, provocations, threats and stalkings. Stuff like that. His access to this type of information is invaluable to people whose safety requires reinforcement."

"How long's he been at it?"

"Years. Before an episode has developed into a matter for the police, people in the public eye often come to him. He advises them on what precautionary measures should be taken. His computer bank also lets him cross-reference any notes received by a client with those of the same type sent to other public figures. He's caught a dozen repeat offenders using this technique." She opened the container of cole slaw and dipped into it. "Of course, if he decides someone is in imminent danger, he calls us in."

"Sort of a private eye with a sub-specialty," Jablonski observed. "You ever worked with him?"

"Couple of times." A sad smile crossed her face. "Isn't it a little bit late to be consulting him on Mikki's behalf?"

"At the moment, she needs all the emotional reinforcement she can get. If Mr. Merriweather can provide useful advice on how to prevent any future battery on Mikki's person, real or imagined, I think it would contribute considerably to her peace of mind and ultimately to the pace of her recovery."

Baxter leaned back and studied Jablonski again. "Refreshing."

"Hmmm?"

"An investigator who isn't in the game just for the bucks."

"Jobs that interest me seem to be few and far between, Sergeant."

"That said, you are nevertheless a gentle man."

Jablonski bowed gallantly. "I trust that will, in no way, impede our working relationship."

"On the contrary. Would you like me to get Ed Merriweather's number for you?"

"That's very kind."

She refolded the packet of butcher paper and slipped it back into the paper bag. "Thanksgiving dinner with you was nice. Such as it was."

"A touch too melodramatic perhaps."

She stood up. "Do you have a card?"

"No. But I'm listed in the West L.A. directory."

"Simple enough. Well, as we say in California: have a nice rest of the day." She leaned down and pinched his left cheek. "I was wrong, Jablonski. Bonkers had nothing on you."

"I'll take that as a compliment, Sergeant Baxter."

"Nancy."

Later, after the policewoman had gone, Jablonski ordered a second cup of coffee. He decided, since he had probably missed Daphne's call at home, he'd better phone Atlantic City and see how things were with his daughter. He got change from the counterman and made his way back to the pay phone.

The flight, Daphne told him, was uneventful and Susie had shown no signs of going into labor as yet. "You know what they're going to call the baby if it's a boy?" his wife asked.

"Jackson?" he asked hopefully.

"Clarence. After Dean's dad."

"What about me, for cris'sake?"

"They have that base covered. If it's a girl they're going to name her Jacqueline."

Jablonski decided to take whatever he could get.

CHAPTER ELEVEN

JUDGING from the amount of traffic speeding along San Vicente Boulevard the Friday after Thanksgiving, it was business as usual for most people. The Honda badly needed an oil change, so Jablonski dropped it off at the Shell station a few blocks west of his office. He made his way through the early morning bustle to the eatery in the basement of his building, where he had a stale doughnut and a cup of cocoa. When he finished breakfast, he took the elevator back up to the lobby and stepped out onto the street. Rounding the corner, he started up the walk adjacent to the structure. Standing outside his office door was a well-dressed youth of twelve or thirteen.

"Mr. Jablonski?" the boy asked.

"That's right."

"My name's Petey Bosworth. If you've got a few minutes, I'd like to interview you for our school paper." Jablonski frowned. "Each month I write a column on someone in the neighborhood. Someone with an unusual or important occupation."

"I dunno."

"The paper's read by over five hundred families in the area."

"Tell me, son, how did I get so lucky?"

"It's like this." The boy leaned in and squinted through his thick tortoise-shell glasses. "I said to myself: 'Look Petey, for recent issues you talked to a doctor, a librarian, an astronomy major, a garbage man . . .' "

"A garbage man?"

"I believe in covering all of society's strata."

"Very democratic."

"The information imparted by these various individuals, although eclectic, wasn't very exciting. What then, I pondered, might grip my readers? I appropriated the Yellow Pages and began my hunt."

"And there I was."

"I was particularly intrigued by the fact that you served twenty-five years with the FBI. I imagine you could regale us with some tall tales."

"If you don't mind my asking, how did you build up such a prodigious vocabulary?"

"Dad requires that we read a new book each week and discuss it at family dinner on Sunday. It's a tradition."

Jablonski unlocked the door to his office and beckoned the boy inside. "How long do you figure this will take?"

"I have a two o'clock deadline this afternoon. I think I could accomplish my mission in half an hour."

"I'm surprised that someone of your obvious resourcefulness and intellect would wait until the last minute to seek out a suitable candidate."

"I cannot tell a lie, Mr. Jablonski. Earlier this week, pursuing my quest alphabetically, I first chose a Mr. Branswagger, primarily because I liked his name, then a Mr. Gregorian." Petey followed the detective into the inner office.

"What was Mr. Gregorian's special appeal?"

"The Gregorian chant." Jablonski looked blank. "A form of ancient liturgical music of the Roman Catholic Church. He sounded classy."

"I see."

"It turned out that both men expected me to compensate them for their time." Jablonski shook his head in disbelief. "Since the exchange of money would be a clear violation of the journalistic code of ethics, I instantly terminated both meetings."

Jablonski sat down behind his desk. "There'll be no charge today," he assured the boy. "Sit down."

"No, thank you. I think better on my feet." Petey paced for several moments before speaking. "How old were you when you decided to go into law enforcement?"

Jablonski scrunched up his lips. "I guess I was about your age."

"Strange, although my father detests the idea, lately I have become more and more preoccupied with the world of the private investigator."

Jablonski said, "In boys, it goes with puberty."

"Are you suggesting that there is a connection between the period when a male matures sexually and the desire to investigate the activities of others?"

"I hadn't thought of it exactly that way, but I suppose there might be." Petey turned and stared out the window, deep in thought. Interrupting his reverie, Jablonski asked, "You want a paper and pencil?"

"Pardon?"

"For notes."

The boy smiled. "That won't be necessary. I have a photographic memory."

"Instead of me," Jablonski continued, "maybe you should be talking to the old lady next door. She's a mind reader. God only knows what the two of you would come up with if you put your heads together."

"I considered that on the way in. For a future column. Psychics are, I believe, highly underrated. But back to you. Would you recall some of the high points of your life in law enforcement?"

"That won't take very long. Most detective work consists of just grinding away." In spite of his disclaimer, Jablonski reminisced for nearly ten minutes about his career. As he spoke, the boy's eyes began to widen. Before he was half finished, Petey had sunk deep into the chair in front of the desk, clearly transported by the revelations of his host.

When Jablonski concluded, Petey jumped up. "This will be the best column I've ever written! You gave me enough for half a page!" He ran around the desk and stuck out his hand. "Before I go, could you tell me what you regard as the single most important quality that a person must possess if he is to become a successful detective?"

"That's a tough one." Jablonski peered up at the ceiling while he sorted out his thoughts. "I suppose I'd put the power of observation at the top of the list."

"Would you elucidate?"

"Most people fail to *notice* things."

"You mean they're not aware of the totality of any given environment?"

"Environment or attitude or action. This is the principle under which magicians operate. Let me give you a couple of other examples: a person who drives through a stop sign because his mind is someplace else; or a diner who doesn't notice how bland the meat on his plate is because the cook smothered it in a sauce. How about Edgar Allan Poe's 'The Purloined Letter'?"

"You're saying that, first and foremost, detectives must be good noticers."

"I think you just made up a new word. But yes, that's the idea."

"Mr. Jablonski, I'm very grateful for your time. If I have any more questions before I turn in the article this afternoon, may I call you?"

"You sure can." The detective pulled over a pad and started to write down his office number.

"You don't have to do that," Petey said. "Just tell me."

Jablonski told him. "I'll give you my home phone, too. In case I decide to have lunch there."

Petey rattled off both numbers. "Correct?"

"One hundred percent. Now remember, keep your eyes open and *observe*."

"You bet, Mr. Jablonski." Petey started to leave.

"And don't forget to send me a copy of the interview."

"Oh, I will! Don't worry."

When he was alone again, Jablonski put his memory to the test by attempting to recall Mikki's home number. After drawing an absolute blank, he finally realized that Shirley had never given it to him. He checked his Rolodex and dialed. After four rings the answering machine picked up. Following the beep, he began to leave a message when a older woman's voice cut in.

"This is Mikki's aunt, Mr. Jablonski. We've had a few people pester us lately, mostly fans who want to talk to Mikki, so I've started to screen our calls."

"A wise move. Is the young lady available to talk?"

"One moment."

Mikki picked up an extension. "Jack, I was just sitting here thinking of you."

"I'm flattered."

"Did you have a nice Thanksgiving?"

"It had its moments. How about you?"

"It was okay. My sister came down from Bakersfield and the gang from the station all showed up for dinner. Except for His Eminence, who sent regrets."

"I saw your cohorts the other night. I must say, the show needs your touch."

"Tell that to the news director."

"Maybe I will. Here's why I called. I'd like your permission to spend a little money."

"Sure. On what?"

"There's a man I heard about named Ed Merriweather. He specializes in advising celebrities on how to protect themselves from the over-adoring public."

"In my case, the horse has already been stolen."

"Not according to your aunt. She says you're getting a few unsolicited phone calls these days."

There was a moment of silence. "Do you know something I don't know?"

"Not at all, Mikki. I just thought you might feel better, I know I would, if you took every precaution possible not only to protect your physical well-being but to preserve your peace of mind as well."

"To tell you the truth, Jack, you'd think some of the nightmares I've been having were out of a book by Stephen King. How much does Mr. Merriweather cost?"

"I have no idea. If he's too expensive, we won't seek his counsel. But I'd like your permission to contact him."

"You got it."

"Good. One more thing, Mikki. I want to spend time with you tomorrow going over the events of the day you were attacked."

"Sure. But what will that prove?"

"Let's find out. Could I finagle another one of those great lunches?"

Mikki laughed. "What would you like Hilda to make?"

"Anything at all?"

"Anything."

"I'm crazy about soufflés. I'm sure your cook can make one, but can she carry it from the kitchen to the patio without it collapsing?"

"We'll eat in the dining room. One o'clock?"

"Perfect."

As Jablonski hung up the phone, he heard the front door open. "Petey?" he called out.

"It's Marla May Willowbrook," a deep female voice announced. "May I enter?"

"By all means," he called out.

The woman, in full gypsy regalia, shuffled into the office. He stood up and made a half bow. "Have my waves been acting up again?"

"On the contrary. You seem to be quite serene."

What then? Jablonski wondered.

The old woman looked around the office. "First time I've ever been in here. I particularly like the beige walls and the hunting prints. Very homey." She turned back to the detective. "Where's Shirley?"

"With your abilities, Miss Willowbrook, I'm surprised you have to ask. She's taking a long weekend."

She inquired, "May I be seated?"

"Of course." Tentatively, the old woman lowered herself into the chair previously occupied by Petey. "As soon as I cross over, you may put forward any question you wish."

"Wha . . . ?"

"Ssssh!" She made a steeple over her bosom with her fingertips and closed her eyes. After what seemed an eternity, her breathing became deeper.

Jablonski figured that was his cue. "Tell me the name of the last visitor I had."

"A young body was recently in this room."

The old fake, Jablonski thought to himself. She saw the kid when he left. "What was his problem?"

Another pause. "The body doesn't know its problem."

What?

"The body will be back."

That ain't good enough. "When?"

"The body will be back."

A safe bet.

"Help the body."

"How can I help the body?"

"Help the body."

Jablonski waited another minute. When nothing more transpired, he cleared his throat. The old woman's eyelids fluttered.

"Are you all right?" he asked solicitously.

She sat up straight. "I'm fine. What did I say?"

"Pardon me?"

"What did I say when I was in the trance?"

"You don't know what you said?"

"Of course not. How could I know?"

"More to the point, how could you *not* know?"

"Communing is a subconscious act. I was hoping I said something to open your mind."

"Why do you think my mind needs opening?"

She drilled the detective with a laserlike gaze. "Together, there is much good ahead for the two of us. I feel it."

"Are you suggesting we team up?"

"When appropriate."

Wait long enough and everything gets down to a buck, Jablonski thought to himself.

Marla May added, "Earlier in my life, I assisted the men in blue."

"Where was that?"

"As a young woman, back in Shaker Heights." Jablonski looked perplexed. "A suburb of Cleveland. A substantial neighborhood. I grew up there."

"If I may pry, what crime did you help them solve?"

"It wasn't exactly a crime. My grandfather had gone shopping in the city center and couldn't remember where he had parked his car. After the authorities failed to find the machine, my mother, one of the very few who respected my gifts, by the way, asked me to intervene."

"And you were able to lead them to it?"

"So to speak." She adjusted the large hoop earring that hung from her right ear. "I'm sure I don't have to tell you that psychics are used regularly by many of the nation's police forces. Unfortunately, they are usually called in when all else had failed and the vibrations have begun to fade."

Jablonski stood up. "I shall certainly keep your kind offer in mind, although I'm afraid there is slight chance that I will ever take you up on it."

Marla May didn't move. "Mr. Jablonski, how often have you been able to solve some problem because of an idea that seemed to come out of thin air?"

"Many times."

"I rest my case."

"What case?"

"Has it ever occurred to you that *you* may have psychic gifts?"

"Never."

"I think there can be no doubt of it. It's just that, compared to mine, yours are underdeveloped." She struggled to her feet. "You get to the truth *ultimately*. I might be able to help you speed things up. Consider me an expediter."

He nodded and thought to himself, I consider you a hustler.

"How unkind of you, Mr. Jablonski," she said, responding to his unspoken assertion. "However, I feel you will see light." She started for the door, tightening the Spanish shawl around her shoulders. "I must return to my sanctuary. I have an inordinately busy weekend." Jablonski followed her into the outer office. At the front door she turned and said, "By the way, there is an answering service on my line. Feel free to call anytime." She let herself out and disappeared down the lane.

The detective picked his car up at the Shell station and stopped by the neighborhood supermarket. After stocking up on supplies, he went home. At the sight of her master, Snoopy performed her usual ritual dance.

"Take it easy, Snoop," he told her, "you'll last longer." The dog followed him into the cottage.

For lunch Jablonski opened a can of vegetable soup. While it was heating, he put together a ham and cheese sandwich. As he was eating, Snoopy sat silently on the floor next to him, her great liquid brown eyes looking up at him beseechingly. "Remember what the book said?" he asked the dog. "You don't get fed from the table."

In response, she scratched her right ear.

Jablonski thought to himself how easy it would be if Marla May was right. He looked down at his pet. "What do you think, Snoop? All these years have I possessed hidden gifts? Is it possible I could crank myself into a trance and come up with the name, address, and social security number of the bum who attacked Mikki?"

Snoopy began whining.

"I see you got the idea. If I could unlock the unknown, we'd be so rich we'd eat like kings. You could have filet mignon every meal. Or caviar."

Without warning, Snoopy jumped up into his lap and gave him a kiss on the mouth.

"You women are all the same. You're only interested in material things." He got up and carried the dog into the kitchen. When he reached up and retrieved a box of doggie treats from the cabinet, she began to bark wildly. "I hear you." He extracted a cookie and held it up. "Now don't take off my hand, okay?"

When he returned to the office, he found that Sergeant Baxter had left Ed Merriweather's telephone number on the answering machine. After dialing, a recorded voice told him the consulting firm was closed for the weekend. Frustrated, he sighed and requested that Mr. Merriweather call him back on Monday.

CHAPTER TWELVE

CLEM Barren didn't have to leave for work until five P.M. Ever since the attack on Mikki, he had spent the four o'clock hour each afternoon, clicker in hand, prowling through the local news programs that aired weekdays on the three network affiliates. He wondered if he would ever again find anyone like his Madonna of the red hair and the soft lips.

Every time he saw her on location, he wanted to go up and put his arms around her tiny waist. But there were always too many people watching.

He changed channels and peered at a thin-faced brunette who was talking to the camera about the latest disaster in the Mideast. Why did they hire *her*? he wondered. She's nothing. *Less* than nothing. He clicked again. This time he came up in the middle of some banter between a male anchor and a pretty young woman with mouse-brown hair. He had noticed her several times in the past few days during his forays across the dial. He waited patiently until she turned and spoke to him. She looked pretty good but she had a problem with her voice. It sounded like it came out of her nose. He moved to another channel. A weather girl was pointing to an oncoming storm front currently over San Francisco. The fact that she was black immediately removed her from consideration. It wasn't that he was prejudiced. He just couldn't imagine himself getting mixed up with someone of a different race. Click. Click. Click.

He shut off the television set and went outside. Using the jerry-built chinning bar he'd erected in his pocket-sized backyard, he pulled himself up fifty times. When he had finished, he took a shower, dressed in a flannel shirt and a pair of rough denims, then set off for work.

After traveling the side streets for several blocks, he joined the traffic flow on Sepulveda Boulevard and headed north. After several blocks he reached down and snapped on the radio. He fished around and found a station that was playing Andy Williams's recording of "Moon River." He hoped things at the restaurant wouldn't be too busy tonight. He wanted to take another look at the ten o'clock news on Channel Three. The blonde with the dimple in her chin was the best bet so far.

But, deep down, he knew he was kidding himself. There'd never again be anyone like Mikki. His beautiful, broken Mikki.

CHAPTER THIRTEEN

EARLY Saturday morning, having failed to hear anything from Daphne concerning their daughter's condition, Jablonski called Atlantic City.

"Nothing's happened," his wife informed him. "Absolutely nothing. But, as you know, forecasting the birth of a child is not an exact science."

"Maybe Marla May Willowbrook could get a better fix on the date."

"Who?"

"That old psychic next door to my office. If you're going to be there until Christmas, it'd relieve my mind to know about it."

"It isn't necessary to get yourself all cranked up, Jack. If you get lonely, you can always fly here and visit for a few days."

"Maybe I will."

Jablonski spent the rest of the morning giving Snoopy an indoctrination course in the art of heeling. After an hour of jerking the poor animal around, he found himself overcome with such pangs of guilt that he took her to the pet store and picked up a bag of special treats. Back in the car, he offered one to Snoopy. She sniffed at it delicately, turned away, and stretched out on the seat. "Go ahead and punish me," Jablonski said wryly.

After returning to the cottage, he filled Snoopy's water bowl and scratched her under the chin. "I'll be back after lunch. Stay out of the begonias." As he pulled away, the puppy was splayed against the gate to the backyard, crying her heart out. He felt like a bastard.

* * *

Mikki looked a lot better than she had the first time he saw her. Her thick red hair was carefully brushed and tied back in a ponytail, and she was wearing an expensive pale blue beaded caftan. The crusts over her facial wounds seemed less formidable and the new bandages that covered her eyes were smaller. More important, she was livelier. When he mentioned this, she replied, "The doctor said I don't have to take that goddamn dope anymore, except at bedtime. Being drugged when you're already depressed is no fun at all."

"I shouldn't think so."

She smiled wanly. "Now I'm only miserable."

At Jablonski's urging, Mikki spent the first part of the meal telling him about life on the modest farm in California's Salinas Valley where she had grown up. She recalled the time after her father died, leaving her mother to struggle with the upbringing of two little girls. She concluded ruefully, "We didn't have too many laughs."

"How old were you when they crowned you Grape Queen?"

"Twenty-one. That was just a local thing. My big break didn't come until three years later when I got picked to be Miss Napa Valley." She felt around the area in front of her until she located the serving spoon. "More soufflé?"

"Absolutely." He held up his plate. "To the left of the casserole dish," he directed. Deftly she ladled out a generous portion. "I'm curious, how did you make the transition from beauty queen to weather girl?"

"Everything's timing. Old Uncle Will was one of the people judging the contest."

"Waterbury, the Channel Ten anchorman?"

"Yes. At the time, the station was looking for a fresh face. He said he'd mention me to the management, if I was interested."

"And everything was on the up and up?"

"If you're wondering whether he made a pass at me, no. Actually, it was sort of refreshing not to get hit on. Will honestly seemed to think I had something special. A few weeks later I got a call from the station. I went down to Los Angeles for an audition. The news director at the time put me on camera and gave me a couple of things to read. I was so raw I didn't know enough to be scared."

"And you got the job."

"Not right away. The woman who was doing weather worked out her contract while they trained me." She sighed. "And now all that's over."

Jablonski ignored her comment. "Sergeant Baxter mentioned that recently you had a boyfriend. What about him?"

"Tommy?"

"She didn't tell me his name. The one who never slept over at your apartment because there was nothing but a single bed in the place."

"We called it quits a couple of months ago."

"Amicably?"

"On the contrary. Tommy was a son of a bitch." She picked up the silver bell from the table and jingled it. "He was in New York the night I got worked over."

"Could he have been mad enough to hire a friend?"

"He wouldn't spend the money. The guy was so goddamn stingy it was sickening. That's why we finally broke up. I'll go Dutch three hundred and sixty-four nights a year but not on my birthday." The cook came in from the kitchen and began removing the plates. "I hope you like the dessert. Tell him, Hilda."

"Prune whip with homemade brownies."

Jablonski cautioned the cook, "Not too much."

Once they were alone again, Mikki asked, "Are you really a shadow of your former self?"

"Perhaps not a shadow."

"I thought you were cute the way you were."

"I'm cuter now." Jablonski shifted his weight. "Any other guys in your life in recent months?"

"Nope. Unless you want to count a rat bastard who date-raped me one night."

Jablonski took out a pad and pencil. "Tell me about him."

Mikki grimaced. "His name is Sabinson. He's a field producer at Channel Ten."

"What's that?"

"Someone who handles remote segments on news shows."

"Without going into detail, where and when did this reprehensible episode take place?"

"In Mexico City. The two of us, and a technical crew, spent a few days down there doing a series of pieces on the drug situation."

"That was the time when your former apartment was appropriated by the bald-headed note writer?"

"Yep."

Jablonski snapped shut the notebook. "Which eliminates Sabinson as your assailant."

"He could never be a suspect. He's skinny and kind of weasel-faced." Mikki sighed. "I wish I'd turned him in."

"Why didn't you?"

"It's too hard to keep that kind of thing quiet. Much as I would have liked to bust his balls, the publicity wouldn't have helped my career any. The bastard knew that."

Hilda brought the desserts.

Mikki asked, "Can the inquisition be put on hold until we've finished lunch?"

"Indeed it can."

Later the cook served coffee on the patio. It was a warm, clear day, with soft Santa Ana winds that carried in the sweet smell of honeysuckle while gently rustling the bushes and the trees.

Mikki observed, "Same kind of weather we had that awful night."

"Where were your aunt and the cook that evening?"

"Both of them have places of their own. I was here alone."

"Now your aunt is staying with you full-time, right?"

"Yes."

"I wonder if you'd ask her to make me copies of the envelopes that the notes came in."

Mikki felt around the top of the small table next to her chair until she located the phone. She punched the intercom button. When her aunt answered, she repeated Jablonski's request.

"What do you want with those, Jack?"

"I'd like to see if there's any sort of pattern."

"Pattern?"

"When the notes were mailed. Where they were mailed." He folded his napkin and sat back in his chair. "Now I want you to walk me through your schedule the day you were attacked."

"Starting when?"

"The moment you opened your big blue eyes that morning."

"How do you know my eyes are blue? You said you didn't watch our show."

"I saw it once or twice."

She took a moment to collect her thoughts. "There was only one thing that sticks out in my mind. And it was scary as hell."

"From the beginning please."

"Okay. Got up. Breakfast. Went to the gym and worked out. Washed my hair. Took a little nap after lunch." She smiled. "A person has to look rested. Then I dressed. Drove to the station."

"What time did you get there?"

"About seven-thirty. Makeup and hair usually take the better part of an hour. From eight-thirty to about nine-fifteen I chatted with the assignment editor and looked at a couple of pieces of tape that I had to narrate that night. Will Waterbury was being honored at some banquet and wasn't going to get to the station until just before airtime, so I had to do the promo."

"What's a promo?"

"Every night at about nine-twenty we do a fifteen-second live insert in one of the commercial breaks in the movie. You know, headlines for the news. Right after that one of the page boys brought an envelope to my dressing room."

"Where did he get it?"

"The guard at the front gate brought it over."

"That's the note that concluded, 'Maybe I'll put my mark on you. Then you'll be mine forever.' "

"It scared the hell out of me. I got so upset I didn't think I could do the show."

"But you did."

She shuddered. "Barely."

"Then what?"

"In the parking lot I discovered my car had a flat tire. I was in the guard station calling the Triple-A when Will stopped and offered to drive me home. I was goddamn grateful because I didn't feel like waiting forty-five minutes for help to arrive."

"Go on."

"On the way home I used his car phone to call the Valley Patrol. I like to have them waiting for me when I arrive, so they can walk through the house to check everything. While they were looking around, I made Will a nightcap. He suggested I ought to take a sleeping pill to quiet myself down and I did. The patrolmen took off. I put on the alarm and Will left through the garden."

"That entrance isn't wired into the system?"

"It is now."

As Jablonski was refilling his coffee cup, he asked, "How about you? More caffeine juice?"

"A touch."

"You left the sliding door to your bedroom open?"

"I love the Santa Anas. Before all this happened, sometimes I used to sleep outside on the patio when it was warm enough."

"What time do you figure you went to sleep?"

"Probably before midnight."

"Because of the medication you were dead to the world ten or fifteen minutes later."

"I must have been. I never heard the dog, and he had a bark on him that would blow you away."

"No one's been able to pinpoint the time of the attack?"

"Not as far as I know." She looked up. "I hear Auntie Belle coming."

A moment later the woman approached and handed Jablonski a manila folder. "I hope you're not tiring out our young lady," she said.

"I'm fine, Belle," Mikki protested. "Talking to Jack makes me feel like maybe there's some hope we'll nail the animal."

"This is everything?" the detective asked the woman.

"Copies of all the envelopes," she replied. "Except for the first one asking for the photo, which we never kept." She leaned down and gave Mikki a hug. "Did you tell Mr. Jablonski what the plastic surgeon said?"

"Good news I hope."

Mikki replied, "Seems maybe I didn't get marked up as badly as everyone first thought. Not that that'll change things much. In my case, half a loaf is the same as none."

"Now you just stop being negative," Belle told her niece. "Things will work out. You'll see."

Mikki turned toward Jablonski. "Will they, Jack?"

The detective paused before he answered. "Quicker, if you'd give yourself a break."

"What's that supposed to mean?"

"Self-pity slows a person down." He stood up. "No charge for the philosophy. I'll be in touch Monday after I talk to the protection expert." He nodded to Aunt Belle. "Madam, a pleasure." He turned back to his client. "Your servant, Mikki. My regards to the chef."

Jablonski helped himself to a chocolate-covered mint from a dish that rested on a shelf near the front door. After unwrapping the foil that encased it, he savored its tangy flavor. He looked around to be sure he was unobserved, then stuffed a half dozen more into his jacket pocket. He rescued his fedora from the coat closet and stepped out into the beautiful California afternoon.

CHAPTER FOURTEEN

As soon as he finished dinner that evening, Jablonski removed the calendar that hung on the kitchen wall and brought it into the living room. After consuming the remaining three mints he had purloined, he cleared off the coffee table and spread out the envelopes that Mikki's aunt had given him. While Snoopy dozed near the baseboard heating element next to the kitchen door, he studied the layout in front of him. The cancellation stamps indicated that each of the notes had been mailed in the 91604 area. He phoned Information and was told that the branch that serviced this section of the city was located on Laurel Canyon Boulevard just south of Ventura Boulevard. Mikki O'Reilly lived less than a mile away.

"Wanna take a ride, Snoop?" Instantly the dog jumped up, ready to go. "We're gonna do a little detecting over in the Valley and then pick up a copy of Sunday's New York *Times*. How does that grab you?" The puppy looked up at him longingly. "I asked you a question. Now talk to me. Speak!"

Snoopy lay down.

After struggling into his jacket, Jablonski decided to forego the fedora. He put the dog in the front seat of the Honda and climbed in next to her. He drove up to Sunset Boulevard and traveled east toward the San Diego Freeway. The Saturday night speeders and exhibition lane changers were considerably more numerous than usual. This prompted Jablonski to hug the curb and hunker down behind the wheel, the better to ignore the frequent blasts from the Porsches and BMWs whose drivers were annoyed that he was exceeding the posted speed limit by only ten miles per hour.

Once in the Valley he turned onto the Ventura Freeway and, several miles later, exited at Laurel Canyon. Shortly after that he was parked in front of the branch post office for the 91604 area. He got out of the car and walked over to one of the several mailboxes that stood on the sidewalk in front of the building. Using a pen light, he leaned down and read the pickup times that were printed on a metal placard. The last collection, Monday through Friday, was five-thirty P.M. The first collection the following morning was six-thirty A.M., except for Saturday and Sunday.

At an all-night pharmacy a block away, he picked up a copy of the New York *Times*. On the drive home he leaned over and told Snoopy, "We may be onto something useful, my girl. The stamps on Mikki's envelopes were all canceled on a weekday in the A.M., which means sometime between midnight and noon."

Snoopy wormed her way up on Jablonski's lap and stuck her head under his jacket. "I know all this is a tad boring, but if you want to live with a detective, you could at least pretend to be interested." The dog dug in deeper. "Very well then, I'll be quiet."

Jablonski recalled, in two of the missives, Mikki's assailant had used the word "night." By extrapolating, he decided this might indicate that the man's pattern was to watch Mikki's show from ten to eleven, sit down at his computer and write her a note, then jump in his car and drop off the envelope at the post office. Probably before midnight. Or maybe he worked late and performed the same routine in some round-the-clock business before stopping by the post office on his way home. In either case, an envelope would sit in the mailbox during the wee small hours of the morning until it was collected at six-thirty A.M.

Back in the cottage Jablonski cross-checked the dates on which his client had received the epistles, as annotated by Aunt Belle, against the dates of the cancelled stamps on the envelopes. In every case the delivery was made the day after the note was mailed.

There was one other option that had to be considered: the attacker hadn't actually posted the letters until the morning *after* he wrote them. But, considering the intimate feelings expressed in the notes, Jablonski found it unlikely that the man would have been able to restrain himself that long.

The detective sat back and sighed in frustration. None of his conclusions was of any value unless Mikki's assailant began writing to her again. If he did that, and followed the same pattern as before, the post office could be staked out weeknights starting at eleven o'clock. Any bald-headed driver who showed up in a small pickup truck with out-of-state plates and a burned-out headlight could be picked up for questioning. Then, if it was indicated, he could be booked for assault. In the event his fingerprints matched up with those on the notes Mikki had received, he was on his way to the slammer. Simple as that.

But the final missive, *Now that your ugly I must give you up,* written after the man had disfigured his love object, seemed to minimize the possibility that he would ever communicate with Mikki again.

Jablonski decided to go to bed. He was midway through the nightly ritual with his electric toothbrush when the phone rang. He turned off the mechanism and hurried into the bedroom.

"Yes?"

A high, tremulous voice said, "Mr. Jablonski?"

"Who's this?" he asked.

"Petey. Petey Bosworth."

"Hello, Petey. How'd the interview turn out?"

The boy ignored the question. "After our meeting, I started thinking about my English teacher, Miss Montgomery."

"What are you talking about?"

"Please. Just listen to me." Abandoning his previously elaborate vocabulary, the words came out in a torrent. "Miss Montgomery's the best teacher in the world. She's sweet and pretty and understanding, always has time for you. On three or four occasions this semester she's come to class sort of banged up. One day she had a black eye. Said she stumbled into a door sill. Another time, when she had a cut above her lip, she told us what a klutz she was. I didn't think too much about it until yesterday after you talked about observing things. I realized that for the past couple of months I'd just been *looking* at Miss Montgomery, but I hadn't been *observant*." He took a breath. "On Wednesday of this week she came to class and her hand was wrapped up in a bandage. She was very tired and sort of pale. After our meeting it occurred to me: maybe all this time her new husband has been beating her up. Last year, before she got married, she was always bright and chipper. But now, she doesn't laugh anymore. Anyway, after I'd turned in my column to the printer, I got in touch with some of my friends and, as of this morning, we've been staking out Miss Montgomery's house."

"You've what?" Jablonski asked incredulously.

"We started at eight. Billy took eight to twelve, Jon twelve to four, Sam four to eight and I'll be on until midnight."

"It's pretty late. What do your parents have to say about this?"

"My parents are on a cruise and won't be home until December tenth."

"Is anyone staying with you?"

"Alicia lives in. She doesn't care. She's old. Goes to bed right after supper."

"I think . . ."

"Please, Mr. Jablonski, listen to me! I'm using an outside pay phone on Pacific Coast Highway near where Chautuaqua comes down the hill. It's about a block from where Miss Montgomery lives. It's a warm night and her windows are open. On and off, since right after dinner, the two of them have been arguing about how much liquor he drinks. A little while ago he batted her around and finally knocked her down. Since then, there hasn't been a sound out of her. I think she's lying on the floor. Maybe dead. He hit her real hard."

"Petey, do you know the exact address of the house?"

"I already called nine-one-one. They said they'd send a squad car and that I should stay here by the phone." There was a sharp intake of breath. "I can see flashing lights about a mile away. Mr. Jablonski, I'm afraid. What if the guy decides to go after me for turning him in?"

"The police won't ask you to accompany them to the door. And they won't use your name. As soon as you have directed them to Miss Montgomery's house, go home."

"But . . ."

"It's an unfortunate fact of life, Petey, certain married people fight a lot. Sometimes the battles can be brutal. Now that you've done your good deed for the day I want you to promise me you'll abandon further surveillance." There was a silence. "Well?"

"I can't promise that, Mr. Jablonski. If you knew Miss Montgomery, you'd understand. She's kind of vulnerable. She needs somebody to take care of her." The boy's tone turned urgent again. "I've got to go now. I was really upset. Thanks for reassuring me."

"Petey . . ." The detective hung up the phone. "Puppy love," he mumbled to himself.

Jablonski adjourned to the bathroom and finished brushing his teeth. He crawled into bed and started to separate the various sections of the *Times*. "You think this newspaper's big and fat out here, Snoop? You ought to see the eastern edition. Twice this size. Guaranteed to give you a hernia or your money back."

He had worked his way through the Arts and Leisure section and half of the Book Review when the telephone rang again. He looked at his watch. Five after eleven.

"Hello?"

"You'll never believe this, Mr. Jablonski."

The detective sighed. "What won't I believe, Petey?"

"Guess who answered the door."

"I can't imagine."

"Miss Montgomery answered the door. I was hiding behind a big tree in the front yard so I could hear everything that anyone said. She told the officers that they must be mistaken. Everything was fine. Then her husband came up behind her and put his arm around her waist." The boy's confusion was total. "What's going on, Mr. Jablonski?"

"I wish I knew how to answer your question, Petey. Just let me say that, when Person *A* loves Person *B* too much, as seems to be the case with your English teacher, Person *A* may get confused about what's right and what's wrong."

"You believe what I told you, don't you?"

"Indeed I do. Now go to sleep."

Petey replied, "I can't. I'm still down on Pacific Coast Highway."

Jablonski adopted a stern tone. "What goes on between Miss Montgomery and her husband is really their business, isn't it? Now I want you to stop spying and go on back home. If Alice, or whatever her name is, wakes up and finds that your bed is empty, she's liable to worry herself to death."

Reluctantly, Petey replied, "Well, okay."

"How far away do you live?"

"About a mile. I've got my bike."

"Be careful. There's a lot of cuckoos loose on Saturday nights."

"What time is it, Mr. Jablonski?"

"Ten after eleven."

"Gee, I better hurry. 'Saturday Night Live' is on in fifteen minutes." The line went dead.

Jablonski folded up the papers and tossed them on the floor and turned out the light. With Daphne away he wondered how he would fill the time Sunday.

CHAPTER FIFTEEN

MONDAY morning, thoroughly tired of being by himself, Jablonski looked forward to the office, where contact with another human being was readily available. Upon arrival, he was dismayed to discover that Shirley wasn't in her appointed spot. His mood quickly changed from disappointment to apprehension when he heard his secretary's voice coming from the inner sanctum.

"Mommy wants you to come out to her desk *now,* Saul. Mr. Jablonski will be here any minute."

"Naaaaaw!" a young child's voice answered.

Good God, the detective wondered, has she brought the sprout to the office? It can't be. But it was. Saul was seated in the big upholstered chair behind the desk, busily scribbling away in a coloring book.

Jablonski cleared his throat. "Good morning. And what have we here?"

"Jack! I know how you feel about kids but this is just one of those things. The woman who works for us . . . her car wouldn't start. Rob couldn't get a sub for his eight o'clock class at UCLA. So either I had to stay home with the baby or bring him here."

"Is Saul's rescue imminent?"

"It's hard to say. Our babysitter doesn't belong to the Triple-A. A friend of hers with cables is going to give Piedad a jump start."

I'd like to give Piedad a jump start, Jablonski thought to himself.

The phone began to ring. Saul picked it up and dropped it on the floor.

Shirley said, "Jack, if you could get that, I'll take the baby outside."

"And kindly close the door," Jablonski directed. He retrieved the instrument. "Hello?"

"This is Ed Merriweather. Is this Mr. Jablonski?"

"The same."

"I'm returning your call of Friday."

"Ah yes. The protection consultant." Jablonski explained his connection with Mikki O'Reilly and requested the earliest possible appointment with the expert.

The man answered, "I'm free at twelve today. Is that too soon?"

"That would be fine."

Merriweather gave him an address in Beverly Hills.

"If I may ask, what is your fee?"

"In view of the fact that your client has already been assaulted, there will be no charge for a consultation. Once she recovers, if she wants to sign up with my company for continuing services, we can discuss money at that point."

"Very generous of you."

"Miss O'Reilly is a great asset to the Channel Ten News," Merriweather said. "I miss her pretty face."

"I'll pass that along," Jablonski promised.

"By the way, I assume you have copies of the notes she received."

"Of course."

"Would you mind bringing them along? I'd like to cross-check them against our data base."

"Excellent!"

Jablonski hung up and dialed Mikki and told her about the appointment he had just arranged. "I'll come by your place later and give you a report."

"Perfect!"

"I need a favor."

"I hope it's something I can do sitting down."

"It is. Give me the names of your associates on the news program."

"You mean the on-the-air people?"

"And any others you dealt with on a daily basis."

"Like the director and the stage manager?"

"Exactly. And the cameramen who went out on the remote broadcasts with you."

"What do you want with that stuff?"

"Maybe one of them saw something that can be of help to us."

"Let me mull for a minute." Presently Mikki dictated a list. "Okay?" she asked when she had finished.

"One more thing. Is there any way you can get a social security number for each of these people?"

"That could be a tough one. Maybe. My makeup lady has a daughter who's a secretary or something in the finance department at the station."

"If you strike out, I can do it. I'm just looking to speed things up."

"Let me give it a shot."

The detective said, "If you're successful, call my secretary." After hanging up, Jablonski studied the list of names. He eliminated several that seemed extraneous, then buzzed Shirley. "Are you available for the day's instructions or are you changing a diaper?"

"What is it you want?"

"Mikki may be phoning in a list of social security numbers. If she does, run them through our computer and see what you come up with."

"Anything else?"

"Get me Sergeant Baxter." Minutes later the intercom buzzed twice. Jablonski picked up. "Good morning, Nancy. I trust you had a pleasant weekend."

"It was passable. How about you, Jablonski? You have any fun?"

"Nothing comes immediately to mind." Jablonski mentioned the nine-one-six-oh-four postmark on the envelopes that Mikki had received. "Did you guys pick up on this?"

"I noticed it, but I didn't think it was relevant."

"It probably isn't, at least not for the moment. I was wondering . . . ?"

"Yes?"

"As far as you've been able to determine, has the cretin who messed up Mikki left his mark on anyone else in the vicinity?"

"There have been a bunch of serious harassment cases, and a few outright threats to people in the public eye, but nothing that's proved to be lethal. At least not in the past six months."

"That's something to be grateful for."

"How's Mikki doing?"

"Better."

"She got dealt a real bad hand." Nancy paused. "You know something, Jablonski. You and I had no business feeling sorry for ourselves."

"What do you mean?"

"Thanksgiving Eve when I ran into you in the deli, I was feeling pretty blue. My eighteen-year-old was visiting his dad down in San Diego. There was nobody to go home to."

"That's tough."

"To my highly trained eye, you weren't bubbling over with joy either, all alone in that booth bent over a plate of turkey. Confess. How close were you to wallowing in despair?"

"I never wallow. I may occasionally bask, luxuriate or, now and then, relish. But I never wallow."

Nancy laughed. "In addition to all your other good qualities, are you going to turn out to be funny?"

"A funny private eye? I think maybe that's an oxymoron. By the way, at noon today I've got a date with your friend Ed Merriweather."

"Tell him hello."

"I'll do that."

"And don't let his phony British accent throw you off. I happen to know he was born in Milwaukee."

Jablonski no sooner had hung up the phone when Saul began screaming offstage. The detective jumped up and ran over to the office door and flung it open.

"What in the hell . . . ?"

"It's nothing," Shirley yelled over the din. "Saul was going to put his finger in the automatic pencil sharpener and I had to give him a tap on the behind."

"If that's what happens when you tap him, I shudder to think of the brouhaha that would result if you gave him a good smack."

Shirley hugged the little boy, who immediately began to calm down. "Rob and I don't believe in hitting children."

"Hitting and smacking are two completely different acts. I'm surprised your psychiatrist husband has failed to grasp the distinction. Or you, for that matter." Jablonski reached into his pocket and produced a five-dollar bill. "Take the tyke out for a nice long walk and buy him something sinful like a double malt with two scoops of pistachio nut."

"Make it ten and I'll stop by the toy store and get him a Teenage Mutant Ninja Turtle game. That'll keep him quiet for half an hour."

"A what?"

"Never mind." Shirley took the five. "I'll go for the balance. We'll be back shortly."

"Please, do not rush. I don't have to leave here until eleven-thirty." Jablonski turned back into his private office and slammed the connecting door.

For the next hour he mentally pawed over the few seemingly inconsequential clues that Mikki's attacker had left behind. Having completed this exercise, he decided that there was absolutely no question about it: both he and the cops were traveling down a road that led nowhere.

* * *

Ed Merriweather's establishment took up the entire second story of a brick building on the corner of Charleyville and Beverly Drive in the heart of Beverly Hills. A discreet mahogany plaque next to the main entrance door bore the legend: Merriweather Consultants. The waiting room was filled with white wicker furniture and the large coffee table was loaded with current issues of various magazines. Tall reddish-orange fake flowers stood proudly in vases that rested on each side of the single imposing window that overlooked the street below. Pastel washes depicting ballerinas in varying poses lined the walls, and soft background music wafted out into the air from unseen speakers.

After the detective had announced himself to the starlet who resided behind the glass partition separating the reception room from the main offices in the rear of the suite, he took a seat. A few minutes later the door to the inner sanctum opened. A sable-coated woman who appeared to be nearing eighty, in spite of the best efforts of what must have been an army of plastic surgeons, stepped into the reception room. She was followed by a thin, effete looking, elegantly dressed man of Jablonski's age.

"Thank you, Mr. Merriweather," she said. "You've made me feel ever so relieved."

"Not to worry, Mrs. Felson," he replied in clipped tones. "I'm quite sure you won't have any more trouble if you follow those few simple suggestions." He opened the front door for her and bowed. After she had disappeared around the corner, Merriweather turned to the visitor. "You must be Jablonski."

The detective struggled to his feet. "Right."

Merriweather held out his hand. "Mrs. Felson is a first for me," he observed, shaking his head. "Her *hairdresser* has received telephoned threats on his life."

"How urbane."

"Apparently the young man has a very prominent and active sexual career. Works both sides of the street. It's brought him much grief."

Jablonski produced the notes Mikki had received. "You wanted to see these?"

Merriweather took them. "I'll have copies made. Wouldn't be a bad idea to see whether Miss O'Reilly's attacker has written anyone else in the area." He swung wide a door that led to the rear section, then dropped the missives off with his secretary for duplication.

Jablonski followed his host down a long corridor off of which half a dozen well-appointed offices opened. In several, the occupants, young men and women, were busily tapping away at computers. "Business is good," he observed.

Merriweather replied, "I don't have to tell you, a lot of what we do is donkey work." He directed his guest into an office at the end of the hall and indicated a Danish modern sofa set against the far wall. "Please. Make yourself comfortable." Merriweather slid into an expensive Eames chair. "Coffee? Or a soft drink?"

"No thanks."

"Well then, to the business at hand. Where would you like me to start?"

"What kind of a data base do you have?"

"There are over seven thousand communications locked away in our secure room and backed up in our computer banks."

"Seven *thousand*!?" the detective responded incredulously.

"Of course, the vast majority of them are of no significance."

"How do you determine which ones are to be taken seriously?"

"Whenever I am first contacted, I consider each case to be potentially dangerous. Then I apply a set of procedures I've refined during the years. Most times it is a comparatively simple matter to separate the innocuous from the hazardous."

Jablonski helped himself to a piece of hard candy from a bowl on the cocktail table. "When I was with the FBI we were occasionally involved with nutcases trying to cozy up to various politicians. But we were pikers compared to you."

"You had Hinckley's attempted assassination of President Reagan," Merriweather pointed out.

Jablonski shook his head. "That was a bad time."

"There was no possible way the authorities could have hooked up the letters the young man wrote to Jodie Foster with what happened later."

"Unfortunately," Jablonski agreed.

"That episode is a perfect example of a person's hostility being displaced from the adored one to an authority figure. By killing the president, Hinckley intended to demonstrate how far he was willing to go in the name of love. Very tricky." Merriweather got up and walked over to the window and looked down at Beverly Drive.

"Other extreme cases that I'm familiar with are equally frightening. A few months back, an actress was shot dead by a man who had been writing to her for over two years. She'd changed residences several times, but that didn't help. When he decided to make his move, he hired a private detective who located the young woman by simply walking into the Department of Motor Vehicles and asking for her address."

"If I recall correctly, a couple of months later the California legislature plugged that loophole."

"Thank God." In response to his secretary's buzz Merriweather crossed over to his desk and flipped a switch. "Hold my calls, please, Lenore." He turned back to Jablonski. "Pretty young women, particularly those in front of the public, are fair game. We had another case out here that was especially macabre. The man came all the way from Scotland and brutally carved up an actress named Theresa Saldana with whom he was obsessed. Fortunately, she survived. Even went on to found an organization called 'Victims for Victims.' The group might be helpful to your client."

"I'll mention it." Jablonski sighed heavily. "What drives people to these insane acts, do you suppose?"

"Only a psychiatrist could tell you. And I'm not sure they always know."

Jablonski took another candy. "Mikki doesn't talk about it much, but I know she's extremely apprehensive that her assailant will try again. What can I tell her that might help put her mind to rest?"

Merriweather pulled open a file drawer in his desk and riffled through some papers. "This is a list of things we recommend to our clients. Most of the suggestions are obvious." He handed a document to Jablonski. "You'd be surprised how many well-known people there are who have never bothered to institute even the most basic procedures to protect themselves from the mentally deranged."

Jablonski looked over the compilation. "Mikki already moved once," he told Merriweather.

"That was *before* she was attacked. She should move again. And even that, as I said, is no guarantee she'll be safe. Almost anyone with the time to invest can probably locate her. A new residence merely increases the odds in her favor."

Jablonski went to the next item on the list. "Her phone isn't unlisted. I know she's had calls from fans as recently as this week."

Merriweather replied, "An easily correctable item. Farther down, you will see that I recommend that whoever opens a principal's mail be trained in the recognition of communications that should be subjected to further evaluation. Also, whoever screens telephone calls should be particularly perceptive."

"To date, Mikki's aunt has apparently been fulfilling these functions. How effectively, I can't say."

"I'd like to evaluate her. Those who *greet* visitors have an even greater challenge, because they must serve both screening and reporting functions and because they are at risk of violence themselves. Within the last year, two guards at one of the big studios were murdered by a man who had come to kill a particular star who was working on the lot at the time."

Jablonski answered, "Something to think about, particularly if Mikki is ever able to return to her job. I suspect that the security at the television station is not of the highest caliber." He read from the paper he was holding. " 'No mail should ever be addressed to a client's residence. Instead, a post office box should be used or the address of a lawyer or other business associate.' "

"That's a key point," Merriweather insisted. "And that includes one's driver's license as well."

"Item six on your list. What do you mean when you say, 'It is dangerous and irresponsible to publish information that makes it easier for those inappropriately pursuing the famous to successfully locate and attack the object of their attention'?"

"Most celebrities have press agents, people who are paid to get their clients' names in the newspapers. Many times they'll release a story about what function so-and-so is scheduled to attend. Things like that can be an invitation to disaster."

Jablonski scanned the other suggestions on Merriweather's list, then folded the paper and put it in his pocket. "Currently Mikki has a good alarm system and a guard who walks the property at night."

"That should reassure her."

"It doesn't seem to be enough to do the trick. My hope is, if I can get her involved in the problems of changing residences again and in instituting some of the other procedures you suggest, she won't spend so much time thinking about herself."

"If there's anything more I can do . . . ."

"I'm obliged. I'll see if I can't get Mikki's Aunt Belle to give you a call."

On their way out to the reception room Merriweather picked up the notes Jablonski had given him and handed them over. "I'll let you know if these lead anywhere."

"Appreciate it."

"Your client's apprehensions are justified, Mr. Jablonski. Whenever one of these fanatics has harrassed or attacked someone and is still at large, it shouldn't be assumed that he's no longer dangerous."

"An ominous thought, Mr. Merriweather," Jablonski observed. "Good day, sir."

CHAPTER SIXTEEN

It had been precisely four fifty-five P.M. on Thanksgiving Eve when the senior vice president of Channel Ten notified Arnold Tolkin, the station's news director, that he wanted to have lunch with him the following Monday. As a consequence, the director spent the entire weekend worrying about how best to answer certain questions that he knew the executive would put to him.

At the moment the news division was holding its own in the L.A. marketplace, so Tolkin, at least theoretically, should have been able to feel some degree of security. But, this wasn't the case. With Mikki O'Reilly out of the game, he knew that the probability of a ratings slip was very real.

The Monday following Thanksgiving, Tolkin, a light-skinned African-American, handsomer than the young Harry Belafonte had been, reported to the station dining room promptly at twelve-thirty. Seated at the elegantly appointed mahogany table, along with senior VP William Mansfield, an Ivy League type, was the station's owner and chairman, C.J. Matthews, a straight-laced, humorless old man. Briefly the news director wondered if, somehow, he had misunderstood the time at which he was to appear and, as a consequence, was late.

Noting the concern on Tolkin's face, the VP reassured him, "Mr. Matthews and I caucused early to discuss some matters not relevant to your department. Please sit down."

While the white-jacketed waiter silently placed plates of wilted spinach and bacon in front of each man, the chairman fired the first round.

"What now, Mr. Tolkin? Since fate has dealt us such a cruel hand, do we continue along with Will Waterbury in the anchor chair, minus Mikki O'Reilly, or do you have something more reassuring to suggest?"

"We're facing quite a challenge, sir," Tolkin said evenly.

"I am aware of that," the old man replied testily. "But we know from past experience what is likely to happen if Will is left all by his lonesome to carry the show." The chairman scooped up a forkful of salad and popped it into his mouth. "You've had nearly a month since Miss O'Reilly's unfortunate encounter to develop an alternative scenario."

After breaking his brain over the weekend, Tolkin had only been able to devise a stop-gap measure, one he hoped would keep top management at bay.

"At the appropriate moment, sir, I plan to introduce Mikki on the ten o'clock strip in a series of guest shots."

"Isn't she going to look sort of weird propped up at the news desk swathed in bandages?" the vice president inquired.

"I plan to send one of our mobile units out to her house, at weekly intervals, and tape interviews on the changes in her condition and state of mind. A sort of running report on how she is fighting her way back to normalcy. Maybe, if she is willing, we might even suggest she ask her assailant to turn himself in."

The two executives exchanged a long look before the chairman broke the silence. "Very imaginative, young man."

Inwardly, Tolkin began to breath more easily. He knew the odds of finding another potential star were practically nil and planned to use the time left to him to look for a new job.

CHAPTER SEVENTEEN

AFTER his meeting with Ed Merriweather, Jablonski had a bite of lunch at an open-air bistro on Beverly Drive, then drove over the hill to the San Fernando Valley, where he spent an hour with Mikki and her Aunt Belle, going over the consultant's suggestions.

"I know it's inconvenient to change residences a second time in six months, but I think it's something you should consider," Jablonski concluded.

"Hell, I don't mind that," Mikki retorted. "I probably would have done it anyway. This place spooks me."

"There are a lot of details involved in a move. Would you like me to discuss all this with your agent, or will you?"

"I'll take care of it," Belle interjected. "Mr. Veck's just as worried about what happens to Mikki as we are."

Jablonski turned back to the young woman. "Has your doctor said when you might be able to have eye surgery?"

"A couple of months. Things have to heal some more before they can try to make repairs."

"You're doing just fine," Aunt Belle said, patting Mikki's hand. She stood up. "If you'll excuse me, I'm going to call Mr. Merriweather and make a date for an indoctrination session."

Mikki waited until she heard her aunt's footsteps fade away on the polished wood floor of the hallway outside the living room. Then she asked wistfully, "You think we're gaining on him, Jack?"

"The creep?" Mikki nodded. "You want it straight?"

"Sure."

"At this point about all I can say is that we're not losing any ground." Jablonski didn't want to tell her that their best shot would come if her assailant decided to start writing letters again. "One more thing. What's the protocol involved in getting an appointment with the anchorman on your program?"

"Will Waterbury is very approachable. All you need is a humble attitude, preceded by a lot of bowing and scraping."

"You're not fond of him."

"He's sort of an institution in this town but, personally, I think he's carried away by the beauty of his own tooting."

Jablonski smiled at her choice of words. "He sounds tiresome."

"What do you expect to get out of Old Windy?"

"You never know. He was the last person who saw you before you were attacked."

"The police already went over that ground. Hell, after they talked to him, Will even did an on-the-air interview with the detective on the case."

"Nancy Baxter?"

"Yep. Friends of mine who saw the piece said it seemed like Will was mainly trying to establish that he had acted properly."

"Meaning?"

"That he did everything right: tucked me into bed, checked the alarm, and locked the back gate on his way out. Stuff like that."

"Why do you think he was so worried?"

"He's *always* worried. About everything. Thinks none of the copywriters know how to compose a lead. That the executive producer doesn't know beans about running a show. Will's a major pain in the ass."

"Thus warned, I shall proceed with caution. Will you pave the way, or should I just forge ahead?"

"Hand me the phone," Mikki directed. Within moments she had left word with the anchorman's secretary that Jablonski would be calling and that she would appreciate it if he was given an appointment. "Go get him, tiger," she told the detective as she hung up.

"Now, if you don't mind, I'd like you to steer me out to the patio. Nothing like a little sun to smooth out the kinks."

Once she was seated in a lounge chair by the pool, Jablonski promised to fill her in on the details of his forthcoming encounter with the anchorman. "Maybe he'll put *me* on television."

"Only if it'll advance his standing as an oracle."

On the way back to his office, Jablonski called Shirley on the car phone. "Expect me in twenty minutes."

"I'll meet you out front," she replied.

Alarmed, he asked, "What's the matter? Did the place burn down?"

"I want to show you the parking facilities I managed to acquire."

As he pulled up at his building on San Vicente, Shirley ran over to his car. "In there," she said, pointing to the gas station next door.

"In where?"

"There. Next to the Coke machine. That's your spot from now on. Twenty feet from your office and only four dollars a day. Saturdays and Sundays free."

"That's twenty bucks a week," Jablonski complained. "A thousand bucks a year!"

Shirley countered, "How much do you think those blinking traffic meters run? At fifty cents an hour you're depositing at *least* that much. Plus, now you'll have a secretary who doesn't spend half her time walking the streets trying to find where you parked your car."

"Very thoughtful," Jablonski acknowledged. After edging the Honda into its new home, he opened the office door and looked around cautiously, girding himself for another encounter with Shirley's small son.

"Saul's not here," his secretary explained.

"A great loss for us all. Kindly phone Will Waterbury's secretary at Channel Ten and get me the earliest appointment the man has available. Then come in and give me a report on your computer search."

While Shirley was making the arrangement he had requested, Jablonski dropped his fedora on the hat rack and repaired to the inner office. He thumbed through several phone slips on his desk. "What did Sergeant Baxter want?"

"She didn't say. Just to return her call." His secretary entered and put down the computer printouts. "Tomorrow at two-thirty."

"Tomorrow at two-thirty what?"

"Mr. Waterbury."

Jablonski picked up the stack of papers. "Anything interesting?"

"Some. I tapped into all the data banks that were pertinent. Apparently the guy you're seeing tomorrow is as clean as a whistle. Couple of minor auto accidents, and a citation for an expired inspection sticker."

Jablonski shuffled through the stack. "I see that Mr. Thomas Smith has had his problems. Which one is he?"

"The black guy who does the sports on Mikki's show."

Jablonski skimmed the sheet. " 'During college . . . history of aggressive behavior with rival players on the football field . . . broke up a few bars while under the influence.' A hothead. Remind me to check on his whereabouts the evening Mikki was roughed up."

"Don't you suppose the cops already did that?"

"Sergeant Baxter was the one I was planning to ask." Jablonski paged to the next report. "Bettina Rawls. She's the lady who Mikki replaced as sub-anchor."

"Miz Rawls doesn't come out so pretty," Shirley commented. "Charged with child abuse back in the early eighties. Put on probation for two years. Do you suppose the TV station is aware of her background?"

"Who knows? That was a spell ago."

"Take a look at the story about Miz Rawls's departure from the show. Seems she didn't leave peaceably."

"Indeed." Jablonski read from a trade paper article. " 'In spite of the denials by Channel Ten's management, Bettina Rawls's agent, Billy Baver, insists his client was pushed out of the sub-anchor spot on the ten o'clock news in a power play instituted by segment reporter Mikki O'Reilly who subsequently replaced her.' Sounds like sour grapes."

Shirley put down several more items in front of Jablonski. "I hope you don't mind. While I was at it, I ran a search on Mikki."

Jablonski's eyes narrowed. "And?"

"See for yourself. Especially the story from the Sacramento *Bee*."

The detective examined the printout. "Would seem our little girl's a pretty tough cookie."

Shirley nodded. "And smart. Imagine getting the winner of the

Miss Napa Valley contest knocked out of the running by announcing that the girl was pregnant.''

"Since Mikki was number two at the time, I can't think of a better way to grab first prize."

Shirley sat down and started giggling.

"What?" Jablonski demanded.

"Look at the last one."

" 'Bikini top worn by Mikki O'Reilly, weather girl on Channel Ten's late news, slipped during last night's program revealing all. Station swamped with phone calls. Five hundred and eighty-two for, twelve against.' " He looked over at his secretary. "Not an accident, I would guess."

"Miss O'Reilly takes pretty good care of Number One."

"A common malady these days." Jablonski pushed the computer printouts across the desk to his secretary. "I've been thinking about those notes Mikki's assailant wrote to her."

"What about them?"

"I find it fascinating that the guy became convinced that Mikki was in love with *him*. Usually these cuckoos only babble on about how much *they* love a particular celebrity."

"Rob and I were talking about that last night at dinner."

"And?"

"And nothing. My husband's not into abnormal psychology. His field is dealing with disturbed children." A twinkle appeared in Jablonski's eyes. "Don't say it, Jack. There's nothing wrong with Saul."

Jablonski made a supplicatory gesture. "I didn't open my mouth."

"You didn't have to."

"Actually, I was wondering if your husband would be interested in reading over the notes Mikki received."

"I'm sure he would."

"Why don't you take the folder home and see if he has any ideas? I'm stuck."

"Okay." Shirley got up and started for the outer office. "You want me to call Sergeant Baxter?"

"No. I'll do it. And close the door please."

Jablonski dug the number of the Valley Precinct out of the Rolodex and dialed. Nancy had gone for the day.

CHAPTER EIGHTEEN

It was almost three o'clock Tuesday morning when Clem Barren pulled into his driveway. Things hadn't gone well at the all-night joint in the San Fernando Valley where he worked as the fast food chef. A water pipe had broken in the tiny restroom in the back of the establishment and an inch of water had collected on the floor before help arrived. Among other things, the mishap shorted out the electrical circuits on the east side of the building, effectively silencing the TV set mounted on the wall over the bar. As a consequence, he hadn't been able to check out Channel Three's blonde, dimpled newscaster as he had planned to do. Fortunately, before leaving for work, he had set his VCR to record the ten o'clock news program on which she appeared, a precautionary measure developed during his relationship with Mikki O'Reilly.

After shedding his clothes, he took a shower. Nude, he walked into the living room, snapped on the television set, and rewound the tape. He picked up the remote control and flopped down into the chair facing the screen. He pushed the start button.

Right after the opening signature, the director dissolved to a close shot of Jill Carlino seated at the anchor desk. "Herb Feldon's off for the night," she said, and launched into the lead story about the latest troubles in Central America. As she spoke to him, the camera slowly zoomed in until her face filled the entire screen.

Clem peered intently at the image, his masculinity flaccid, hoping that he would get aroused. Mikki had never failed him. Whenever he was with her, inside of a few seconds, he was always hard as a rock.

He tried concentrating on Jill Carlino's lips, but he might as well have been looking at a dish of Jello. After a while he gave up in disgust. The girl has no spirit, he decided. None at all. Worse, her eyes are like those of a shark, dull, empty. She isn't talking to me. She's reading.

He watched for another minute then, pointing the remote control at the VCR, he stopped the tape and rewound it. He went over and located the composite tape of his favorite clips from past news shows on which Mikki had appeared.

An instant after she popped up on the screen, his manhood began to assert itself.

CHAPTER NINETEEN

THE next morning, with the puppy in tow, Jablonski made his way up the lane to his office. As they passed Marla May Willowbrook's chamber, the door opened and the old woman stepped outside. The dog took one look at her garish costume and began to growl.

"Don't be alarmed," Jablonski told the psychic. "Snoopy's never seen a gypsy before."

"She is sweet and will bring you a great deal of happiness," Marla May announced. "She will also be pregnant before the first of the year."

"Not if I have anything to say about it."

"Be forewarned, she's an adventuress."

The detective made a move toward his door. "I'll keep my eye on her."

"Mr. Jablonski, you've forgotten our chat, haven't you?"

He turned back. "Of course, I haven't."

"You are missing a great opportunity. Together we could accomplish much. One plus one could equal three." She stepped inside and closed the door.

Shirley was on the phone when he walked into the outer office. "Hang on a second," she told the caller, and reached for the hold button. "It's Sergeant Baxter."

"Here," Jablonski said, handing his secretary the leash.

"God, she's adorable!" Shirley knelt down and tickled the puppy behind the ear. "Where's he been hiding you, sweetheart?"

Jablonski hurried into his office. "Her name's Snoopy and she has to be walked every two hours."

"After parking meter duty, it'll be a pleasure."

"Close the door." The detective leaned over the desk and picked up the phone. "Nancy, good morning!"

"How you doin', Jablonski?"

He hadn't left his name the previous afternoon when he'd telephoned and wondered what prompted her call. "I'm fine. How's by you?"

"Just trying to keep up with the body count. Three unsuspecting citizens bit the dust last night during a drive-by shooting. It's a hell of a world, isn't it? Your wife still in the east?"

"She is."

There was just the slightest pause. "You busy tonight?"

"Well . . . no."

"I belong to sort of an informal club that takes aerobic class every Tuesday after work. Four of the women from the station and their boyfriends and husbands."

"I hope you're not talking about exercise."

"It wouldn't kill you. Anyway, when we're finished, we always go to this little Italian joint down the block. Since you're alone, I thought you might be interested in joining us."

"That's very kind, but jumping up and down is for people with pogo sticks."

"You could meet us at the restaurant after."

Since Daphne's departure Jablonski had found the evenings to be a drag. "I guess I could."

"We never know *exactly* what time we're gonna finish, so maybe you better meet me at the Health Helpers. It's on Sepulveda north of Ventura, west side of the street. You can't miss it. About seven."

"Alright. By the way, while I have you on the line, when you checked out the people Mikki worked with, did you turn up anything that I might be able to use?"

"Zip. All the folks seemed to be reasonably clean."

"Seemed?"

"We didn't push too hard because everyone had substantial alibis and no discernible motives."

"I see. Any more DMVs check in?"

"Half a dozen. Also zip."

Jablonski sighed. "Goddamn, it's frustrating sitting around hoping for a break."

"Cops do it all the time, Jablonski. Dress casual. See you later."

As the detective was sitting down behind his desk, Shirley knocked and entered.

"What's Snoopy up to?" he asked.

"She's taking a nap."

"The pup sleeps a lot in the daytime. I wish she'd get it into her head that that's what the nights are for."

"With you at the office she's alone. What do you expect her to do?" She gestured toward her desk outside. "While you were on with Sergeant Baxter, Mr. Merriweather called."

"And?"

"And nothing. He wasn't able to match up Mikki's notes with anything in his files."

"Damn!" Jablonski growled. He pointed to a chair. "Sit. Tell me something. When someone says to dress casual, what does that mean?"

"In California casual means . . ." She shrugged. "Anything goes."

"Like what?"

"If it's the beach, jeans or shorts and sneakers."

"How about a restaurant in town?"

"A sports jacket and no tie, or maybe a sweater. Depends on the place. Why?"

"Sergeant Baxter invited me to join her and some friends for dinner tonight. She said to dress casual."

"What have you got in your closet?"

"None of the above."

"Back to the guy with the diamond in his nose." Shirley stood up. "Is that all?"

Jablonski grunted. "For now. Don't forget to take Snoopy for a walk around eleven."

Jablonski was amazed at the size of the complex that housed Channel Ten. There were a dozen beige buildings, most of them two or three stories high, and a parking lot large enough to hold more than five hundred automobiles. Four huge satellite dishes were pointed skyward, seeking out and sending the signals that were the station's lifeblood.

The detective identified himself to an ancient guard at the front gate. After the man had spent an interminable period shuffling through a stack of passes, Jablonski was finally admitted to the premises. Finding the parking slot assigned to him was even more time consuming. He drove down row after row of parked cars trying to locate number 210. Just before he was ready to call it quits and return to the guard shack, he discovered the spot. It was almost two forty-five when he entered the anteroom occupied by Will Waterbury's secretary.

"I'm sorry I'm a little late. That's some obstacle course you've got out there."

"I had you down for thirty minutes," the tight-lipped matron behind the desk responded. "Half your time is gone."

"I guess I'll have to talk fast."

She leaned over and flipped a switch on the intercom on her desk. Waterbury's voice came booming out into the room.

"Is that Mr. Jablonski?"

"It is."

"Come in, sir." There was a click.

"Through that door," the secretary directed.

Waterbury's office was a perfect model for the working newspaperman. The furniture needed polishing and the rug was scuffed. Most of the dozens of plaques that hung on the walls, announcing past honors, were slightly askew and the desk was littered with stacks of paper. Even the single window overlooking the helipad was suitably smudged. To Waterbury's right an old Remington portable rested on a stand. Several television monitors, quietly chattering, stood on a long table behind him. Each was tuned to a different station. Nearby, a police radio scanner completed the electronic lineup.

When Waterbury got up and extended his hand, he turned out to be considerably shorter than Jablonski had expected. And a lot more fidgety. The well-teased hairdo the anchorman featured when he held forth on the tube was in disarray. His coat hung off the back of his chair and his shirtsleeves were rolled halfway up his arms. He looked like somebody's visiting uncle from Dubuque.

"I understand you have been hired by Miss Mikki," he began.

"That is correct."

"What a tragedy. She's a fine young lady. I hope you can help her."

"I hope so, too."

"Careful when you sit down. The chair is somewhat rickety."

Waterbury was right. In addition, the cane seat had just enough holes in it to make things interesting.

"Does Miss Mikki feel the authorities are being negligent, Mr. Jablonski?"

Once he had settled himself, the detective answered. "As you are well aware, Mr. Waterbury, the police are undermanned and overworked. They have more pressing problems than the disfigurement of a young woman, even one as attractive and celebrated as Mikki O'Reilly. To answer your question, I'd say she wants to feel that no corner remains unswept."

Waterbury selected a pipe from a collection in a rack on his desk, wet his lips, and stuck it into his mouth. "I don't smoke. Merely a nervous habit left over from my youth. Fire away, Mr. Jablonski."

"Couple of things I find puzzling. I'm told that the night of the attack, the note Mikki received was *delivered* to the station."

"That's right."

"To the guard shack in the parking lot."

"Yes."

"And nobody actually *saw* the messenger?"

"Apparently not. The letter was discovered on top of the only desk in the place. By one of the guards."

Jablonski nodded. "There were *two* officers and neither of them saw anyone enter the shack?"

"Seems a bit hard to believe, but that's apparently the case."

"Both men were in residence, so to speak, the entire time. No coffee breaks?"

"I believe so."

"Could it be possible that someone delivered the letter earlier in the day and it just sat on the desk for a couple of hours?"

"That doesn't work. Old Dan, he was the shift chief, told the police he ate his supper at the desk when he came on duty about four o'clock. There was no letter."

"The communication just appeared out of thin air."

Waterbury said, "I don't follow you. Why are you so curious as to *how* the letter arrived? Isn't the fact it was a threat, a threat that was later carried out, more important?"

"I'm allergic to loose ends." Jablonski stood up and scratched his backside. "You ought to get that chair fixed. I hope you don't mind if I stand."

"Not at all. Sorry."

"When you and Mikki arrived at her place the local patrol was already waiting there."

"Yes. They went in with us and did a quick sweep of the house and departed."

"How quick a sweep?"

"Maybe three or four minutes."

"Could it be possible the assailant had hidden himself somewhere in the house and avoided discovery?"

"I hadn't thought of that," Waterbury admitted, "but it doesn't seem likely."

"Because of the Doberman?"

"Exactly. Raven was a fierce watchdog."

Jablonski pursed his lips. "According to the newspaper reports I researched, there wasn't so much as a fingerprint anywhere in the residence that might be connected to the letter writer."

"Surely he wore gloves."

"If so, the night he attacked Mikki appears to be the only time he took such precautions. Think back. He planted a palm print on the half-open window of her car when he tried to shove in a package. When he abandoned her apartment it was plastered with his prints.

One must assume that all the notes he wrote had at least one or two of his fingerprints on them."

The anchorman said, "But wouldn't he be more careful if he was planning to inflict bodily harm?"

"Maybe. A final thing. Because Mikki turned on the alarm *before* you departed the house that night, you were forced to leave via the garden to keep from setting it off."

"That's right."

"I know you've been asked this a dozen times, but are you certain that you locked the garden door?"

"I think I did. I'm quite sure."

"But you're not positive?"

"As positive as I can be."

Jablonski was silent for a moment. "There were no scratches on the outside knob. I examined it myself."

"What does that signify?"

"The lack of any markings indicates one of three things: the door was unlocked, the assailant had a key, or he picked the lock. If it was the latter, he was a professional."

"How do you reach that conclusion?"

"Have you ever tried to pick a lock, Mr. Waterbury?"

The anchorman chuckled. "I'm afraid not."

"Unless you know the ropes, it's a pretty difficult thing to do. An amateur would leave traces of his work and probably wouldn't have succeeded anyhow."

"So accepting that I did, in fact, lock the inside knob on the garden door, the intruder used a key."

"I see no other reasonable alternative. We must then assume that, during some earlier exploration of the premises, Mikki's assailant managed to steal a key to the back gate. If you will recall, he has a history of moving in where he doesn't belong."

"He could have stolen the key days, or even weeks, earlier," Waterbury suggested.

Jablonski sighed. "If only you had neglected to lock the door, it would be such a simple matter to develop a workable scenario."

Waterbury nodded. "The attacker could simply have walked in and, after doing the deed, locked the door and walked out."

"Exactly."

The anchorman stood up and stretched. "Did you know, Mr.

Jablonski, that for about ten minutes the police considered me a possible suspect?"

"Probably because you were the last person known to have been alone with Mikki."

"That, and the fact I suggested she take a sleeping pill. They posited I could have waited in the living room or out in the patio area until the drug took effect."

Jablonski interjected, "You're certainly strong enough to have overpowered her. And it's logical that your fingerprints would be found all over the place, as they were."

"I thank God I was home in bed with my wife about the time the neighbors heard Mikki screaming."

The detective turned to leave. "Well, thank you for your help."

On the way to his car, Jablonski ran into a line of eager visitors, four deep, waiting to watch the taping of a sitcom with the improbable title, "Jesse and the Yo-yo." Briefly he envied them their abandonment to the simpler pleasures of life.

CHAPTER TWENTY

JABLONSKI was attempting to tie a Windsor knot in his necktie while balancing the phone on his shoulder. He told his daughter, "Never mind what the doctors are saying, Susie. What do *you* think?"

"I really believe the baby's coming soon, Daddy. Any minute."

"What's 'any minute'?"

"Maybe in the next forty-eight hours."

Jablonski sighed. "Day after tomorrow it'll be a week your mother's been there."

"I know. I would have gone nuts without her." The detective heard his wife's voice in the background. His daughter said, "Mom wants to talk to you."

After a short pause Daphne came on the line. "What time is it in California, Jack?"

"It's three hours earlier than New Jersey. Just like the last time you called. Why can't you get that straight, for God's sake?"

"Because I keep forgetting whether the difference is three hours plus or three hours minus."

"Here it's plus. There it's minus."

"That's what's confusing. Have you had your dinner yet?"

Jablonski tightened the knot in his necktie. "Nope. I got invited out."

"How nice for you. By whom?"

"Sergeant Baxter. Works in the Valley Division. She's assigned to the Mikki O'Reilly case."

"Should I be worried?"

"Maybe. She's taller than you, and you know how I go for big broads. She has long blonde hair down to the middle of her back and wears four-inch spike heels. Told me she was a go-go dancer before she joined the force. But what the hell, Daph, we've had twenty-five good years together."

"Just remember that California is a community property state. I get half."

" 'Course, if you were here, I wouldn't be so vulnerable."

"You are many things, Jack, but vulnerable isn't one of them. I should be home in a week. Have fun."

Jablonski hung up the phone and picked up the nubbly beige sweater he had bought on his way home from Channel Ten. He showed it to Snoopy. "Well, what do you think?"

The puppy looked up and began to pant.

"That good, eh?" He slipped on the garment and peered into the bedroom mirror. Having long been a slave to the formality of the FBI, with its dark blue suits and thin, plain ties, he was pleased with how he looked.

"It's a new me, Snoop."

He fed the dog her dinner and put her out in the backyard. Then he returned to the bathroom, washed his face, and applied a few drops of a new toilet water purchased at the same time he picked out the sweater. He sniffed. I smell like a goddamn rosebush, he decided. He patted some cold water on his cheeks and attempted to wipe away the scent.

On his way out to the car, Snoopy looked up at him hopefully. "Be good, my dear. I won't be late."

The Health Helpers building was at least a hundred feet long and was constructed of concrete blocks that were painted a pale yellow. On the top of the structure a large, garish neon sign stood emblazoned against the clear, dark night sky. While waiting for the traffic signal to change, Jablonski determined that the endlessly jerking lines of light on the display portrayed a giant flexing his biceps. The detective pulled around back and stopped in the parking lot. Upon closer examination, the architecture looked more like a storage facility than a place dedicated to the improvement of the human body.

He found a parking space near the entrance. As he stepped inside the building, he was almost flattened by the sound of a hard rock beat ricocheting off the plaster walls. Drawn toward the source of the music, he soon arrived at an open double door that led into a very large room with a low ceiling. It was filled with groaning, sweating men and women ranging in age from mid-teens to early seventies. Facing the door at the far end, a muscular young man stood on a raised platform vigorously directing the calisthenics. It took Jablonski the better part of a minute to identify Nancy Baxter.

What he saw was a revelation. Stripped down to a skintight pink leotard, the sweat glistening on the back of her neck and her arms as she moved, Nancy was a knockout, a body double for Jane Fonda. In spite of himself, Jablonski felt a momentary stirring just south of the border.

He edged his way around the room until he found a chair near the front. Moments later, he caught Nancy's eye.

She mouthed the words, "Ten minutes."

He replied in kind, "I'll wait."

Later, outside the workout room, after the people in Nancy's group had switched into street clothes, introductions were made. To Jablonski the three younger women seemed more or less interchangeable except for the fact that one of them wore a wedding ring. Their escorts, two with imposing moustaches, all with impressive physiques, appeared to be in their mid- to late twenties.

"Remember Dick?" Nancy asked Jablonski, indicating a stocky brunette with a broken nose. "He's the one who carted off the would-be knifer from the deli."

"Didn't recognize you without your badge," the detective replied.

"Nancy said you're FBI," the young man said admiringly. "I'd like to get a shot at that kind of duty."

"A law degree's a big help," Jablonski pointed out.

"I'm going to school nights. Except Tuesdays." He laughed and took his girl friend by the arm. "Let's eat!"

"You can ride with me," Nancy told Jablonski. "I'll drive you back after dinner so you can pick up your car."

The meal was a triumph—tri-colored pasta, veal chops, a savory salad of arugula and endive, and a mixture of Italian sherbets. The place was dark and intimate, containing only about a dozen tables. The owner, a Mr. Mastantonio, was given to shouting at the single waiter on duty whenever he perceived that things weren't proceeding on schedule.

"Don't let him bother you," Nancy counseled Jablonski. "It's part of his act. Vincenzo once told me that if he didn't shout, people wouldn't know he was Italian."

Among the eight of them, they consumed nearly four bottles of red wine.

After the check had been brought to the table, Dick asked, "What's a hundred and forty-seven divided by eight?"

"Is that with or without tip?" Jablonski wanted to know.

"With."

"Eighteen bills and change," the detective fired back, reaching for his wallet.

Impressed, Nancy asked, "How'd you do that so fast?"

"Bribery. When I was twelve, my grandmother on my father's side promised to take me to Yellowstone Park if I got an A in math." He put two twenties on the table.

"You're heavy there, Jablonski," Nancy said, pushing one of the bills back to him. "We all go Dutch."

The detective shook his head. "Man or boy, I never let a female pick up a tab."

Nancy retrieved one of Jablonski's twenties, leaned over and pulled out the neckline of his sweater, and tucked the bill into his shirt pocket.

"You smell good," she announced.

She opened her purse and contributed to the rapidly building pot in the center of the table.

After the goodnights were finished, the two of them climbed into her car and made the short trip back to Health Helpers. She pulled to a stop near the entrance door and adjusted the ignition key, silencing the engine but leaving juice for the radio. Then she fiddled with the dial until she found a station that was playing soft middle-of-the-road music. "I'm full up."

"How about me?" Jablonski countered. "And I didn't lose four pounds before dinner doing aerobics."

She drummed her fingers on the steering wheel in time with the music. "How long's your wife going to be back east?"

" 'Bout a week, I guess." Suddenly nervous, Jablonski felt like he was sixteen years old again in the back seat of his father's Ford with Carolyn Schmidt.

A gust of wind scattered a collection of debris across the deserted parking lot, momentarily claiming his attention. He glanced over at Nancy. Her eyes were closed, and the rays from the street lamps outside highlighted the contours of her face. He knew that the prudent thing to do was to get out of the car. Instead, he let the music continue uninterrupted for a few moments before he spoke again.

"You have some pretty nice friends."

"They like you, too." She hummed along with the radio. " 'Yesterday' is one of my all-time favorites. I love the Beatles, don't you?"

"Actually, I never got their message."

"You probably like Barry Manilow and Englebert what's-his-name."

"His name is Humperdinck and, in my book, he's right up there with Robert Goulet."

"Yuck."

"What's the matter with Robert Goulet?"

"He sounds like he has sinus trouble." She sat up in her seat and faced the detective. "It seems like it's going to take some time and effort to get you up to speed, Jablonski."

"Hmmm?"

She reached over and removed his hat. "Who else but a middle-aged ex-FBI man would wear a fedora with a sweater?" She mussed his hair. "Is that why I find you kind of sexy?"

"I bet you say that to all the boys."

She leaned in closer. "I hate boys."

Jablonski chose his words carefully. "Tell you the truth, Nancy. I'm sort of an old dog now. I don't come down off the porch much anymore."

She played with his ear. "Then maybe I'll have to come up there and join you."

Jablonski swallowed hard and retrieved his hat. "It's past my bedtime. Thanks for a terrific evening." He got out of the car and closed the door.

Nancy rolled down the window on the passenger side. "Is there something wrong with me?" she asked, a smile playing across her lips.

"Nothing that I have uncovered thus far." He tipped his hat and strolled nonchalantly to his car.

It wasn't until he was halfway home that he realized that neither of them had mentioned the Mikki O'Reilly case.

CHAPTER TWENTY-ONE

THE following morning, distraught and somewhat disheveled, an hour after she was due, Shirley came bounding into the office.

She told Jablonski, "I know it's ten-fifteen, but Piedad threatened to quit and I had to do some fancy talking to get her calmed down."

"What now?"

"Saul painted the beagle blue."

Jablonski pursed his lips. "Dark blue or light blue?"

"Come on, Jack. This isn't funny. The house is a mess." She swept up the contents of the out basket. "Luckily it was a watercolor paint." She departed for the outer office, where Jablonski could hear the sounds of the coffeemaker being loaded and turned on.

"I'll have some Sweet 'n Low," the detective called out.

Shirley stuck her head in the door. "What's the matter with sugar? You look fine."

"I *am* fine. But last night I consumed a meal of such gargantuan proportions that I find a demonstration of restraint to be an absolute necessity. I also skipped breakfast." He put his feet up on the desk. "Has your husband reached any conclusions about the notes you took home?"

"He thinks he's onto something, but he doesn't want to discuss it yet. He's spent the last two nights in the library."

"I await his pleasure."

The telephone rang. A moment later, Jablonski's buzzer sounded. "Our client on one."

"Miss Mikki, good morning," the detective said cheerfully.

"Let me guess," she replied. "You've talked to Will Waterbury. He's the only one who calls me that."

"Indeed I did."

"Was he helpful?"

"Let's just say certain things are less blurred than they were before."

"I'm glad."

"You sound pretty chipper."

Mikki replied, "I'm really excited! I called to tell you Arnold Tolkin phoned a few minutes ago and said he wants me to do an interview today for the ten o'clock news. Out here at the house, by the pool."

"Which one is Arnold Tolkin?"

"The news director. My boss." She giggled. "William the Conqueror will not be happy."

"Do you know where in the program you'll appear?"

"Arnold said right after the second commercial."

"What time is that?"

Shirley set a steaming cup of coffee at Jablonski's elbow.

Mikki answered, "Ten-twenty, give or take. Call me tonight when it's over. I want to know what you think."

"I'll do that."

"I'm going to drape myself in a patio lounger and wear my new emerald green bathing suit. It has a French cut up to here. The folks'll be so busy looking at my legs no one will have time to feel sorry for me."

Good for you, Jablonski thought to himself.

"You want me to mention your name?" Mikki asked.

"A little free publicity couldn't hurt."

"*Adios,* then, Big Jack. We'll talk later."

In the late afternoon Petey Bosworth came steaming into the office without bothering to identify himself to Shirley. He walked right in on Jablonski, who was flat on the floor behind his desk doing push-ups.

"Mr. Jablonski, I have to talk to you."

Surprised by the sudden interruption, the detective stopped what he was doing and looked up. "Stand by, Petey, I'm almost finished."

"It's awful important."

Jablonski resumed exercising. "Eighteen. Nineteen. Twenty." He stood up.

Shirley appeared in the doorway, a quizzical look on her face. She pointed to Petey. "A friend?"

"It's okay. This is Mr. Bosworth, the young man I told you about." He turned to the boy. "What's up?"

Petey's lip began to tremble. "Miss Montgomery didn't come to school today."

Jablonski led him to a chair and motioned to Shirley to leave them alone. "I guess there's more to it."

The boy stared at the floor. "Yes."

"You said you wanted to talk to me. I'm listening."

He looked up at Jablonski. "You won't be mad?"

"Should I be?"

Petey swallowed. "Maybe."

For a moment Jablonski studied the downeast lad. "You've continued to watch your teacher's house?"

The boy nodded. "I . . . I couldn't help it."

"Evenings, I assume?"

"From the time her husband comes home from work until they go to bed. The other guys gave up. But I just couldn't."

Jablonski sighed. "When did you say your parents were coming back from their vacation?"

"Not for a while."

The detective sank into his big chair. "So your teacher didn't show up today. Do you have any idea why?"

"Ever since Miss Montgomery's husband pushed her around last Saturday, he's been good to her. Until last night. Then he had a bunch of drinks before dinner. About the time they were having dessert, he started yelling."

"About what?"

"I couldn't tell exactly. The windows were open but I was too far away to make anything out. Anyway, she yelled back and then he reached across the table and slapped her so hard her chair fell over backwards." Petey's eyes misted over. "She got up and ran out of the house and jumped into her car. She was bleeding, Mr. Jablonski."

"Easy does it, son." He opened the bottom drawer in his desk and pulled out a box of Kleenex. "Here."

After the boy had regained control of himself, he concluded, "Then she drove away. I called the police like I did before, but the man on the phone said there was nothing they could do." The pain in Petey's eyes was palpable. "Why didn't they want to help?"

Jablonski got up and walked around to Petey's chair and lowered himself to one knee. "If Miss Montgomery was able to drive herself away, the police would assume she wasn't seriously injured. Besides, she was the one who was attacked. She would have to lodge the complaint against her husband."

Upon hearing Jablonski's rationale, Petey burst into tears.

It had been a long time since Jablonski had cried, longer than he could remember, and the boy's outburst made him uncomfortable. He said, "It'll be okay, Petey. It'll be okay."

"No it *won't*!" the boy exploded. "Miss Montgomery married a terrible man. Some night . . . some night he'll hit her so hard she'll be dead. And nobody will do anything to stop him!"

Jablonski patted Petey on the shoulder and got to his feet. "Did you wait around after Miss Montgomery left?" The boy nodded. "Did she come back?"

" 'Bout an hour later. She went right upstairs."

"Did her husband start after her again?"

"He was passed out in front of the TV."

It's tough to be young, Jablonski reminded himself. Especially when you're all alone. "I'll make a deal with you." Petey looked up expectantly. "You have to promise me you'll go home now and *stay* home, or it's no dice. Will you do that?" Petey nodded. "Honest to God?"

"Honest to God."

"Okay. You go to school tomorrow morning. If Miss Montgomery doesn't show up for class, you call me at my place first thing. I'll go over to her house and see if maybe I can't have a talk with her." Jablonski wondered what he was getting himself into.

"How about tonight?" Petey persisted. "What if her husband hits her again?"

"Grownups are funny, Petey. A man does something bad to his wife, then he feels guilty. He turns around and tries to make up for what he's done: buys flowers or perfume or something like that. I have a hunch Miss Montgomery's husband will be nice to her this evening."

"Why isn't he nice to begin with?"

"Why, indeed?"

Petey took a handful of tissues and blew his nose. "Thanks, Mr. Jablonski."

"Where do you live?"

"Bundy, north of Sunset. I've got my bike."

"Suppose we go across the street and get you a hot fudge sundae. Then I'll drive you *and* your bike up the hill."

Petey smiled wanly. "You don't trust me."

"I certainly do. It's just that you've been through a lot today. You should conserve your strength."

"If you think so."

"I'm sure of it." Jablonski opened the door to the outer office. "I shall return presently, Shirley. My young friend and I are going over to the ice cream parlor."

"Bring me back a smidgen of pralines and cream."

"How much is a smidgen?" the detective asked.

Petey explained. "More than a particle and less than a dab."

"Whatever happened to the metric scale?" Jablonski wondered aloud. "By the by, my boy, when do I see my name in print?"

"The paper comes out Friday. I think I've written you as a remarkable and fascinating character."

"Sounds about right." Jablonski opened the office door. "Two things I've never been are rich and famous. Perhaps, at long last, you have taken care of the latter."

As the door closed, Shirley rolled her eyes.

CHAPTER TWENTY-TWO

It was just after nine-fifteen P.M. when the Charles Bronson movie on Channel Ten was interrupted for an endless stream of commercials. While they were unspooling, Clem Barren was putting the finishing touches on a plate of ham and eggs for the establishment's only customer, an unshaven, surly type seated at a corner table. The waitress was busy on the phone in the rear, so he carried the plate over and put it down in front of the man.

As Clem turned away he heard Will Waterbury's voice mention Mikki O'Reilly's name. He stopped dead in his tracks and looked up at the screen.

"... will be with us in an exclusive interview during the ten o'clock news tonight ..."

"Do you have some ketchup?" the customer asked.

"Ssssh!" Clem snapped.

"Hey, I ..."

"SHUT UP!"

"... also the latest on the conflict in Central Europe." The movie resumed.

The suddenly furious patron yelled, "Give me some goddamn ketchup or I'll break your fucking head!"

Clem wheeled around and pulled the man up out of his seat and pinned him in a painful arm lock. Then, cruelly increasing the pressure, he propelled him toward the front door. Without a word, he shoved his victim out onto the street, where the man stumbled and fell into the gutter. Clem slammed the door and picked up the plateful of ham and eggs and dumped the contents into the garbage can behind the counter.

"What was that all about?" the young, gum-chewing waitress asked when she had finished her phone call.

"Nothin'."

The girl shrugged and busied herself wiping off the now abandoned table and replacing the silverware setting.

My God, Clem thought. What is Mikki going to say?

He cursed himself. If only he'd set the timer on his VCR to Channel Ten instead of Channel Seven when he left for work. He wondered if he should pretend to be sick and race home. There was always the danger that the restaurant would fill up with people at the time Mikki's interview began and he wouldn't be able to watch.

He had to hear what she said. He *had* to.

Although the night was cool, by the time ten o'clock arrived, Clem was covered with sweat. His mouth was dry and his heart was frantically banging away in his chest. When he heard the show's opening signature, he hurried to a booth on the opposite side of the room and slid in. Any customers who showed up, well, fuck 'em.

The benevolent visage of Will Waterbury leaned toward the camera as he began his report about a three-point-two earthquake that had hit the city of Anaheim.

Who *gives* a shit? Clem asked himself.

Next he had to endure a long drawn-out story about a drug bust that the L.A. police chief pronounced "the biggest in the history of the city." This was followed with a venomous series of exchanges between members of the city council concerning the acceptability of another high-rise building in the Wilshire corridor. Just when Clem was positive that Mikki would appear, the initial pod of ads was teased by Will Waterbury with a promise of *"the first television appearance of our own Mikki O'Reilly. Stay tuned."*

The commercials were interminable, and so was the consumer reports section and the excerpts from a speech the president had made to the United Nations. Now, Clem urged, as the chief executive was winding up. NOW! But it wasn't to be. Waterbury repeated the tease for Mikki's appearance *"right after these messages."*

The bastards, Clem fumed. The dirty rotten prick sons of bitches! Stringing me along.

A few minutes later, an old lady wandered in off the street and took her place at the counter. "Coffee," she said to the waitress. "And a sweet roll."

When Clem heard the order he breathed easier.

Finally Will Waterbury announced, *"And now for the interview you've all been waiting for. I went out to Mikki's house this afternoon and chatted with her."*

Instantly the screen was filled with a long shot of Mikki O'Reilly, poolside, dressed seductively in a sexy bathing suit. As the camera zoomed in, Clem Barren felt light-headed. Jesus, God, don't let me pass out! he thought to himself, grasping the tabletop for support.

"How do you feel, Mikki?" Will Waterbury asked.

"I'm so glad to be here with you," she responded. She turned to the camera.

Suddenly, it was just like old times. Clem knew, behind the dark glasses, she was looking right at him.

CHAPTER TWENTY-THREE

SNOOPY brought her favorite tennis ball and dropped it at Jablonski's feet.

"Not now, my girl. You'll have to wait until Mikki's finished."

The young woman's red hair glistened in the afternoon sun. It reached down to her shoulders in graceful folds, framing her tiny, freckled face. There was a light breeze that stirred the bushes in the background.

". . . when can we expect to have you back with us?" Waterbury was asking.

"That's hard to say, Will. Tentatively, both the corneal implants to restore my sight and the plastic surgery on my face are planned for sometime in February."

"That's very encouraging. I know you'll be as good as new and every one of us down here at Channel Ten is rooting for you."

"The doctors are hopeful. That's all I can say."

"Is everyone taking good care of you?"

"They certainly are. I'm particularly grateful to Mr. Jack Jablonski."

Waterbury said, *"He's the private investigator whose help you enlisted."*

"That's right. The inaction on the part of the police seems to indicate that they're stuck. It's very reassuring to have an ex-FBI man with twenty-five years experience on my side. You can imagine how much I want the perpetrator locked up behind bars."

Jablonski beamed. "Hear that, Snoop? They'll be breaking down my doors tomorrow."

The interview continued for another minute and consisted mainly of an enumeration by Waterbury of the people who wanted their good wishes conveyed to Mikki.

"Now be sure to take care of yourself," the anchorman said in conclusion.

"I will." Mikki stood up, showing off her model-perfect figure. She waved. *"Bye-bye."*

Jablonski snapped off the set and picked up the tennis ball. "Go for it," he instructed, flinging the object into the far recesses of the bedroom. The puppy eagerly scampered away. As the detective reached for the phone to dial Mikki, it rang.

"Let me guess," he said into the instrument.

"Well," Mikki asked breathlessly. "How did you like it?"

"I found the part about Jack Jablonski to be particularly compelling. I hope the cops don't get sore because you said they were dragging their feet."

"Let 'em *get* sore. It's true, isn't it?"

"They're faced with the same problem I have: not enough to go on."

Mikki got down to the important stuff. "How do you think I looked?"

"Ravishing."

A phone bell sounded in the distance. "There's my other line, Jack. I'll talk to you later."

As Jablonski was hanging up, he noticed Snoopy sitting patiently, the tennis ball in her mouth.

"You did it right the last time. Drop it, Snoop. That's part of the routine, remember? As the throw*ee,* you locate the object, you bring it back, and then you deposit it on the floor at the throw*er's* feet. Remember?"

Snoopy made no move to cooperate. Jablonski reached down and attempted to dislodge the ball from the puppy's mouth. Instantly this became a game, Snoopy pulling in one direction, Jablonski in another. After a while the dog tired of the exertion required to keep the object and relinquished it to her master.

"You need a refresher course in retrieving," the detective observed. "It's almost ten-thirty. Would you like your cookie before retiring?"

The sound of the word "cookie" caused Snoopy to fly out into the kitchen and go into a circular holding pattern while Jablonski fought to open the obstinate top on the new box of treats.

"There. Now go to your bed."

Five minutes later both dog and master were sound asleep.

The next morning, when he was halfway through his shower, Jablonski heard the phone begin to ring. Dripping wet and cursing audibly, he hurried into the bedroom and, after drying his hands, picked up the instrument. He wondered if it was Daphne with news of their new grandchild.

"Hello?"

Petey Bosworth announced, "Miss Montgomery didn't show up."

"Wait a minute," the detective ordered. He returned to the bathroom and removed the terry cloth robe hanging on the back of the door. Before re-establishing contact with the youth, he slipped into it.

"Are you sure?"

"There was a substitute. Miss Montgomery won't be in today."

Damn, Jablonski thought to himself.

"Remember what you promised?" Petey asked, his voice laced with hope.

"I remember. What's the lady's address?"

Petey gave the detective directions to the house, then said, "Can I come over to your office at lunchtime and find out what happened?"

"Sure."

After hanging up, Jablonski wandered back to the bathroom. How, he wondered, do I knock on the door of a woman I've never met and inquire into the violent behavior of her husband? I have no warrant. I have no right to go meddling. I don't even know, for *sure,* that Petey's imagination hasn't been inflamed by his fast-flowing pre-adolescent juices.

He combed his hair, then spent ten minutes with the barbells before feeding the puppy her breakfast. Finally, he prepared himself an English muffin smothered in butter and honey. When he finished, he put the dishes in the sink and left a message on the answering machine in his office, telling his secretary that he would be delayed.

Miss Montgomery and her husband lived on a side street a quarter of a block west of a busily traveled artery that led down to the beaches below the Pacific Palisades. A huge pepper tree, its branches flowing with feathery fronds, was firmly anchored in the middle of the lawn. The couple's small split-level dwelling was fronted by carefully-kept flower beds that bristled with birds of paradise and calla lilies. On one side of their residence stood a vacant house with a "For Sale" sign out front; on the other, the framework of a new abode in the mid-stage of construction.

Jablonski parked his car across the street and studied the scene. Since there were no neighbors adjacent to the house, the couple's altercations could be carried out unheard and unobserved.

The detective got out of his car and nervously adjusted his fedora. I'm not a goddamn buttinsky, he told himself for the tenth time since leaving home.

Seeing the Toyota station wagon standing in the driveway, he wondered if the husband had left for work. He checked his watch. It was nine thirty-five. He decided the car probably belonged to the teacher.

As he stepped out into the street, the front door to the residence opened. A petite young woman in her early thirties emerged and started down the front walk carrying what appeared to be a letter. She and Jablonski arrived at the curbside mail box together. He doffed his fedora and made a small bow.

"Miss Montgomery?"

"Yes," she replied nervously.

"My name's Jack Jablonski and I'm a friend of Petey Bosworth's."

The smile she gave the detective wasn't quite small enough to hide the fact that her right lateral incisor was missing. In addition, her otherwise attractive face was marred by a black-and-blue mark under her left eye and an angry-looking scab that led from the left side of her mouth down to her chin.

"Petey's a lovely boy. Is he in some kind of trouble?" She popped the note into the mailbox.

"No, but he thinks you are."

Involuntarily she raised her hands to her face. "I'm fine," she said abruptly, and started back up the walk. "Tell him I'm fine."

Jablonski caught her by the arm. "Forgive me, but your appearance suggests the contrary."

"I had a nasty fall off a stool in the kitchen," she said defiantly.

Their eyes locked for a long moment before Jablonski spoke. "Petey's worried sick about you. So much so that he's been watching your house nearly every night for a week."

"He's *what*?!"

"He saw what your husband did last Saturday and again night before last."

"I don't know what you're talking about," she snapped. She ran up the steps and disappeared in the house.

"Miss Montgomery," he called out. "Please. I think you should talk to me." He followed and paused at the open front door. He knocked on the jamb. "Miss Montgomery?" There was no answer. He knocked again and stepped into the front hall, closing the door behind him. He looked into the living room.

The young woman was sitting on the sofa, her face in her hands, crying silently.

He crossed into the room and lowered himself onto a footstool that stood nearby. Several minutes went by before she was able to calm herself.

Slowly she sat up. Her widely spaced brown eyes were filled with pain. "I'm sorry. This is all so humiliating."

"I believe my next line is, 'Would you like to discuss it?' "

"Who are you, Mister . . . ?"

"Jablonski."

She asked fearfully, "You're not connected with the school district?"

"No." Jablonski produced his identification.

"A private investigator. Petey hired a private investigator," she said unbelievingly.

Jablonski quickly explained the circumstances surrounding his involvement with the young man.

"Frankly, the boy is infatuated with you. He has noted your various absences from class since your marriage and the excuses you gave for them. He suspected that your husband was maltreating you and took it upon himself to investigate further. Twice in the last few days he has seen your husband knock you around. Petey is very, very upset and, with his family out of town on a cruise, feels he has no one to talk to. He asked me to intervene. I was extremely reticent to do so but, now that I have, I hope that I may be of some service."

She smiled wanly. "You're an adult, Mr. Jablonski. You understand that this is something my husband and I have to work out."

The detective nodded. "I do indeed."

"The beating he gave me Tuesday night was the last straw. When it was over I drove myself to a psychiatrist friend who helped put me back together both emotionally and physically, at least for the time being. The next morning I convinced Steve, that's my husband, that either he would join Alcoholics Anonymous without any more excuses *and* that he and I would start a regimen with a marriage counsellor, or I was leaving."

"That sounds promising."

"Believe me, Mr. Jablonski, from now on, if my husband even *looks* at me strangely, I'm out of here."

"I'm happy to hear that." The detective stood up. "What do you think I should tell Petey? He's coming over to my office at noon."

"Just say that everything's going to be okay. Tomorrow after class I intend to reassure him myself." She walked Jablonski to the door.

"Please don't hesitate to call me if I can be of any help." The detective dug his card out of his wallet and handed it to her.

"Thanks, but I don't think that will be necessary."

Jablonski tipped his fedora and started down the walk. As he was crossing the street he flashed back on Miss Bolte, his math teacher in junior high. She had wavy black hair and eyes that twinkled. She wore rouge on her high cheekbones and tight dresses that showed off her figure. He remembered the time he came to bid her goodbye when she was about to transfer to another school in the district. He felt a twinge when he recalled that day. Jesus, he mused to himself, she must be seventy by now! But even that thought couldn't erase the memory of how he had felt when she leaned down and kissed him on the forehead.

He turned around and looked in the direction of the teacher's house. The young woman was still standing in the open doorway. He waved. She waved back then stepped inside.

Jablonski wondered whether Petey would remember Miss Montgomery forty years from now.

As her boss walked in, Shirley said, "Sergeant Baxter just called. She's very anxious to talk to you."

"Get her." He started into his office. "Did you watch the segment with Mikki on the Channel Ten News last night?"

"Of course. We already had a couple of inquiries as a result of it."

He flopped down into his chair and waited for the two buzzes signaling that his call was ready.

"Morning," he said brightly.

"Is that with or without the letter *U*?"

"Sorry?"

"Morning, as in 'Good Morning,' is a salutation. *Mourning,* on the other hand, is a synonym for grieving. And that's what I'm doing right now, Jablonski, grieving."

"Let me guess. Your boss didn't like what Mikki said last night concerning the efforts being exerted on her behalf by the LAPD."

"My captain is just this side of a cardiac arrest. Your client's remark reflected badly on all hands, starting with yours truly."

"That is to be regretted. Is there some way I can make amends?"

"Maybe you'd like to hear the rest before you try to butter me up."

"I'm serious, Nancy."

"So'm I. The boss also had a few choice observations about ex-FBI men who muck about in his territory."

"How can I redeem myself?"

"With him, no way. With me, a nice candlelight dinner might get things back on the track."

Which track, Jablonski wondered to himself. The thought of being alone with Nancy made him somewhat anxious. "Dinner?" he repeated.

Shirley appeared in the doorway and delivered a series of semaphore signals.

"Wait a minute," the detective ordered. He put Nancy on hold. "What?"

"I was going to ask you to dinner at our house tonight," Shirley said.

"Need I remind you again of my dislike of small children?"

"My husband has dug up some interesting research on the type of guy who wrote those notes to Mikki. Since Rob's busy most of every day, dinner seemed like a good idea."

Saved by the bell! Jablonski thought. "Could I bring Sergeant Baxter?"

"Why not? God knows she's an interested party."

Jablonski punched the button on line one. "I've got a better idea, Nancy." After explaining the reason for it, he extended Shirley's invitation to the sergeant.

Nancy said, "Okay by me. I don't get out of here until seven-thirty. Is that okay?"

"I'm sure it is."

"Will you pick me up in the parking lot at the station? My son has the car."

"Absolutely." After hanging up, Jablonski wandered back into the outer office and tossed his fedora on the hat rack.

"In a word, what did your husband discover about Mikki's attacker?"

"The man seems to possess all the symptoms of a rare and interesting disease."

"Does it have a name?"

"Indeed it does. It's called erotomania."

CHAPTER TWENTY-FOUR

Rob and Shirley Bernstein-Mandlebaum lived in Encino, north of Los Angeles, a thriving business and residential locality in the San Fernando Valley that possesses neither discernible boundaries nor singular topography. Because of this lack of uniqueness it looks exactly like a dozen other communities in the area, bearing such varied names as Studio City, Woodland Hills and Tarzana.

The Mandlebaums' modest two-story house, covered in white clapboard, was situated on a quiet side street a dozen blocks west of the San Diego Freeway. The abode featured an overhanging roof covered with fire-retardant, slate gray shingles. A large television antenna sat on the dwelling's ridge line and below it stood a small brick chimney. The double-hung windows across the front were bordered by green shutters and the sidewalk leading up to the front door, as well as much of the lawn, was littered with a variety of toys.

Jablonski, after getting out of the Honda, spotted the playthings and reacted with alarm. "Shirley didn't tell me she had more than one child," he complained, pointing at the shambles. "Looks like a goddamn brood lives here."

"Not necessarily," Nancy replied. "A two-year-old can accumulate an awful lot of stuff in a very short time."

Jablonski walked around and opened the passenger door. He leaned in and popped the glove compartment. "In addition to being highly motivated, the kid is very inquisitive. You better check the artillery."

"Good idea." Nancy removed the .38 from her purse and placed it in the nook.

Jablonski assisted his date to her feet and locked the car. "Remember," he told her, "it's Shirley and Rob."

The doorbell chimed the first four notes of "Joy to the World." As Jablonski was about to comment on the musical taste of their hosts, an extremely tall, thin, gawky man with a prominent Adam's apple swung open the door.

"Hi! I'm Rob." He stuck out his hand to Sergeant Baxter. "And you must be Nancy. Please, come in." He stepped aside, allowing the woman to enter. "And, finally, I have the pleasure of meeting the famous Jack Jablonski. Shirley has told me so much about you."

"Likewise," the detective responded. "Nice of you to give us a hand."

Saul ran in from the dining room and collided with Jablonski. The toddler extended his arms and said something that sounded like "Hop."

"He wants you to pick him up," Rob explained.

Jablonski stared down at the child.

"Go ahead," Nancy said. "He won't bite."

"The hell he won't."

"He wants to give you a goodnight kiss, Jack," Shirley announced as she appeared on the landing at the top of the stairs.

Cautiously, like he was handling a dead squirrel, Jablonski picked up the child. Saul planted a wet smacker right on the detective's nose, then started squirming violently.

"Now he wants you to put him down," Rob explained.

Relieved, Jablonski placed the boy on the floor. "Where's the blue beagle you told me about?"

Shirley came the rest of the way down the steps. "In the kitchen." She turned to Sergeant Baxter. "You're Nancy. We've talked."

"We sure have. Thanks for inviting me."

"I hope you like pizza, Nancy. Rob just picked up a great one on his way home."

"I *love* pizza," Nancy said.

"First I've got to put the baby to sleep," the hostess announced. She turned to Saul. "Beddy-by." At the sound of those two words, the tot started screaming. Then he threw himself on the floor. Ignoring this display, Shirley started toward the kitchen. "Be right back."

Jablonski turned to Rob and shouted over the din. "I'm interested, Doctor, to see how one in your line of work deals with a situation like this."

"Whenever possible, I leave tantrums and soiled diapers to the female of the species. Women are far better equipped to handle such crises."

"A man after my own heart," Jablonski declared.

Nancy shook her head and tossed a look at the ceiling.

Shirley, trailed by a forlorn-looking beagle, returned with the toddler's bottle. She reached down and picked up her distraught son. "Make our guests a drink, Rob. We'll eat in fifteen minutes." She shoved the bottle in Saul's mouth and started upstairs. Before she had reached the landing only the sounds of ingestion could be heard.

"What did I tell you, Jack?" Rob asked.

The detective responded admiringly, "You should write a book."

"I already have. Two of them, in fact. Psych texts."

Nancy asked, "Anything about this erotomania Jack mentioned?"

Rob laughed. "I wish there had been. Then I might have gotten some sleep the last couple of nights."

Nancy looked puzzled.

Jablonski explained, "He's been busy researching at the UCLA library." He looked down at the dog, who was busily sniffing away. "He smells Snoopy, my cocker spaniel. Tell me, Rob, what do you call this animal?"

"Beagle. And it's a she."

"I know it's a beagle. I just wanted to know her name."

"That's what we call her: Beagle. Or Beegie for short."

Jablonski walked into the living room and plopped down on the sofa. "Come here, girl." The dog scurried over and jumped up into his lap.

"She's very affectionate," Rob explained. "If you don't encourage her, she'll go away."

The detective gave the animal a thorough scratching behind her ears. "She's cute as a button but, I hate to tell you, I've got the Queen at home."

Rob went over to the bar. "What'll it be, Nancy?"

"Do you have some white wine?"

"You bet. A great California chardonnay." He looked at Jablonski. "Jack?"

"Personally, I was raised on something stronger. Scotch?"
"Light or dark?"
"Surprise me."

During most of the meal Jablonski was the center of attention. At the urging of the others, he described several of the cases in which he had been involved during his years with the FBI. It wasn't until Shirley was pouring after-dinner coffee that the detective finally brought the conversation around to the business at hand.

"Enough of a walk down memory lane. I know I speak for Sergeant Baxter when I say that we are hugely curious to hear what Rob has to tell us."

Nancy said, "I asked the department psychiatrist about erotomania and he said he never heard of it."

Rob reached over to the sideboard and pulled off a thin manila folder containing several pages of notes. "I'm not surprised. This particular disease was first documented in 1921 and, through the years, I don't think more than a hundred cases have made their way into the literature, if that many." He thumbed through the material and selected a page. "Here's a good description of it.

" 'When romantic delusions occur *without any other sign of serious mental disturbance,* the diagnosis is erotomania.' "

"I can't believe that there have only been a hundred cases reported in the last seventy years," Nancy interjected. "Seems like every other week I hear about some poor soul falling in love with a celebrity and then calling her up or writing her letters. Or worse. I know for a fact that Ed Merriweather has thousands of letters in his files."

"Let me explain," Rob continued. "The poor soul you mention, actually the typical case, *first falls in love* without giving much, if any, thought to how the love object feels about him. On the other hand, the *initial* aberration of the erotomaniac is that some God- or Goddess-like figure *loves him* and it's to that love he responds."

Jablonski said, "And you think that's what we have in Mikki's case."

"I do. The minute your man decided Miss O'Reilly *loved him* he started writing to her." Rob pulled out the sheaf of notes written to Mikki. "Listen. March fourteenth: 'I know how you feel about me.' April fourth: 'You must be lonely. When are you coming back?' May fifth: 'I could see you looking around trying to find me.' May twenty-fourth: 'People who love each other shouldn't hide from each other.' July twentieth: 'Our love for each other will take us through anything.' August first: 'More and more I feel the magic coming out of your eyes. I love your love.' " Rob dropped the notes on the table.

Nancy said, "Talk about nutty."

"Anything else?" Jablonski asked.

Shirley said, "Tell them about the telephone calls, Rob."

"The *lack* of them interests me." He flipped over a page. "There's something else. Very seldom, *very seldom,* do erotomaniacs resort to violence. Remember, this type of delusional person is *without any other signs of serious mental disturbance.* The others who go around stabbing and shooting and slashing are, without exception, psychotics."

Jablonski interrupted. "What you're saying is that, after demonstrating relatively inhibited behavior for months and months, the act of throwing acid into Miss O'Reilly's face doesn't fit the usual pattern."

"It really doesn't," Rob replied. "But then psychiatry isn't an exact science."

The four of them sat quietly for a few moments.

"What's the personality profile of a typical erotomaniac?" Jablonski asked the psychiatrist.

"The majority of people with these delusions are withdrawn and lonely. Many have had few sexual encounters and, according to the literature that I dug up, some are notably unattractive. Combine these elements and you can readily see why they fixate on others of superior status, looks, or authority."

Shirley got up. "I don't know about the rest of you, but I could use some hot coffee."

"A welcome idea," Jablonski responded. "And just a sliver of that peach pie, if there still is some."

"Coming up," Shirley answered.

Nancy asked the hostess, "You need some help?"

"Thanks. You could pile up a few plates and tote them on out."

When they were alone Jablonski said, "Barring some unforeseen piece of luck, we don't have much of a chance to nail the guy who damaged Mikki. Unless . . ." The detective pondered briefly. "Unless we could think of a way to get him back into the fray."

"The way his last note reads, I don't think there's much chance of that. It would seem to me that he's separated himself from the young woman permanently."

"If and when the lady recovers and returns to the broadcast, maybe that will change the ground rules."

The psychiatrist nodded. "Maybe. How is she coming along?" Jablonski repeated the latest medical bulletin from Mikki. "Sounds moderately hopeful. Corneal transplants aren't usually a big deal and the plastic surgeons are performing miracles these days."

"Let us hope so," Jablonski responded fervently.

The women returned from the kitchen. Nancy placed a piece of pie in front of Jablonski. "Eat hearty."

"That's not a sliver," Jablonski complained.

Nancy turned to the doctor. "What causes a person to become an erotomaniac?"

"There's no broad agreement on a single psychodynamic explanation," Rob replied. "In the research I went through, most of the authors were impressed by the patients' lonely, isolated lives and their extreme dependence on their parents. One theory that appeared regularly was that the patient felt himself to have been plucked from obscurity and singled out for the object's love. This suggests that erotomaniacal delusions serve narcissistic needs, perhaps being expressed as the delusion of being loved because that is the ultimate form of approval."

"Can you put that in simpler terms?" Nancy asked.

The doctor smiled. "No."

"Let me try," Jablonski volunteered. "Guy lives alone. Guy feels lonesome and neglected. Guy decides Miss Wonderful loves him. Guy feels better."

Nancy said, "This is all fascinating, but where it leads I can't imagine."

"Patience," Jablonski said. "We may yet find out."

During the drive to Nancy's house in nearby Burbank, she sat sedately on the passenger side of the front seat and stared out the window.

After a dozen blocks of silence Jablonski inquired, "Something I said?"

"Hmmm?"

"All of a sudden you're so quiet."

She sighed. "Too bad you're so thoroughly married, Jablonski. I'll bet, when we get home, you're not even going to give me a goodnight kiss."

"Before we get down to specifics, would you mind if I asked you a question?"

"Go ahead."

"Why me?"

"Why you what?"

"I am a plump, fifty-five-year-old gentleman of modest physical attributes, clearly set in my ways. What possible attraction could I hold for an unattached, bright, well-formed creature such as yourself?"

"Why don't you just accept your good fortune, and stop thinking of me as an unsolved case?"

"I wish I could, but I'm unaccustomed to being pursued by the opposite sex."

Nancy thought for a minute. "The day you walked into the station I thought you were kind of adorable."

Jablonski waited. "That's it?"

"That's all it takes."

"Are you often overcome with such feelings as the result of a chance encounter?"

"I'm not a bimbo, Jablonski, if that's what you mean."

"Nothing could be farther from my mind."

She pointed to the first intersection ahead. "Turn left. Then how about I cook dinner Saturday night? At your house."

"At *my* house?"

"My son is having some of his friends over." She indicated a red brick apartment building at the end of the block, then removed her .38 from the glove compartment and put it in her purse. "I promise to leave this at home. You'll be perfectly safe."

"Well . . ."

"Relax. Whatever happens, happens. Or not, as the case may be."

As he pulled the car to a stop, Nancy leaned over and gave him a peck on the cheek. "What do you say?"

"I guess I can handle that. What do you want me to buy?"

"We'll go shopping in the afternoon. See you around five."

Jablonski spent most of the ride home telling himself that there was nothing wrong with a home-cooked meal and a little female companionship.

CHAPTER TWENTY-FIVE

JABLONSKI pulled the Honda into his garage and got out and stretched. It took a moment for him to realize that the usual sounds produced by the puppy upon his arrival were not to be heard. He started for the gate to the back yard.

"Snoop? Where you hiding, pal?" There was no response. "Snoopy, come!"

Quickly he returned to his car and helped himself to the flashlight. "Snoopy?"

He stepped into the yard and shined the light back and forth over the area. When he failed to spot the dog, he turned the beam to the bottom of the fence and traced along the perimeter. Halfway down Snoopy had dug a deep hole. In her effort to escape under the barrier, her collar had caught on one of the strands. Thus trapped, she apparently worked her way out of the restraint and had run away.

Heartsick, Jablonski picked up the collar and examined the disk listing his address and phone number. He flipped to Snoopy's license, then fingered the circlet that verified her inoculation against rabies. Dear God, he thought, it's almost midnight and she's out there someplace without a shred of identification. Even if she is lucky enough to get picked up, her rescuer would have no way of knowing whom to call. Goddamnit, he fumed, gritting his teeth.

"Snoopy, come!" he shouted into the night. "Snoopy, come!"

After an hour of fruitless search he returned to his street. As he approached his house a flicker of hope burned inside his chest. Maybe she's come back, he thought. Maybe!

"Snoopy? You there, girl? Snoop?"

But there was no response.

He left the side gate ajar in case she decided to return. After unlocking the back door to the kitchen and propping it halfway open with the West L.A. phone book, he placed a doggie treat on the rug beside Snoopy's basket.

It was a bad night. He slept fitfully and every time he awakened he leaned over and looked down to see whether the animal had wandered back. But her basket was always empty. Before seven o'clock the next morning he rolled out of bed, exhausted and discouraged.

At least, he thought to himself, it's daylight. Maybe now I'll have better luck.

He skipped breakfast and arrived at the office half an hour early. He checked with the West Los Angeles animal shelter. No dice.

Shirley was scarcely through the door when he began barking orders. "Snoopy ran away last night while I was at your house. Bring your book in here."

"What happened?"

"She dug a hole under the fence and snagged her collar. She's wandering around somewhere in my neighborhood without any identification. First, call the L.A. *Times* and see how soon we can get an ad in. Second, go to the printer down the block and order about fifty signs, eleven by fourteen, describing the dog, giving my phone number, and offering a reward. Put a rush on the order." Temporarily out of steam, he sank back in his chair.

Shirley walked around the desk and put her hand on Jablonski's shoulder. "Don't drive yourself crazy, Jack."

"I wish I knew what to do." He shrugged helplessly.

"I have an idea. Why not take your car and canvass the neighborhood? Maybe one of the jogging fraternity saw Snoopy. Or, what the hell, you might get lucky and see her wandering around someplace."

Jablonski thought for a minute. "Sure. Why not?" He got up and shuffled toward the door.

* * *

When the detective returned to the office more than three hours, later it wasn't necessary to inquire how his quest had gone. Failure was written all over his face.

"Nothing," Jablonski mumbled.

"I'm truly sorry," Shirley responded. She paused momentarily then said, "Mikki called a few minutes ago. Another letter came in the mail this morning."

This news visibly stiffened the detective's spine. "The creep is back in business?"

"Apparently."

"Call her and say I'm on the way over, and also not to mess up the note. There may be prints."

"She said she was sure her aunt handled everything correctly. It seems that the lady is taking lessons from that celebrity protector you interviewed."

"Did either of them call the cops?"

"Not yet. They're waiting to hear from you."

At the front door to the office Jablonski turned to Shirley. "Did you take care of the stuff for Snoopy?"

"All done. The cards will be ready at four o'clock. In the meantime, we'll keep our fingers crossed."

"Screw crossed fingers and all other varieties of black magic. The only way we're gonna get Snoopy back is by covering every base. I'll do another sweep of the neighborhood later today and put up the signs."

The newly arrived note read, *"I was watching the movie on your station when they said youd be interviewed on the news. I cant believe your on the television again. Ill be watching every night from now on. It was a terrible thing what happened to you. You are so gorgeous even when I cant look into your eyes. When you stood up and said goodnight your beautiful body just called out to me."*

Mikki and Aunt Belle watched as Jablonski picked up the tweezers from the dining room table and flipped the letter over. There was nothing written on the back.

"The guy is positively loquacious in this one," he observed. He leaned down and examined the envelope in which the missive had been mailed. "Like the others, same zip code as yours. Same A.M. postmark. Most likely deposited in the box in the wee small hours Thursday morning."

Mikki wondered, "How do you interpret, 'It was a terrible thing what happened to you'?"

Jablonski hunched up his shoulders. "Sounds almost apologetic, like he's guilty about what he did."

Aunt Belle spoke up. "That line about Mikki's body calling out to him. *That* gives me the creeps."

"How do you think I feel?" the young woman asked.

The detective took a few minutes to tell them what he and Sergeant Baxter had learned from Shirley's husband the previous evening.

"Incidentally, Mikki," Jablonski continued, "the line about your body calling out to him is similar to a statement in an earlier note. The one where he said he felt the magic coming out of your eyes. According to the doctor, this kind of language absolutely indicates someone who's erotomaniacal."

"And you say those lost souls aren't supposed to be violent." She smiled wanly. "Except sometimes. I guess I'm a 'sometimes.'"

"It would seem so."

"And now the creature is sorry for what he did," Aunt Belle said, shaking her head. "It's all so cruel and pointless."

"I considered staking out the post office," Jablonski observed ruefully. "I wish I had."

"Don't torture yourself, Jack. The attack on me was over a month ago. For all we knew, the guy who did it could have gone to the moon."

Jablonski sighed. "Have you found a new place to live? With this latest development I would think it's essential that you move as quickly as possible."

Aunt Belle answered. "We haven't had any luck so far, but Mr. Merriweather thinks that by adding round-the-clock guards and changing all the locks Mikki's safe enough for now."

"He's the expert," the detective acknowledged.

Mikki said, "Belle, make a note of our new phone number for Mr. Jablonski."

"I already gave it to his secretary."

For the first time during the meeting, the detective slumped back in his chair and breathed a sigh of relief. "At last we're onto something. The next time Baldy writes a letter, he's mine."

"But it could be weeks, or maybe months, before he decides to do that," Aunt Belle pointed out.

"Not if we force the issue." He took Mikki by the hand. "You have to be interviewed on the air again. And the sooner the better. Can you set that up?"

"I can try. To have me on the show *once* is one thing. But a second time so soon, I don't know how Arnold will feel about that."

"Tell your news director he could end up with an exclusive when the cops pinch your attacker."

Mikki smiled broadly. "That ought to do it." She thought for a moment. "What time is it?"

Aunt Belle looked up at the small clock over the swinging door to the kitchen. "Coming up on three."

"Damn!" Mikki mumbled. "Probably too late for tonight's show. I could try to get Arnold to schedule it for Monday."

"That's time enough," Jablonski replied. "Can I borrow your phone? I want to tell Sergeant Baxter about the latest note and also what I have in mind for dropping a net on your pursuer. The police will want to be in on this."

Mikki said, "There's a phone in the hall. Around to your right."

"After I work out the details, should I coordinate with Arnold Tolkin at your station?"

"Yes. I'll tell him you'll be calling."

As he walked toward his car, Jablonski found himself thinking about Snoopy. He decided to stop by his house before going back to the office. There's just a chance, he told himself, maybe an off-chance, that she came home and was waiting for him.

Shirley was stacking the newly printed signs against a chair in the outer office when a dejected Jablonski entered.

"They finished these an hour early," she explained. "They were just delivered."

"I want to make a couple of calls before I go on the prowl again," he responded grumpily.

Shirley followed him into the inner sanctum. "You may not have to."

"Not have to what?"

"Go on the prowl again."

Jablonski's eyes brightened. "Did you hear something?" he asked eagerly.

"Yeah, I did."

"Well, spit it out!"

"I think I sort of know where Snoopy is."

"Where?" he demanded.

"Sit down, Jack," she suggested. "This needs a preface."

After the detective had seated himself, Shirley continued. "Now don't get excited."

"Who's excited?" Jablonski demanded.

"I took your microcassette recorder, the one you dictate into, over to Marla May's. I wanted to be sure I got all the details right."

Jablonski slammed his fedora down on the desk. "You're going to tell me Marla May Willowbrook, that ancient bagful of superstitions and sappiness, has pretended to pinpoint the whereabouts of my dog? Give me a goddamn break."

"Not exactly pinpoint."

"What then?"

"Will you at least listen to what she said?"

Jablonski sighed deeply. "I don't believe this."

His secretary placed the dictating machine on the desk and pushed the play button. "You'll find this interesting."

"Nothing's impossible," Marla May was saying. *"Napoleon had it right: 'Impossibility is a word only to be found in the dictionary of fools.' Did you discover the animal's birth date?"*

"Yes. We keep her pedigree papers in the office files."

"Don't tell me now. Wait until I'm in the trance."

"For God's sake," Jablonski moaned.

"Sssssh!"

"I recall meeting the dog one day with Mr. Jablonski. That will make things considerably easier."

"Let's man the pumps," Jablonski growled. "It's getting too thin to shovel."

"Animals are psychic. How do you think the swallows know when to come back to Capistrano?"

There followed a rustling of cloth that Jablonski presumed was the green taffeta dress that the Madame favored.

"*I'm told my breathing is very shallow and rhythmic when I have reached the trance-like state. Wait until then to ask your questions.*"

"It took her about three minutes to go under," Shirley explained. "Shall I fast forward?"

"Please," Jablonski said resignedly.

"I think she really gets onto something. You'll be surprised."

"I can hardly wait."

Shirley stared at Jablonski as the microcassette hummed. "You don't have to clench your teeth."

"I'm not clenching my teeth."

"Then how come the muscles in your jaw are rippling?" She stopped the tape and rewound it to a specific point. "Listen. First you'll hear me lay it out for her."

"*Miss Willowbrook, I am looking for a small black cocker spaniel female named Snoopy, born on March second of this year in Banning, California. Is the dog still alive?*"

A long pause was followed by Marla May's measured, almost unintelligible response, "*The body is alive.*"

Jablonski sat up. "What's this about a body?"

"Listen!"

"*Where is the body now?*"

Another pause. "*The body is happy.*"

"*Where is the body now?*"

Marla May didn't speak for ten seconds. "*The body is in the country house.*"

"*The body is out in the country in a house?*"

"*The body is in the country house.*"

"*Does the body want to come home?*"

"*The body is happy.*"

"She's a goddamn broken record," Jablonski complained.

"*Will I find the body?*" Shirley asked.

Another insufferable pause. "*No.*"

"*But the body is safe?*"

"*The body is alive and happy in the country house.*"

"*Thank you. That's all I have to ask.*"

Marla May coughed her way back to consciousness. "*What did I say, Shirley?*"

"You don't know?"

"Of course not."

"You said that the dog is alive and happy in the country house."

"I hope that is helpful."

"I don't know. Maybe my boss can figure it out." The tape cut off.

"Well, what do you think?" Shirley asked Jablonski.

"I think it's a crock. The old broad was just trying to give you your money's worth."

"She didn't charge me and your misogyny is overpowering."

Jablonski said, "Get me Nancy Baxter."

"Yes, *sir!*" Shirley responded, flouncing out of the room.

"You don't have to get sore," he called out. "I can't help it if I'm upset."

"I'm not sore. I'm disappointed." A moment later his buzzer sounded twice.

"Nancy, hi. How did you do with your captain?"

"He won't cooperate," the sergeant replied.

"What are you saying?" Jablonski replied, suddenly agitated. "This is the first decent chance we've had to drop a net on the bum who wrecked Mikki."

"He says what you propose is as full of holes as a Swiss cheese. Claims we don't have enough manpower to cover the post office for twelve hours on the off chance that the guy shows up."

"He'll *show* up," Jablonski insisted.

"He also feels that there's at least a fifty-fifty chance the letters were mailed in some post office box within the zip code, not at the main headquarters. As far as he's concerned, you're spinning your wheels."

"He's still pissed off at what Mikki said on TV about the cops."

"Maybe."

"Guess I'll just have to go forward without you guys." He hung up and adjusted his fedora. In the outer office he picked up an armful of signs.

"Did you think to get a hammer and nails?"

"Better. I got some big thumb tacks." Shirley handed him the box. "Remember to display those things where there's a stoplight. Drivers can't read worth a damn when they're zooming along. I'll put one up in the supermarket and another over your parking place in the gas station."

"Thanks."
"See you Monday."
"Good hunting, Jack."

CHAPTER TWENTY-SIX

AFTER he had loaded up the Honda, Jablonski pawed through the various maps of Los Angeles that he kept in the glove compartment and located the one that covered the Brentwood area. Since there was no logical way to develop a strategy for posting the signs, he arbitrarily decided to work in an ever-widening square, using his house as the center point.

Even though he continued to believe Shirley's visit to Marla May's sanctuary was an exercise in wishful thinking, his mind kept churning over the psychic's words, "The body is in the country house." She had said it three times on the tape exactly that way. Not "in *a* country house," but "in *the* country house." He mulled this over at some length. Did she mean the *country* house as opposed to the *modern* house, or the *ranch* house? Considering the Madame's utterance in this light, he had to admit that it might not be entirely frivolous.

He began to consider what architectural characteristics *"the country house"* might have. English? French? What? He decided that he would concentrate on the various residences along his route to determine if one of them met the psychic's description.

A half hour later he happened across a thatched dwelling of the type often seen in Cornwall and Wales. By now, because of his continuing exertions, his appearance was that of a motorist whose car had broken down alongside the highway: no jacket, tie down, hair thoroughly windblown. Worse, he suspected he had a wild look in his eyes.

He took a minute to get his breath before ringing the doorbell of the abode. After a suitable pause he heard the safety chain being connected. Slowly the door opened.

Through the crack a short, plump Mexican maid asked, "Sí?"

At some length the detective explained his mission.

When he finished, the woman replied, *"Yo no comprendo Ingles."*

"Dog," Jablonski said desperately, making the single syllable sound like two. "Dog." For one wild moment he considered barking, but he was afraid of scaring the woman out of her senses.

An eight-year-old boy appeared in the background. *"Por favor, Maria,"* he said, moving the maid to one side. "What is it, sir?"

Again Jablonski went through his routine.

"I'm sorry, sir. We have no animals. My mother is allergic to cats and dogs." As an afterthought he added, "And birds."

After soliciting a promise from the youth that he would keep his eyes open, Jablonski gave him his card and thanked him.

At the end of the day, his supply of placards exhausted and his spirits at their lowest ebb since he took on Mikki's case, he decided to go home. He was driving down Twenty-sixth Street, a principal north-south artery in Brentwood, when, for no particular reason, he decided to turn into a quiet, tree-lined street. In order to study the expensive domiciles dotting the area, he drove slowly, pausing for a prolonged period at each of the several intersections he had to cross. But nothing caught his attention until he turned into the street that led down to San Vicente Boulevard, a block to the south.

On his left, several hundred yards away, stood the most beautiful reproduction of a French country farmhouse he had ever seen. From its craggy stone exterior to the design of its slate covered roof, it was a perfect example of the architect's art. The fence bordering the place, the planting, the leaded glass windows, everything was perfect.

Hurriedly Jablonski pulled up across the street and parked. The wide driveway that fronted the residence was covered with clay bricks of irregular shapes. He got out of the Honda and crossed the street. He peered through the slim bars of the gate, admiring the grassy, circular mound on which a stand of birch trees had been planted.

At one side of the vehicle entrance stood an inverted L-shaped bar that held a box containing a call button and a keypad used to activate the gate. With his pulse rate climbing, Jablonski gave the button half a dozen sharp jabs.

What the hell is the matter with me? he asked himself. Am I so desperate to find Snoopy that I've embraced Marla May's free-floating trumpery?

Before he could answer himself, a handsome, middle-aged woman in a white, four-door Mercedes pulled up.

"Can I help you?" she inquired.

As Jablonski was outlining his dilemma, the woman's face broke into a warm smile.

"Your puppy's here."

Jablonski could scarcely believe his good fortune.

"We heard her scratching at the dining room door last night while we were having dinner. She's adorable."

"I can't begin to tell you how relieved I am," the detective admitted. He sighed happily.

"Forgive me. I'm Valerie Harkness."

"Jablonski. Jackson Jablonski. Please excuse the way I look, Mrs. Harkness. I've been running all over the neighborhood for the past couple of hours posting notices about Snoopy."

"Is that her name? We've been calling her Blackie and it worked just fine."

"You could call her Mabel and she'd come running. She's too affectionate for her own good."

The woman laughed. "I don't think so. But why are we standing out here?"

"Why, indeed?"

The woman leaned out toward the keypad and punched in the combination. Slowly, the gate opened.

"Come along, Mr. Jablonski."

The detective followed the Mercedes to a stop, then opened the door for Snoopy's savior. As Mrs. Harkness inserted the key into the front door, the sound of paws scurrying across a polished wooden floor could be heard.

"That's your puppy," the woman said.

Carefully she pushed open the heavy portal. As the crack widened, Snoopy wriggled through, her stubby tail vibrating as fast as a hummingbird's wings. The detective knelt down to pick up the animal who, upon feeling human contact, proceeded to go berserk. While licking her master's hands and face and whining happily, she proceeded once again to demonstrate the depth of her affection. This time she peed on his shirt.

Jablonski sighed ruefully, "I wish she didn't love me so much."

On the short drive back to his house he considered the preceding events. There was no getting around the fact that he never would have had the opportunity to tinker with the meaning of the phrase "the country house" if it hadn't been for Shirley's session with Marla May Willowbrook. The fact that he apparently guessed what the old woman meant by it was, in itself, a sheer piece of luck. But there were other occurrences (coincidences?) equally as intriguing.

Why, he wondered, did he arbitrarily make a left turn off of Twenty-sixth Street? Never before, while driving home, had he selected that route. And what caused him to swing right at the fourth intersection, the cross street on which the Harkness home stood? He'd never done that either. The more he thought about the whole episode, the more bizarre it seemed.

The first thing Jablonski did when he got home was to change his shirt. Then he phoned Shirley and told her of his good fortune.

"So it turns out Marla May's not so batty after all," his secretary suggested.

"I'm not sure I'd go quite that far. Do me a favor. On your way out, drop in and extend my apologies for any past doubts I may have exhibited concerning her abilities. Also tell her I'm in her debt."

"Why don't you tell her yourself?" his secretary asked. "I think she'd be thrilled."

"You're right. I should. Happy weekend."

When he had finished his conversation he prepared a dish of food for Snoopy.

"I don't know when you ate last, but what the hell."

While the animal was devouring the lamb, rice, and kibble mixture, the detective busied himself locating the telephone number of a local establishment that specialized in the installation of fences. He arranged for its artisans to arrive first thing the following morning and extend the bottom of the barricade in his backyard eight inches deeper into the ground, thus preventing another escape by his pet.

Finally he called Mikki and learned that she had been able to arrange for a second interview that would be aired Monday night. Also that Channel Ten's news director had given his enthusiastic approval for a team to accompany Jablonski during the stakeout of the 91604 area post office following the program.

Things are beginning to come together, the detective thought to himself.

He poured a stiff drink of Cutty Sark scotch and called Daphne to report on his adventure with Snoopy.

"I don't know what I'd do without that puppy," his wife said. "Thank the good Lord things worked out the way they did."

"Speaking of things working out, what news on the baby front?"

"It'll be any minute now. There's no question in my mind about that."

"How do you know?"

"I know."

Jablonski was wise enough not to pursue the subject any further.

After hanging up, he realized he hadn't mentioned the fact that Nancy Baxter would be cooking dinner for him tomorrow night. Right here. In the Jablonski kitchen.

Briefly, he wondered what Shirley's husband Rob would have to say about the omission.

CHAPTER TWENTY-SEVEN

SATURDAY morning, while Jablonski was explaining to the men from the fence company what he wanted done in the back yard, Petey Bosworth showed up with an armful of copies of his school newspaper.

"Hot off the press yesterday," the youth announced. "How many would you like?"

"I'll have to read what you wrote before I can make a decision," the detective replied. "If it's favorable, I'll take a couple. If it's a pan, I'll buy the whole stack just to keep the story off the street."

Petey handed Jablonski a copy. "Page five. I asked for page two but it was already filled up."

"How many pages in the paper?"

"Six. But, at least, you're up at the top left." As Jablonski began to thumb through the publication, Petey added, "There's one more thing. They spelled your name wrong. I write in longhand and I guess my *J*'s look like *Y*'s."

The detective read aloud, " 'Jack Yablonski, former FBI man, sets up shop in Brentwood.' How come they got the *J* right on Jack?"

"Prob'ly the computer operator never heard of anyone named Yack."

"Before this turns into a comedy routine, why don't we go into the kitchen and brew up a pot of cocoa? Or is there something else you'd prefer?"

"Actually I'd like a Perrier if you have one."

"I've got some soda."

Petey shook his head. "It's not the same."

While the boy played with the puppy, Jablonski prepared the cocoa. When he had finished, he sat down at the kitchen table and read through the article.

"What do you think?" Petey asked, taking the chair across from Jablonski.

"I never said 'To prevail over the Forces of Evil is one of Life's most profound delights,' or 'Unraveling a knotty case is like enjoying a glass of fine wine.' "

"I will readily admit to fabrication in those two instances. But since most of your answers were almost overwhelmingly straightforward, I thought the spice of elaboration was indicated. Are you offended?"

"On the contrary. In this part of town, a newcomer who sounds like William Buckley ought to be welcomed with open arms." Jablonski filled each of their cups. "Did Miss Montgomery show up at school yesterday?"

"Yes, she did." Petey added a spoonful of sugar to his cocoa. "She also asked to me stay after class."

"Indeed?"

"She thanked me for being concerned about her and told me that her husband was going to start a regimen to bring his alcoholism under control." He took a sip. "Wow, is that hot!" He blew into his cup. "I wish I felt reassured."

"What's that supposed to mean?"

"He isn't going to start treatment until next week. And there's still tonight to get through."

"What's so special about tonight?"

"It's Saturday."

"So?"

"Surely, Mr. Jablonski, you of all people must know that violent crime reaches its peak each weekend, particularly on this night."

"We're not talking about crack houses or drive-by shootings here, Petey. Alcoholism is a problem that many families have to deal with. It can be tragic; that's for damn sure. But do I have to remind you again that this sad fact doesn't give the rest of us a license to stick our noses into other people's business?"

Petey looked away. "I can't help worrying. The way Miss Montgomery's husband kept hitting her . . ." The boy shuddered.

Jablonski decided it was time to deliver the *coup de grace*. "Petey you have a bad case of puppy love. This condition has caused your judgment to become distorted and, if I'm not mistaken, has produced a multitude of intense feelings in you for which there is, as yet, no satisfactory outlet. That includes spying.

"In spite of the fact that Miss Montgomery embodies all that is tender, desirable and exciting, there is no point to your continuing pursuit of her. She is an older married lady and her relationship to you is that of teacher to pupil. Do I make myself clear?"

The boy looked sheepish. "I guess so."

"Go out and fall in love with someone your own age."

"Nobody's come along yet."

"You're twelve and you're impatient. Also your hormones are starting to act up. But you'll survive. Most of us have."

Petey stood up and stuck out his hand. "I wish my dad would talk to me like this."

"You feel better?"

"Yeah. As long as I don't think about Miss Montgomery, I'm okay."

"Good. Don't think about her."

"Trouble is when I try to concentrate on other things, she keeps intruding."

"Tell her to buzz off."

"I don't know if that will work."

Jablonski put the cups in the sink. "Give it a shot." He showed the youth to the door. "Remember, if you ever need me, especially while your folks are out of town, I'll be right here."

"Thanks. I will."

The job on the backyard fence was a simple one and the laborers finished it shortly before one o'clock.

"Your puppy will never get out of here," the team leader assured Jablonski.

"It is devoutly to be hoped," the detective replied.

Following the workmen's departure, Jablonski made himself a grilled cheese sandwich. Then, since nothing was scheduled for the rest of the afternoon until Nancy's arrival, he decided to drive to his office and dictate answers to some of the inquiries he had received as a result of Mikki's plug during the evening news. In the process, if Marla May Willowbrook happened to be in residence, he planned to visit with her.

As he started up the lane toward his office door, he discovered the old woman busily dusting the several pots of ivy that sat on the inside ledge of the window that fronted her small enterprise.

"Miss Willowbrook," he called out.

She opened the door. "Good afternoon, Mr. Jablonski. And, for your information, it's *Mrs.* Willowbrook, although my husband passed over many years ago."

Jablonski considered asking if she still kept in touch with him but decided that would start the conversation off on the wrong tone. Instead he said, "Of course. I should have noticed the wedding ring."

"Shirley told me the good news about your dog. Have I made a believer out of you?"

Jablonski smiled. "I don't know if I'd go quite that far. But, after yesterday's adventure, I'm willing to concede there are some things that cannot be explained by simple logic alone."

"Many things, Mr. Jablonski." She beckoned to the detective. "Won't you come in? My next client isn't due for half an hour."

Her quarters were cramped, approximately eight by ten feet. The walls were covered in deep, red velvet and the various pieces of furniture looked as if they had survived for half a century.

"I'm pleased to find you here on a Saturday," he told her. "I didn't want to wait a whole weekend before thanking you for your assistance."

"You're entirely welcome." She pointed to an ancient Chesterfield sofa. "Please." She sat down at circular table upon which a six-inch crystal ball and several sticks of incense rested. "Actually Saturday is my busiest time. Particularly in the evening."

"Really? I would have thought that people out for a good time would be more inclined to concentrate on the pleasures of the moment, rather than in what the future might hold."

"Happily, I have become somewhat of a cult figure in the neighborhood. As you may have noticed, there are several nightspots nearby that cater to the young. The teenagers, in particular, keep me very busy."

The detective smiled politely. "I'm curious, Mrs. Willowbrook, how you first discovered you possessed the gift of clairvoyance?"

The old woman lit a stick of incense. She placed it, base down, in a slim silver container on the table.

"It was as a young child that I first realized that God had made me special. One night, when I was in second grade, I fell asleep while reading a new book my mother had given me. It was called *Rebecca of Sunnybrook Farm*. Perhaps you've heard of it."

"Indeed I have, although I have never partaken personally."

"A perfectly charming tale. I had only gotten through two chapters before I drifted off. The next morning, when I woke up, I knew the entire story by heart and could even quote lines from it word for word."

"I find that hard to believe."

"But it's true. I must have actually slept *on* the book. The mind functions on more levels than you can know."

"It would certainly seem so."

The old woman leaned forward in her chair. "How many people who experienced true psychic phenomena were judged insane and put behind locked doors, simply because other people couldn't accept the truth of what had happened? How many 'witches' [she spit out the word] were drowned or burned at the stake before man came to understand that just because something couldn't be explained by an established scientific law, it wasn't necessarily evil?" Marla May pointed a bony finger at him. "I feel you are less hostile toward my calling today, Mr. Jablonski. That is an important step forward."

"If so, it's all thanks to your good offices, Mrs. Willowbrook."

"Come closer."

The detective took the chair across from the old woman.

"Do you know what mythology tells us?" she whispered.

"No," he whispered back. "What?"

"There was a conference of the gods at the moment the Universe was formed. One god said, 'Let's give man the same power of comprehension that we possess.' Another asked, 'Where shall we conceal this priceless gift?' A third god said, 'Let's hide the gift where man will never think to look for it . . . within his own mind.' Consider, Mr. Jablonski: why did you alter your normal driving route yesterday?"

"The answer to that continues to elude me."

"Well, it shouldn't elude you any longer. You have gifts too. Yesterday you demonstrated them."

The detective shook his head doubtfully. " 'Jackson Jablonski, The Prognosticative Investigator.' Aren't you afraid I'll put you out of business, Mrs. Willowbrook?"

"There is no danger of that. My prowess exceeds yours by any measure you care to apply. That is why I continue to remind you of what a happy and productive association ours could be."

Jablonski said, "I speak with great sincerity this time, Mrs. Willowbrook. Your abilities are not to be taken lightly."

The old woman studied him for a long moment. "I believe you. And, in case you care, I feel you are in for a very exciting evening."

"Would you care to elaborate?"

She looked at her watch. "I'm afraid there isn't time."

CHAPTER TWENTY-EIGHT

LATE Saturday afternoon Nancy Baxter pulled up in front of Jablonski's house and tooted her horn twice. When he appeared in the front doorway she called out, "Shopping time! Your car or mine?"

"Mine. I know the neighborhood."

Jablonski watched as she slid out from behind the wheel and started across the lawn toward him.

She was dressed in a light blue velveteen skirt and a pale yellow blouse. Her high heeled shoes were dark blue and a matching purse was carelessly slung over her shoulder. To top things off, a pair of huge white circlets hung from her ears.

"I'm surprised, Nancy. I thought we were going to have dinner here."

"Who said we weren't?"

"An outfit as fancy as yours belongs in the best restaurant in town."

"When I get through in your kitchen, it'll *be* the best restaurant in town. I hope you're hungry."

"Starving. I haven't eaten since lunch. What's on the menu?"

"Is there a decent grocery store in these parts? Not a supermarket, but a place that carries the *crème de la crème*?"

"There's one in the Palisades. Ten minutes from here."

An hour later they returned, loaded down with four shopping bags.

"We *should* have gone to a restaurant," Jablonski groused. "I'm already in for ninety-three bananas."

"That's not my fault," Nancy replied. "I didn't tell you to go for two bottles of twenty-five-buck wine."

"Considering the trouble you're going to, it's the least I could do."

Jablonski gave Snoopy her dinner and then indicated her basket near the stove. "Go take a nice, long nap."

The couple consumed the first bottle during the hour and a half it took Nancy to prepare dinner. In spite of the glow provided by the pungent chardonnay, Jablonski had difficulty adjusting to the sight of his guest wearing one of Daphne's aprons and was relieved when she finally shed the garment.

As Nancy was dishing up the first course, she inquired, "How about some candlelight?"

Jablonski brushed aside the idea. "I don't think we have any candles."

"I can't believe that." She began rummaging through the drawers in the cabinet near the refrigerator. A moment later she produced two long, slender tapers. "Ta da! Now how about holders?"

"Holders?"

"The little things with the hole in the middle where you stick the candles. Remember?"

"To tell you the truth, Nancy, when I eat, I like to see what I'm doing."

"We'll leave a light on in the living room."

Jablonski sighed. "They're up with the wine glasses, I think."

After locating the objects, she handed them to Jablonski. "Be creative."

As he was lighting the candles there was a distant rumble of thunder.

"Goody. It's going to rain," Nancy observed. She placed two platefuls of snails on the table. "Maybe we can have a fire later."

Clearly, Jablonski thought to himself, Nancy Baxter takes no prisoners.

He opened the second bottle of wine and sampled it. "Highly satisfactory," he observed. After filling both their glasses he leaned over his plate and savored the aroma of the appetizer. "These critters smell so fine, it'd be a shame to eat them."

"Don't keep me in suspense."

Jablonski popped a snail into his mouth and closed his eyes. "Ummm MMM!"

Although it didn't seem possible, the meal only got better from this point on. A consommé with croutons was followed by a mixed green salad.

"Save room," Nancy cautioned.

"Have no fear," Jablonski said, rubbing his hands together. "Bring on the main course."

"Not yet. First some lemon *sorbet* to cleanse your palate."

"I've never had my palate cleansed before. I trust you'll be gentle."

To follow the tartness of the *sorbet,* she had prepared stuffed chicken breasts and mixed vegetables. As Jablonski was helping himself to some of the tender meat, a blinding flash of lightning lit up the neighborhood.

"Hang onto your hat," he told his companion. "The next sound you hear will be a doozie." A second later a tremendous clap of thunder shook the kitchen windows.

Nancy commented, "Storm's right overhead."

At that point the heavens opened and the rain came pelting down.

"Did you close the windows in your car?" Jablonski asked.

"Yes."

"Thank God for small favors."

During dinner Jablonski managed to keep the conversation more or less centered on the Mikki O'Reilly case. He emphasized his displeasure at the parochial attitude of local police departments in general and the intransigence of Nancy's commanding officer in particular. By the time they had finished the last of the wine, neither one of them was feeling any pain.

As she was clearing the dishes from the main course, Nancy inquired, "Did you ever ask yourself why I wanted to make dinner tonight?"

"The question occurred to me."

" 'The way to a man's heart is through his stomach.' Right?"

"I've heard it said."

"How'm I doing?"

Actually she was doing a lot better than Jablonski was prepared to admit.

"Stand by for the final touch," she announced.

Minutes later she produced a peach Melba that turned out to be extraordinary.

When he was done, Jablonski reclined in his chair and said wistfully, "That was so good, I could lick my plate."

"Go right ahead," Nancy replied. "And when you're finished, if you like, you can lick mine."

While Jablonski was trying to figure out a suitable response to this suggestion, someone began pounding on the front door. The noise woke Snoopy out of a sound sleep and triggered the puppy into a paroxysm of high-pitched barking.

"Who the hell is that?" Nancy asked, clearly annoyed.

The detective got up and started toward the hall. "I don't have the faintest idea." He snapped on the porch light and peered out of the peephole in the door. "Jesus!" He flung open the door. "What are *you* doing here?"

Petey Bosworth looked half drowned. He sputtered, "I couldn't call because somebody had busted up the telephone I used the other night." Another flash of lightning ripped the sky followed immediately by a crack of thunder.

"Get in here!" Jablonski ordered. The youth stepped across the threshold and fought to get his breath. "Nancy, there's a linen closet at the top of the steps. Bring something we can use to dry the kid off." As the woman hurried to comply, Jablonski closed the door and turned to Petey. "You've been spying on Miss Montgomery again. In spite of everything I said."

"I couldn't help it," the boy admitted. He began to tremble. "Something just made me do it."

Jablonski shook his head. "Okay, tell me what happened."

"I . . . I . . ." Suddenly Petey started gagging.

"Easy, now. Easy."

Nancy hurried down the stairs carrying a bundle of towels.

"Help me get him out of these wet clothes," Jablonski ordered.

Petey pulled away. "There's no time for that!"

Nancy said, "Could someone tell me . . ."

The detective made hurried introductions. "What's the matter, Petey? Talk to me."

With great effort the boy collected himself. "I . . . I think something awful's happened to Miss Montgomery."

"You *think*? I don't understand."

Nancy looked puzzled. "Who's . . . ?"

"I'll tell you later," Jablonski told her. "Come on, Petey, what the hell is it?"

Because of the youth's agitated state, the torrent of words that followed were nearly unintelligible. "Like I told you . . . was worried about tonight being Saturday . . . wanted to be sure Miss Montgomery's husband wouldn't start drinking again . . . do something bad to her so 'bout seven-thirty I rode over to their place on my bike . . . hadn't started raining. Before she came downstairs, I saw him go over to the bar . . . pour a glassful of something out of a square kind of bottle."

Jablonski interrupted, "A *glassful*?"

". . . think so . . . looked like it. When he heard her coming he put the top back on the bottle . . . sort of eased his way out into the front hall. When they came out to get into the car . . . he said they should hurry up or they'd be late . . . for their reservation at Vlaminck's."

"The restaurant across from the Mart on Twenty-sixth Street?"

"Yes. She asked him if he'd had a drink . . . He told her no. She was trying to sound real cheery. I could tell . . . said she was looking forward to having a date with him." Petey stopped for a moment to take a big breath. ". . . decided I better wait until they got home.

You know . . . to be sure she was okay . . . few minutes after that, it started pouring. Then about fifteen minutes ago, he came back."

"*He?*"

"I figured Miss Montgomery was still in the car. Her husband was real drunk. Staggered up the front steps and everything . . . When he was inside, I snuck over and looked inside to see if she was okay. She wasn't there."

Jablonski sighed. "Petey, she and her husband probably had a fight in the restaurant and Miss Montgomery went off someplace without him. Like the last time when she ran away. Remember?"

"There was a shoe, Mr. Jablonski."

"What?"

"One of Miss Montgomery's shoes was on the floor by the front seat."

For the first time Nancy intruded. "Did she have a coat on when she left the house, Petey?"

"No. That's another thing. She was wearing a real silky kind of red dress."

Nancy turned to Jablonski. "Why would the lady run off into the pouring rain in a skimpy gown with only one shoe on?"

Jablonski pondered for a moment. "Maybe she never left the restaurant. Or, even more intriguing, maybe she never even got there."

Petey begged, "You've got to do something, Mr. Jablonski! I know there's something really wrong."

Nancy asked the boy, "Did you happen to notice if she was carrying a purse?"

"No. But, if she was, it had to be real small because she was kind of twirling around and waving her arms up and down on the way to the car."

Nancy said, "I don't understand."

"She was, you know, kind of dancing." He paused. "Happy like."

Jablonski turned to his date. "Nancy, you're the cop. Call Vlaminck's and see whether the couple ever showed up. If they did, approximately what time did they arrive and when did they leave?"

"What does she look like, Petey?" Nancy asked.

"She's beautiful. Tall, willowy, with a real tiny nose."

Jablonski intervened. "The lady's about five-four, mouse brown hair. Green eyes. A hundred twenty. Has a beauty mark on the lower right side of her face just above the jaw line."

"Got it."

As the sergeant disappeared into the kitchen, Jablonski began peeling off the youth's jacket and shirt. "C'mon now," the detective ordered. "Cooperate." Petey took one of the bath towels and started wiping himself off. "And dry your hair."

"Forget about me!" the boy pleaded. "Her husband did something awful to Miss Montgomery. I know it! We've got to get going!"

"Where is it you think we should go?" Jablonski asked patiently.

"I don't *know*! But we just can't stand around here!"

"Steady down, Petey. What time was it when the man came back to the house?"

"I can tell you to the second. Seventeen minutes past nine."

The detective looked at his watch. "Just over a half hour ago." He heard the policewoman hang up the phone. "Come with me." In the doorway Jablonski almost collided with his guest. "Sorry, Nancy. What'd you find out?"

"The Martinellis were at Vlaminck's." Petey looked confused. "Martinelli is Miss Montgomery's married name. He had two martinis before dinner and a lot of wine with. She had hardly anything to drink. During the meal the husband kept getting louder and louder. When he asked for the check, she said she wanted to drive the car. Martinelli apparently got furious and started screaming at her . . ."

"See?" Petey interposed. "He always yelled at her before he hit her."

Nancy continued, "The *maître d'* was very happy when the couple finally left."

Jablonski asked, "Could he recall what time that was?"

"Martinelli paid with a credit card. I had the cashier look up the restaurant's copy of the computer printout. It read eight fifty-three P.M."

"Anything else?"

"Some. Apparently there's a glass door that leads to the street. The two of them stood outside in the pouring rain. Martinelli had hold of his wife by both arms and was calling her every name in the book. At one point she broke away from him and ran across the street into the Mart's parking lot, which, the *maître d'* said, was practically deserted. Martinelli ran after her."

"Then?" Jablonski demanded.

"Then nothing. Another couple arrived for dinner and had to be seated. The next time he looked out the window, there was no sign of either of the Martinellis. After that he forgot all about them until I phoned."

Jablonski suddenly looked worried.

"What is it, Jablonski?"

"Their dinner check was rung up at eight fifty-three. Figure another five or six minutes to complete the paperwork and for Martinelli's verbal abuse in front of the restaurant. That takes us to nine bells. Even in a downpour like we're having tonight, it wouldn't take longer than about ten or twelve minutes to drive from the Mart's parking lot on Twenty-sixth Street to the Martinelli residence."

"He got back there at exactly nine-seventeen," Petey repeated eagerly.

Nancy said, "That leaves approximately five minutes unaccounted for. Why don't I call dispatch and see if the lady used nine-one-one? Or if, God forbid, somebody phoned to report a female in trouble who fills her description."

"Good idea." Nancy hurried away. "Follow me, Petey." Jablonski started up the hall steps. "We're going to get you into some dry clothes before we do another thing." He looked back at the youth. "They may be a little large, but they're better than nothing."

"But Mr. Jablonski . . ."

"No buts."

"Okay. But, after I change, then what are we going to do?"

"If the police haven't heard *from* or *about* your teacher, we're going to drive to the restaurant and follow the most direct route back to her house."

"What's that supposed to prove?" Petey asked, disconcerted.

"I have a hunch that Miss Montgomery's husband drove off, leaving her standing in the parking lot. After a minute or two she probably started to walk home."

"No, Mr. Jablonski, you're wrong!"

"Petey," the detective said patiently, "your teacher was wearing a silk dress, was minus a shoe, and maybe wasn't carrying a purse. Her options were pretty limited."

As the boy slid into Jablonski's new sweater, Nancy called from below. "Jablonski?"

"We're coming." As they started down the steps, he asked, "Well?"

"No luck."

The detective reiterated what he planned to do. "I hope you have a few umbrellas," she said.

"Right there," he replied, indicating the antique stand by the door. "Let's go." At the detective's command the boy didn't move. "What is it, Petey? What's the matter?"

"I'm afraid, Mr. Jablonski."

"Don't be. Miss Montgomery's probably halfway back to her house by now."

The boy shook his head sadly. "I don't think so. I don't know why, but I don't think so."

CHAPTER TWENTY-NINE

" 'INTO each life some rain must fall,' is a reasonable proposition," Jablonski observed, peering ahead of the car, "but this is lunatic." The wipers, wildly flipping back and forth, were no match for the torrents of water that threatened to engulf the vehicle. Even at twenty-five miles per hour the sloshing of the hub-cap-deep puddles onto the windshield continually blinded the detective.

Ten minutes later, while carefully navigating up Twenty-sixth Street, the threesome passed the empty parking lot adjacent to the Brentwood Country Mart, a varied collection of small businesses that serviced the well-to-do residents of the area. Jablonski pulled up across from Vlaminck's, one block south of San Vicente Boulevard.

"Okay," he said. "We start here." He took a moment to check the immediate vicinity. "I've got to concentrate on driving, so Petey you watch out of the right windows. Nancy, you take the other side."

"You'll have to go very slowly, Jablonski," she informed him. "The visibility is damn near nil."

As they turned out into the deserted street, the detective suddenly felt that they were on a futile quest. The wind was gusting violently, at times seeming to reach near hurricane force. The occasional tree was uprooted and the stoplights at the corner intersection had ceased to function.

"We'll turn left at San Vicente, then work our way down to Seventh Street," he explained. "That's the most direct route, the way she would have gone. Then right on Seventh. The Martinellis live halfway down the hill that leads to the beach."

As the car crawled along the boulevard Nancy waited several minutes before reporting, "There's not a soul out tonight, Jablonski. Nobody."

"Patience," the detective suggested.

Petey's nose was glued to the right rear window and his breath had begun to cloud up the glass. He made a circular motion with the sleeve of his sweater and cleared a spot so he could see better. Suddenly he stiffened.

"Look," he cried, "up ahead by that parked van. Isn't that somebody?"

When they were abreast of the vehicle, it became apparent that what seemed to be a person was an isolated bush at the edge of a driveway to which a piece of newspaper had attached itself.

"This is crazy," Nancy announced. "Anybody out there would be blown away."

Jablonski sighed. "You're probably right but, since we've come this far, we might as well continue." He squinted into the onrushing curtains of water. "I can't see the light at Seventh Street. Where are we now?"

Petey piped up, "We just passed Eleventh."

Where they needed to turn and head down the hill toward the beach, a trough in the pavement had caused a pool of water to back up to a height of several feet.

"If you drive through that mess you could lose your brakes, Jablonski," Nancy said nervously.

"Maybe not." Carefully the detective eased the Honda through the obstacle and out the other side. Then, while pumping the brake pedal with his left foot, he applied pressure to the accelerator. "This'll dry out the pads."

"Put the shift in low," Nancy urged.

"We'll be fine," Jablonski insisted. "Keep your eyeballs outside the window."

"Over there!" Petey yelled.

Jablonski slowed to a stop. "Where?"

"There. At the corner."

"He's right," Nancy interposed. "Something's moving."

"Miss Montgomery's place is only two more blocks down," Petey added hopefully.

Carefully Jablonski released the pressure on the brakes and the Honda rolled forward. Moments later the threesome were able to discern that the object of their attention was a woman struggling valiantly against the fury of the elements.

Nancy said, "She has a raincoat, Petey. I don't think that's your teacher."

"I guess not," the boy answered sadly.

She lowered her window halfway. "Hello! Can we help?" she called.

The woman looked over. "Yes, please!" With great difficulty she made her way to the vehicle. "Believe it or not, I ran out of gas up above. There wasn't a soul around to assist me."

"Petey, open your door," Jablonski directed. "Get in," he told the woman.

"Tomorrow I'm having a car phone installed." She pulled the door closed behind her. "I didn't think I could walk another step."

"Where do you live?" the detective asked.

"In the middle of the next block."

As Jablonski pulled up in front of her house she said, "I'm ever so much obliged," then turned and ran up the sidewalk.

Just as the detective was about to start down the hill again, a Yellow Cab passed on his left throwing a cascade of water up against the side of the Honda.

"Bastard," Jablonski growled, brushing off the drops of water that had been flung through the crack in the window on the driver's side.

"Look!" Petey whispered, pointing ahead. "The taxi's stopping in front of Miss Montgomery's."

Both Jablonski and his companion stiffened. "What the hell!" Nancy exclaimed.

" 'What the hell,' indeed." Jablonski turned out into the street. As they passed the Martinelli house, a man lugging a heavy suitcase ran out. Reaching over the back seat, the cab driver unlatched the door and the man threw the bag onto the seat and climbed in.

"Petey, can you get a look? Is that Miss Montgomery's husband?"

The boy shook his head. "I can't tell for sure, Mr. Jablonski. I think so."

The cab honked and started down the hill. The detective turned back toward the curb and let the vehicle pass.

"Would you roll down your window again?" Jablonski asked Nancy. He stopped the Honda and peered through the sheet of rain. "Not a light in the joint, as far as I can tell." He glanced over at the dark blue BMW 325i parked in the driveway. "Petey, is that Mr. Martinelli's car?"

"Yes."

Jablonski removed a flashlight from the compartment at his side. Then he pulled down his fedora and turned to the boy.

"Hand me a bumbershoot. It's time to get wet."

"She's not here," Petey said plaintively. "She never came home."

"Maybe somebody gave her a lift, like we did with that lady."

"Do you want me to come with you?" Nancy asked.

"I don't think you better. I may have to do something illegal."

He stepped out of the car and opened the umbrella. Instantly, the wind blew it inside out and ripped it from his grasp. Before he had time to appropriate a second one, he was soaked through to the skin. Turning toward the sidewalk, he stepped into the ankle-deep torrent of water that was roaring down the hill. It overflowed into his Florsheims causing him to make a squeaky, sloshing sound as he hurried toward the BMW. The door on the driver's side was unlocked. He examined the interior of the car thoroughly. There was no shoe anywhere. He wondered if Martinelli had removed it or whether Petey had just been imagining things. After slamming the door he crossed to the garage and pulled up the sliding panel. A Toyota station wagon sat inside.

He produced the flashlight from his pocket and opened the tailgate. There were a few schoolbooks scattered around. Also a pile of test papers bound with a rubber band. Gloves. Some men's shirts in a cellophane bag. A six-pack of Diet Coke.

He closed the panel. After panning the beam of light around the garage he located a door that, presumably, led into the house. He tried the knob. No dice. After leaning down and examining the lock, he removed the slim wallet he always carried in his inner jacket pocket and selected a sharp instrument. He inserted it into the keyhole. Moments later, the door swung open.

"Hello!" he called. "Anybody home?" He stepped into the kitchen. "Miss Montgomery? It's Jack Jablonski." No response.

Systematically he began to search the house. After ten minutes spent checking all the rooms and closets it became apparent that the teacher had never returned from her dinner date. He hurried into the front hall and snapped on the porch light, then opened the door and motioned to Nancy and Petey.

"What is it?" the policewoman asked, as she and Petey burst into the hall.

"The lady's not here," he said brusquely.

"I *told* you something happened to her," Petey wailed.

"I'm beginning to believe you," Jablonski admitted.

"For all we know," Nancy insisted, "the lady *did* have a purse and located a phone and called a friend to come pick her up. Or she might even have gone back to the restaurant. I didn't tell the owner where I was calling from so he wouldn't have known how to notify me."

"Nancy, at the risk of offending, may I say that you're sounding like a cop. At this point, in similar cases, the police tend not to involve themselves, operating on the supposition that things will work themselves out."

Somewhat tentatively, she replied, "And they usually do."

Jablonski cocked his head. "In this instance you don't sound like you're convinced they will."

"Maybe I'm not. Totally."

Petey's eyes began to brim over as he looked up at the detective. "Please, Mr. Jablonski."

He put his arm around the boy's shoulders before turning back to his companion. "Nancy, call Yellow Cab in Santa Monica and ask them where the pickup at this address was going."

"My guess would be the airport."

"And you would no doubt be right. But *where* at the airport. Which airline?"

Nancy reached down and dialed Information. After getting the number she called the Yellow Cab dispatcher in the area and identified herself.

While the policewoman was thus engaged Petey asked Jablonski, "Are you going to have Mr. Martinelli arrested?"

"Let's see what Sergeant Baxter finds out."

Nancy hung up the phone. "American."

Jablonski thought for a minute. "With the weather like it is, two things are for sure. First, it's going to take Mr. Martinelli a good hour to get out to the airport. Second, his flight will probably be delayed by at least the same amount of time."

Nancy asked, "So?"

"My guess is he won't be going anywhere before midnight." He looked at his watch. "An hour and a half from now."

Jablonski sat down next to the phone table. Almost half a minute went by before he spoke again. "We have three obvious choices. We can place a formal call to the *gendarmes* and ask them to pick up Mr. Martinelli which, as I pointed out, they won't do because they will dismiss our suspicions as being insubstantial; or, we can jump in the car and traipse out to LAX and try to locate the gent ourselves in the hope of discovering what happened to his wife; or, we can pack it in for the night and hope for the best."

"There's got to be *something* else we can do, Mr. Jablonski," Petey implored.

"Maybe there is. But it's a very long shot, one Sergeant Baxter will, I'm afraid, find it difficult to countenance."

"What are you talking about, Jablonski?"

"Remember the saga of Snoopy with which I regaled you this afternoon?"

"Sure, but what's that got to . . . ?" Nancy stared at the detective, open-mouthed. "Consulting a fortune teller? You wouldn't."

"If there was one other single damn thing I could think of to do, I wouldn't."

"Jablonski, you're out of your mind! Besides, where the hell you are going to find the Madame at this time on a Saturday night?"

"It so happens that I know exactly where Marla May Willowbrook is." He stood up. "Based on recent past history, it's certainly a possibility that Miss Montgomery has suffered at the hands of her husband. There is also the fact that Mr. Martinelli may soon vanish into thin air, so to speak. Consequently, outlandish as it may sound, an unorthodox approach may be our best shot."

Petey checked in. "I think it's a great idea, Mr. Jablonski!"

"Consider, Nancy. The old lady helped me find a dog. A person should be less of a challenge." He crossed to the door and snapped off the hall light. "Come on."

CHAPTER THIRTY

THE storm was beginning to abate somewhat as Jablonski pulled the Honda into an empty parking spot in front of the building that housed his office. He turned around to the boy.

"Petey, I just thought of something. Do you, by any chance, know when Miss Montgomery's birthday is?"

"What's that got to do with anything?" Nancy demanded.

"According to the tape Shirley brought back from her session with the Lady Willowbrook, it helps when a psychic knows the time and place of a subject's birth."

"You're losing it, Jablonski."

"Well, Petey, do you?"

"Our English class had a birthday party for Miss Montgomery earlier this year, right after school started. It was on a . . . the last day of September. September thirtieth."

"I'll bet, because she's a woman, she only admitted to being over twenty-one."

Nancy made a face.

"Actually, Mr. Jablonski, Miss Montgomery made a big fuss about being thirty because her birthday happened to be on the thirtieth. I don't know for sure where she was born, but one time she said Chicago was her home town. Does that mean she was born there?"

"Close enough," Jablonski replied. "Does your teacher have a first name?"

"Mary."

Jablonski unhooked his seat belt. "Nancy, from personal experience I happen to know that Madame Willowbrook is super sensitive. Since you're a non-believer, as well as an emanator of hostile vibes, you could be a serious liability. It's best that you stay here in the car with Petey."

"For God's sake, Jablonski, can't we even wait in your place?"

"The waves you're putting out will go right through the office walls. Believe me, I know what I'm talking about."

Before Nancy could respond, Jablonski removed himself from the Honda and headed for the psychic's chamber. As he approached her front door, a teenage couple came out into the lane and hurried down toward the boulevard. Madame Willowbrook, a sou'wester tied under her chin, was just slipping into a yellow slicker when the detective knocked.

"Do you have a moment?" he asked.

"Mr. Jablonski! I was just closing up shop, so to speak. Was my prediction valid? Has your evening been exciting?"

"Precisely why I am here, Mrs Willowbrook." Jablonski closed the door behind him. "You expressed a wish to become associated with me at the appropriate time."

"I certainly did."

"That time has come."

Marla May made a sweeping gesture. "Be seated at the table, Mr. Jablonski. I must get out of these rain togs and compose myself." She hung the slicker on the back of the door and began to untie her hat. "I'm gratified that you have finally accepted the fact that the unknown can, upon occasion, be successfully penetrated."

"I still have one niggling doubt. How would you define the difference between 'successfully penetrated' and coincidence?"

"There is no such thing as coincidence, Mr. Jablonski. Things sometimes coincide."

"That seems a narrow distinction." The detective leaned in toward the old woman. "In any event, Mrs. Willowbrook, we must forge ahead. We are under certain time constraints."

"My contribution, if indeed I am able to make one, can only come after I enter a trance. Under pressure, there is no guarantee when or even *if* I will be able to escape the bonds of the conscious state."

Jablonski nodded helplessly. The old woman adjusted the illumination. After lighting a piece of incense she sat down at the table and closed her eyes. Moments later her head began to nod slowly back and forth.

He waited for what he considered an appropriate interval, then asked softly, "Are you ready, Mrs. Willowbrook?"

Without interrupting her ritual the old woman replied, "Hush. You will know when to speak."

Jablonski wished he hadn't drunk all that wine earlier. He licked his lips and tried to work up a swallow of saliva. Impatiently, he examined the tassels that hung from the nearby floor lamp. After counting them five times without ever coming up with two identical answers, he looked over at the psychic. Her chin rested on her chest and her breathing was deep and regular.

"Mrs. Willowbrook?"

"Yeeees?"

"I am trying to locate a woman named Mary Montgomery. She was born in Chicago on September thirtieth, nineteen sixty-one."

He waited patiently but, after almost a minute, no response was forthcoming.

"Mrs. Willowbrook?"

"Yeeees?"

He repeated the facts. "Can you help me locate Miss Mary Montgomery?"

"Yeeees." The old woman's breathing accelerated. "The body is . . . The body is . . ."

"Where, Mrs. Willowbrook, where is the body?"

"The body is in danger."

Jablonski tensed up. "Much danger?"

"The body is in . . . grave danger."

He chose his words with care. "I must know the exact location of the body. *Exactly* where is Miss Mary Montgomery's body? Can you tell me?"

Pause. "Yeeees."

"Where is the body?"

"In a box."

"What kind of a box?"

Pause. "A strong box."

"The body is in a strongbox?"

"A strong *box*."

Jablonski wondered where he should go from this point. "Is the body outside in the rain?"

"Yeeees . . . and no."

"What color is the box?"

Pause. "Black. The body is in a black box."

"The body is in grave danger in a strong black box partly outside in the rain."

"Yeeees."

Jablonski recalled the dark blue BMW 325i parked under the big tree in the driveway of Mary Montgomery's house.

"Thank you, Mrs. Willowbrook." He got up. "Thank you very much. You have, I believe, saved the day." He leaned over her and whispered, "You can wake up now."

Not getting any reaction, he wondered briefly whether he should take the psychic by the shoulder and shake her. On second thought, fearing this might somehow upset her subconscious processes, he decided to leave well enough alone. Quickly he made his way outside, leaving the old woman sitting in her chair, still in a trance.

Spotting Jablonski hurrying along the lane, both Nancy and the boy rolled down their windows.

"Is Miss Montgomery all right?" Petey demanded.

The detective ignored the question. "We've got to go into my office. I need a hand." The threesome retraced Jablonski's steps. "If I read Mrs. Willowbrook right, the young woman has literally been under our noses."

"What'd the old lady say?" Nancy asked.

Jablonski paraphrased. "Miss Montgomery is in a strong, black box probably outside in the rain."

The policewoman shook her head. "I don't get it."

"How about the trunk of the BMW?"

"Jesus," Nancy murmured, her eyes nearly popping out of her head.

"Shakes you up, doesn't it?"

"Miss Montgomery's dead?" Petey asked tremulously.

"No, no, no! Mrs. Willowbrook said your teacher's in *danger*. I take that to mean she's alive." He opened the door to his office and snapped on the lights. "My talents at breaking and entering are limited to garden variety door locks. To get a car trunk open we need a locksmith. How about your people, Nancy?"

"The police require probable cause before they'll stick their noses into something, and the word of an old lady in a trance wouldn't be good enough." She pointed to the phone. "It's illegal, but it might be a lot quicker if we could locate a locksmith in the neighborhood."

"Fair enough. The West L.A. phone book's in the top left hand drawer of my secretary's desk. You take A through M. I'll get the rest of the alphabet. A lot of these people advertise they're available twenty-four hours a day." He started for the inner office. "Sing out if you get a bite. We want a guy there pronto."

"What can I do?" Petey asked.

"Sit tight," Jablonski replied. "You may turn into a hero pretty soon."

"I don't care about that. I just want Miss Montgomery to be okay."

After grabbing his phone book, Jablonski sat down at his desk and turned to the Yellow Pages. Laboriously he located "Locksmiths" and worked down to the N's. While he was dialing his initial selection, Nancy appeared in the doorway.

"Hit the jackpot on the second call."

"How long?" the detective asked.

"If we hurry, we may beat the guy."

On the way out, Jablonski glanced through Marla May Willowbrook's window. The old lady was exactly as he had left her a few minutes earlier. Is she alright? he wondered. Is there any likelihood a prolonged trance could do permanent damage to her somewhat fragile faculties?

Petey pulled on the detective's sleeve. "C'mon!" the boy ordered.

The steady rain had turned into intermittent showers as they drove back down San Vicente. Many of the indentations in the street still held enough water to douse the car thoroughly each time it hit a puddle. No one spoke a word during the short trip.

A small van was waiting in front of the Martinelli residence. As the Honda pulled up and stopped, a short, dark man sporting a scraggly, oversize moustache stepped out of the vehicle and walked over to Nancy.

"You Miss Baxter?"

"Yes."

"I'm Bob Adams." He indicated the BMW. "Is that the car?" Nancy nodded. "You neglected to mention the nature of the emergency."

Jablonski took charge. "Never mind that. Let's move." The group walked over to the BMW. "How long will this take?"

"Not long." He produced a set of keys and a flashlight from his pocket. After flipping through the collection he selected one and inserted it into the trunk lock. It didn't work.

"Hurry up!" Petey demanded.

On the fourth key a click was heard. The locksmith lifted the top of the trunk and shined his flashlight into the interior. Except for a pair of work gloves, a set of jumper cables and a spare tire, it was empty.

"Damnit!" Jablonski exploded.

"That'll be fifty dollars," the man announced. "Saturday night is double time."

Frustrated, Nancy sighed. "Okay, Jablonski, where does this leave us?"

"Let me think."

"Credit card or cash?" the locksmith persisted.

Jablonski peeled off two twenties and a ten. "Give me a receipt," he directed.

The man returned to his van to complete the paperwork. The detective took Nancy by the elbow and guided her to the Honda.

"Use the car phone and call the West L.A. detectives again. See if there's any late news on the lady."

"Okay."

"What if there isn't?" Petey asked anxiously.

Jablonski sighed. "Then she's fine and is with some friend or relative, or . . ." The detective shrugged helplessly.

The locksmith presented Jablonski with the receipt he had requested. As the man drove away, Nancy stuck her head out of the Honda.

"Not a word."

The boy collapsed against the side of the vehicle and began sobbing. Jablonski knelt down to comfort him. "Easy does it, pal."

The tears streamed down his face. "She was such a nice lady, Mr. Jablonski."

"Let's keep things in the present tense, Petey. We don't know for sure that your teacher's in trouble." He took the boy by the shoulders. "Now, more than ever before, each of us needs to keep a level head and concentrate on the job at hand."

"I guess so."

Jablonski walked around and slid into the driver's seat. He spoke softly to his companion so as not to be overheard by the youth. "Let's examine the dark side. If Martinelli did anything bad to his wife, it probably happened in the parking lot at the Brentwood Mart."

"What are you suggesting?"

"The guy was always whacking her around. Maybe he hit her too hard."

"Then stuffed her into a strong, black box? In a parking lot?"

"You can't take Marla May too literally." Jablonski's eyes narrowed. "There are a bunch of food stalls in the mart. Where do they dump their garbage?"

"What?"

"A dumpster. A garbage dumpster is a strong, black box." He called out to the youth. "Petey, get in."

"Where are we going?" the boy asked.

"Hopefully, to find your teacher."

Five minutes later the threesome roared into the Brentwood Mart's deserted parking lot. Jablonski steered the Honda into a space in the middle of the site and pointed to a small, solid structure that stood adjacent to the alley. It was made of cinder blocks that had been painted a light yellow to blend in with the bank building fifty feet away. The inset wall facing them was six feet square and the sides that extended to the alley's border were approximately eight feet long.

"Come on!" Jablonski shouted. The threesome piled out of the Honda.

The part of the structure facing the alley was open, as was the top.

Both spaces were protected by a coarse wire fencing. Jablonski yanked back the double gate and shined his flashlight into the interior. Standing there was a garbage dumpster.

"Nancy, bring the car over here and point it so we have some light!" Jablonski ordered. While she hurried to comply, the detective turned to Petey. "I could use a hand. We've got to move this thing outside where we can get at it."

After three attempts the heavy receptacle rolled into the alley. Nancy positioned the car so that the brights made a direct hit on the front of the dumpster. Jablonski folded back the metal lid. Garbage had been heaped right up to the top and the stench was overpowering. Nancy joined the detective and the two of them began to paw through the mess.

There was a moan.

"Jesus!" Jablonski exclaimed. "She's buried in here!"

Urged on by Petey, who wasn't tall enough to be of any assistance, the two adults threw handful after handful of garbage into the alley. Within seconds they had uncovered the teacher.

"Call the paramedics, Nancy."

"Aren't you going to pull her out?" Petey demanded.

"We need help for that. I'm going to try and turn her over so she's face up," Jablonski replied. "I don't know how badly she may be hurt and I don't want to create any additional problems." Carefully, he moved the young woman into a more comfortable position.

Petey asked, "Is she breathing okay?"

The detective nodded. He didn't tell the boy how pale and drawn the teacher appeared or that she had a fierce-looking wound above her right temple.

"Does she know we're here?"

"No, Petey. Mercifully, she's unconscious."

Moments later Nancy rejoined Jablonski. "On their way." She leaned into the dumpster and brushed the matted strands of hair away from the young woman's face. "I also called West L.A. detectives and told them to see that Martinelli was intercepted at the airport and placed in custody. They're dispatching a black-and-white to us."

"Good."

"What will they do to her husband, Mr. Jablonski?"

"They'll put him in jail, Petey. And probably get him in an alcohol treatment program."

"How long will he be there?"

"Hard to say."

The young woman moaned again. Jablonski picked up her wrist and tried to find a pulse. Nancy glanced over at him.

"I don't know," he said softly. "It's pretty weak."

Less than a minute went by before the wail of a siren could be heard approaching the area. Jablonski said, "Those medics are fast."

"The fire station's not very far away," Nancy explained. "Up on Sunset."

The paramedics, both in their early thirties, were a complete contrast in types. The driver of the red-and-white ambulance was thin and intense and constantly flexed his fingers when his hands weren't otherwise occupied. The team leader was almost six feet four and was built like a torpedo, firm and fully packed. He wore his sandy hair in a crew cut and the sleeves of his uniform could barely contain his biceps. After he had examined the teacher, the redhead turned to his assistant.

"That's a real bad head wound. Her pulse is thready and her blood pressure is way low. She may need neurosurgery. Get on the horn and see if Saint John's can handle this." He turned to the others. "That's the closest hospital. Down on Santa Monica and Twentieth."

While the junior partner called in for instructions, the big man opened the back doors to the van and removed a stretcher that he placed on the ground in front of the dumpster. Then he reached inside the receptacle and, with practiced gentleness, lifted out the young woman. When Petey saw his teacher's limp body, he paled.

Afraid they were about to have another casualty on their hands, Jablonski said to the boy, "Go over and wait in my car. There's nothing more you can do now. My guess is you've saved Miss Montgomery's life."

As Petey drifted away, the two paramedics picked up the stretcher and slid it into the van. The team leader got into the back with the battered woman and pulled the doors shut. The driver ran around to the front, jumped in and started up the vehicle. As the growling siren on the ambulance wound up, it mixed with the high-pitched wail of a black-and-white that sped up Twenty-sixth Street and skidded to a stop in the parking lot. Two police officers hopped out and made their way over to Jablonski and Nancy.

After identifying herself, Nancy filled in the two young men on what had transpired, intentionally omitting any reference to Marla May Willowbrook.

"That is one lucky lady," the swarthy member of the team said. "A private collection service picks up the Mart's garbage on Sunday mornings. Early." He pointed. "The driver would have stopped here, guided his fork lift under the dumpster, raised it up over the truck's cab and spilled the contents into the back without taking any notice."

The second cop added, "Then out to the landfill in the Valley and goodbye world." He shook his head sadly. "You wonder what people will think of next." He turned to Nancy and Jablonski. "Afraid you'll both have to come down to the station and make a statement."

"Sure," Jablonski said.

The swarthy cop told his partner, "I'll stay here until the detectives arrive to check things out. The sergeant and her friend can follow you back to the precinct house."

"First we have to drop off the twelve-year-old who's been with us," Nancy said. "You certainly won't need him."

"Whatever you say, Sarge."

On their way to Petey's house Jablonski complimented the boy on sticking to his instincts. "If you hadn't held firm, I don't like to think what would have happened."

"Thanks. How about Miss Montgomery?" he asked anxiously. "Will she be okay?"

"I hope so. Call the hospital in the morning. They won't be able to tell you anything before then."

"I will." From the back seat Petey leaned forward and stuck his head between the two adults. "You guys are cool. I think we made a pretty good team."

After finishing up at the precinct station, it was nearly one A.M. when Nancy and Jablonski pulled into his driveway. She leaned over and kissed him on the cheek, an act Jablonski prayed would mark the conclusion to the evening's entertainment.

Nancy sighed. "I hope you won't mind if I don't come in. I'm pooped and my hangover needs to be put to bed."

"I sympathize, my dear. My condition, at this point, is also beyond fragile."

She got out of the car. "I'll be back in the morning to help with the dishes."

Feeling totally incapable of participating in another episode of the mating game at such an early date, Jablonski replied, somewhat grandly, "That won't be necessary. I am perfectly capable of handling things."

"Oh, but I *want* to!" Nancy insisted. "Wait'll you see what I did to the kitchen. It's a mess."

Jablonski swallowed. "Okay. But not too early."

Before going inside, the detective watched Nancy's car disappear around the corner. As he prepared to unlock the kitchen door, he realized that, in his haste to leave, he had neglected to confine Snoopy to the backyard. He hesitated to think what awaited him as a result of his carelessness.

He had scarcely cracked the door when the puppy made a mad dash toward her favorite bush and proceeded to perform like a trouper. After clawing the appropriate amount of grass upon her deposit, she trotted over to Jablonski and sat down. She looked up as if to say, "Well, let's hear it for the kid."

The detective gave her a round of applause and assured her of his undying affection. "Now, perhaps, a cookie?" he asked. Barking joyously at the sound of this combination of syllables, she darted inside.

Nancy was right. The kitchen looked as if it had been worked over by a pair of grizzly bears imported especially for the occasion from the Pacific Northwest. Once he had recovered from the shock, he noticed that the light on the telephone answering machine was flashing. He pushed the playback button.

Daphne's voice came booming out into the room. "It's three A.M. here in Atlantic City. Out there it's either midnight or six o'clock in the morning. I'm so excited that I can't figure out which. Where are you anyway, Jack? The big news is that you're a grandfather! Susie's just fine! She gave birth to little Jacqueline just about two hours ago. The baby weighed seven pounds, six ounces, and is the spittin' image of you when you were tiny."

Jesus! Jablonski thought. The poor kid.

"I'm going to bed now. Don't call me. I'll call you after I get some sleep." There was a short pause. "Oh yes. If everything goes as planned, Susie will be leaving the hospital day after tomorrow. I'll probably stay with her until the end of the week." Another pause. "Where are you, Jack? Did you turn off the phone or are you out gallivanting? Remember, don't call tonight. You can tell me tomorrow." The line went dead.

On his way upstairs Jablonski realized that Daphne's news had so invigorated him that he didn't feel tired or hung over anymore. Recalling how much he had been taken with his own daughter when she was growing up, he found himself eagerly anticipating the idea of being involved in a repeat of the process, even if it could only be on an occasional basis.

He decided that first thing Monday he would open one of those college accounts the investment brokers had recently been advertising. By the time little Jackie graduated from high school, a university education would probably cost over a hundred thousand dollars.

CHAPTER THIRTY-ONE

At nine-thirty Sunday morning the shrilling of the phone woke Jablonski out of a sound sleep. With his eyes still closed, he pawed around the top of the bedside table until he located the instrument.

"Yeah?"

"Jack, it's Mikki. Are you awake?"

Alarmed, he sat up. "Is something the matter?"

"No. Everything's fine. That was some adventure you had last night."

"How'd you hear about it?"

"The news director at the station just phoned. He's anxious to reach the kid who tagged along with you and Sergeant Baxter."

"Who told *him*?"

"He has his sources."

"What's Tolkin want with the boy?"

"Sunday is a slow news day. Unless something else breaks in the meantime, Arnold plans to lead with the Martinelli story on tonight's show. He thinks the young man is the core of the piece. Wants to do a segment."

"His name's Petey Bosworth. He lives on Bundy, north of Sunset. Tell Tolkin to take it easy with him. Petey's parents are out of town."

"Okay, I will. Arnold also wanted me to ask if you'd like to be interviewed."

"I would not. As you know, I'm already in enough trouble with the cops." Jablonski kicked off the covers and stood up. "Do you know if the boys in blue ever picked up Martinelli?"

"They sure as hell did. The bastard was so relieved to find out his wife was still alive that he told them everything."

Jablonski raised an eyebrow. "Which was?"

"It seems that, after dinner, the couple was alone in the parking lot, fighting like crazy. His wife called him a dirty name and he whacked her. She lost her balance, slipped, and fell down and hit her head on the front fender of their car. Apparently he was staggering drunk. When he couldn't revive her, he decided she was dead. He panicked and loaded her into the dumpster. Then he took off."

"Did Tolkin say where he was headed?"

"London."

Jablonski took a moment to digest all this information. "No question about it, Mrs. Martinelli is one lucky lady."

"Didn't sound to me like it was all luck, Jack. As I understand it, if it hadn't been for you, she would have been a goner."

"It was a group effort."

"But you located the body."

"*Technically,* I located the body. Actually, there's more to it."

"You want to tell me?"

"No. And if you push me, I'll take the Fifth."

"Sounds kinky. One more thing, Jack. Could you come over here today at one o'clock? Turns out that's the only time there's a crew available to tape the spot you wanted for the Monday night show. I'd like to be sure that I do everything right."

"I wouldn't miss it."

"You want Hilda to prepare lunch?"

"Under no circumstances. Last night I ate so much that, when I got on my scale, a card came out that read, 'One at a time, please.' "

"Jack?"

"Hmmm?"

"That joke's older than you are."

"Quite possibly." Snoopy began pulling on his pajama leg. "I am being summoned to chores by an irresistible object. So, with your permission, I'll sign off."

Jablonski hurried downstairs to prepare Snoopy's breakfast. For a moment, when he entered the kitchen, he thought he was in the wrong house. The place was spotless. He looked down at the puppy. "Some watchdog you are."

Propped up on the sink was a note from Nancy which read, "You're not the only one who can pick a lock. I hope I put everything back in the right places. I had to come so early because I forgot I have a lunch date with my mom in Palm Springs. I'm going to try and get assigned to the graveyard shift starting tomorrow night, in case you need any backup during the stakeout. Love, Nancy."

There was a P.S. "You haven't heard the last of me."

After feeding Snoopy, Jablonski called the hospital in Atlantic City and chatted with his daughter and Daphne.

As she was about to sign off, his wife said, "I finally figured out it was midnight when I phoned last night. Where were you?"

Jablonski decided on a literal response. "At that precise moment I was in the West Los Angeles precinct station making a statement."

"Did you get in some kind of trouble, Jack?"

"No, I didn't. But I think I came pretty close."

"Oh, dear. You must tell me all about it when I get back."

"It's of no consequence, my love."

"You sure?"

"Absolutely."

After twenty-five years of marriage Jablonski knew better than to open a second front.

* * *

Jablonski wasn't surprised to discover that there was no love lost between Mikki and Max Sabinson, the segment producer who had raped her during the Mexico City shoot some months previous. Most of their conversation was carried on through half-clenched jaws and in sharply cutting tones. Jablonski took an instant dislike to the man.

The threesome was seated on the L-shaped sofa in the O'Reilly living room, surrounded by blazing lamps of various sizes that a hugely fat cameraman was constantly adjusting.

At one point Mikki told the producer, "I think I'd rather have the fireplace wall as a background."

"It's too goddamn busy," Sabinson hissed. "Besides, the lights are all set up for this angle."

"Well, unset them," Mikki snapped.

"Sorry. They're staying where they are."

"If you don't move the lights, Max, you're gonna be making a silent movie today."

In the interest of hurrying things up, Jablonski intervened. "Isn't there some sort of a compromise possible?"

"The word 'compromise' isn't in Miss O'Reilly's vocabulary, Mr. Jablonski," the producer answered sarcastically. "She's an expert on everything from lighting to makeup to camera angles. Whenever I go on a shoot with her, I'm ashamed to take Channel Ten's money."

"Fuck you, Max, and move the lights," Mikki ordered.

Sabinson smiled. "Maybe I should just go out to the kitchen and have a beer while you wrap this thing up."

"Maybe you should." She turned to the cameraman. "Willy, if I scoot over to my right, is it a lot of trouble to reset things?"

"Not at all, Mick," the fat man answered.

Sabinson shrugged. "Personally I don't really give a shit." He swiveled around to the detective. "You should understand, Mr. Jablonski, Mikki gets her kicks trying to embarrass my ass in front of strangers. Though it's unfortunate that she can't see what she's doing anymore, it's a pleasure to watch her screw herself up."

While the technical setup was being changed, the makeup girl stepped in and powdered Mikki's forehead.

"How do I look, Rosie?" Mikki asked.

"Real good, babe. Smashing."

"Jack, I hope and pray that the son of a bitch who wrote those notes is watching tomorrow."

"I'm counting on it."

"Arnold told me they were planning to promo my segment twice in the movie ahead of the newscast."

"I don't like to be pushy," Sabinson interrupted, "but I've got a hot date. Willy, you ready?"

"Yeah," the fat man replied. He picked up the camera.

"You feel comfortable with the routine we worked out?" Jablonski asked Mikki.

"Perfectly." She smiled and cocked her head. "I wonder how Will Waterbury feels about all this. Not that it matters."

"He thinks it's a crock," Sabinson told her. "To him, this whole business is amateur night. He said you're gonna look like some distraught mother in Bakersfield pleading for her lost child. Incidentally, I agree with him." He looked toward the camera. "Roll 'em, Willy."

The fat man rechecked focus while the sound engineer extended a microphone over Mikki's head. Sabinson held up a small slate in front of the young woman's face. On it was written "O'Reilly Reward, Take One."

"Unless you want to appear on television with our superstar, you better step over there," Sabinson told the detective. Jablonski positioned himself off to one side.

"Tape is rolling," the cameraman declared.

"O'Reilly Reward, take one," Sabinson called out. He pulled the marker out of the shot.

"Okay, Mikki, we have speed," the fat man said. "Anytime."

Mikki arched her back and began to speak.

CHAPTER THIRTY-TWO

Since Channel Ten was, in effect, putting a mobile unit under Jablonski's command on Monday night following the telecast of Mikki's segment, Arnold Tolkin had requested that the detective conduct a briefing session to coordinate all the details. To this end Jablonski joined the news director and members of the station's staff in the conference room prior to airtime. The news team consisted of Max Sabinson, the segment producer, Estella Gomez, the on-the-spot reporter, a cameraman, and an audio engineer.

Jablonski started out by saying, "There's no guarantee this scheme will work. If it does, we'll bag the guy and you'll get an exclusive. If it doesn't, we've wasted a night staking out the post office on Laurel Canyon."

Sabinson, who had been slumped in a chair in the corner with his eyes closed, asked, "How come the cops aren't in on this?"

"Because they think it's a waste of time." Jablonski was glad that Nancy had wangled herself onto the graveyard shift, because she already knew what was going down and wouldn't need a long explanation if he suddenly needed help. "The plan is simple enough. In front of the post office on Laurel Canyon near Ventura, mailboxes have been installed on both sides of the boulevard for use by passing drivers. Your news van will be parked adjacent to the main building. You'll watch the line of boxes nearest you. I'll be in my car on the opposite side of the street, keeping those drops under observation."

Sabinson butted in. "Since we'll be pointed in different directions, one of us will have to make a U-turn in order to follow the guy if he shows up. Depending on traffic, that could be tricky."

"We'll have walkie-talkies and both vehicles are equipped with car phones. If anybody gets lost during the pursuit, it should be easy enough to close up the gap."

The news director interrupted. "Let me reiterate the key points. You'll be looking for a small pickup truck with out-of-state plates. Possibly one of its headlights is dark. Mikki described the guy who accosted her in our parking lot some months back as 'a large man with a bald head.' "

Sabinson asked, "Tell me, Mr. Jablonski, isn't it reasonable to assume that more than one small truck with out-of-state plates could show up tonight?"

"Of course," the detective responded patiently. "But if there's a woman at the wheel, or a teenage kid, or a couple in the cab, it's not the vehicle we're looking for. A medium-sized truck, or a brand new one wouldn't qualify either."

The producer shook his head. "There are mailboxes all over the Valley. Why are you so certain this bum uses the main post office?"

"It's a hunch. According to the experts, he's probably a loner. If he's in a writing mood after watching Mikki on TV, he sits down at his computer and knocks a note off to her. It follows that someone with a compulsion like his would make every effort to assure that his letter was delivered as quickly as possible."

Begrudgingly Sabinson answered, "Maybe."

"The main post office offers a faster way to get the missive moving than if he used some corner mailbox."

"Anything else?" Tolkin asked.

Estella Gomez piped up, "Arnold, do you want me to do a running audio commentary as soon as we make contact with the guy?"

"Absolutely," the news director answered.

"While we're following him, it'll be tough to get any decent pictures," the cameraman pointed out. "Unless we're lucky with the source light while we're stopped at a traffic signal."

"Do what you can," Tolkin directed. "In any event, the important part of the story isn't on the road. It'll be at wherever he ends up."

"You must be careful not to let him see you holding a camera," Jablonski cautioned. "Until I'm able to confront our quarry and ascertain he's the one we're looking for, we're all candidates for a harassment suit, or something even more exotic."

"Okay," Sabinson said, "let's roll."

As the group filed out, Tolkin said, "Good luck, Jack. Bag the bastard."

Jablonski nodded. "Let's hope Miss O'Reilly works her magic tonight."

Ever since he had written Mikki the previous week, Clem Barren had faithfully watched the late news on Channel Ten in the hope that she would turn up again. In the unlikely event that he might be swamped with orders at the time of the telecast, he had always set the timer on the VCR at his house to record each program. Because it was a Monday night, business was slower than usual. At nine fifty-five he poured himself a cup of black coffee and laced it with three fingers of brandy from a bottle that he kept locked up in a nook in the service closet. Then he sat down at the counter.

As the station break unfolded, he heard Will Waterbury announce Mikki's upcoming appearance. At the mention of her name he felt a tightness in his chest.

The young waitress approached. "Clem, I've got to go potty. Will you cover for me?"

He grunted, never taking his eyes off the screen for a moment. It was an eternity, almost fifteen minutes, before Mikki appeared. In the interim, the waitress had returned and taken the seat next to him. She sat silently until it was time for Mikki's spot to begin. At that point she asked, "Why do you always look at the news? There's never anything on."

"Ssssh!" he demanded.

Mikki was dressed in a dark blue turtleneck over which she wore a cranberry-colored blouse. There was a tiny pearl in each earlobe and a single gold chain hung around her neck. The television lights focused on her dark, reddish hair made it gleam. The scars on her face had been softened with makeup, but the bandages on her eyes and the dark glasses covering them made Clem uncomfortable.

"Again I want to thank all of you who have written to me," Mikki began.

She really means me, Clem thought.

"I'm here tonight to talk about something that moves me very deeply. The management of Channel Ten announced today that they are posting a reward of twenty-five thousand dollars for any information leading to the capture of the man who assaulted me so viciously."

"The bastard," the waitress commented.

"Ever since the night of the attack I've wondered, over and over, what kind of a monster would do a thing like this. What perverse satisfaction could someone possibly get from throwing a dose of acid on me while I was alone in my house asleep?"

The camera moved in until Mikki's face filled the screen.

"Whoever it was, I can feel you watching me right now and I want to talk to you."

Clem pulled at his collar.

"According to your letters, you think I'm in love with you. You tell me how much you love me. Would you like to know what I think? I think you are a sad, lonely man who is desperately ill. Before your compulsions drive you to do something equally as loathsome to someone else, I urge you to turn yourself in. If you would do this, for me, I would forgive you. I know, in my heart, that you would undo the whole dreadful experience if you could. Show me that you are willing to prove your love. Show me that you are a man."

The station logo filled the screen. After a short teaser promoting several of the stories yet to come, a dog food commercial began to unspool. Clem walked around behind the counter and reached up and turned off the TV set.

"Leave it on," the waitress complained. "I want to see who America's ten worst-dressed women are."

"It'll be in the papers tomorrow," he mumbled.

A group of teenagers burst in and sat down at the large table in the corner by the window. Their appetites were as enormous as their conversation was loud. Clem was kept so busy for the next half hour that he was unable to formulate any kind of a plan. If they would only leave, he thought to himself, if they would just hurry up and get the hell out of here, I could figure out what to do.

When the assemblage had finally finished their hamburgers, double fries, Cokes, and various desserts, as well as their discussion of the evening's basketball game, they filed out into the night. As the waitress cleaned up the mess the customers had left behind, Clem appropriated a glass from underneath the counter and helped himself to a double shot of brandy.

"You're hittin' that stuff pretty good tonight," the young waitress observed, popping a piece of bubble gum into her mouth. "What's the matter?"

"What's the matter is none of your fucking business."

"Okay. I just figured maybe talking about it would help."

"It?"

"Whatever is bothering you."

He knocked back the contents of the glass and slammed it down on the counter. "There's fucking nothing that's bothering me. You satisfied?"

"Sure, Clem," she said, retreating to the room in the back that housed the dishwasher, a large freezer and the owner's desk. As she loaded the dirty dishes, she was careful not to slop any water on the old model computer and printer that sat nearby. As she worked, she wondered what went on in Clem's head. He hardly ever said anything, and when he did it was always something angry.

Shortly before eleven P.M. Channel Ten's Mobile Unit 3, a Ford van with the identification on its sides carefully masked, was in place on the east side of Laurel Canyon in front of the post office. Near the curbing, extending for a distance of twenty feet in front of the vehicle, were six mailboxes spaced out at intervals of a foot, their snouts protruding outward, ready to accommodate passing drivers. Max Sabinson and Estella Gomez sat in the front seat with the audio technician who was also acting as driver. At this precise moment an ancient Chevrolet Impala, bright yellow with thoroughly dented fenders, came from behind them and stopped at the depository farthest away.

"Not a hell of a lot of business at this hour," the audio man commented.

"That'll make it easier to spot the asshole," Sabinson responded. He checked his watch. "Two after eleven. The show's over."

Estella Gomez, the on-the-spot reporter, lit up a cigarillo. "How long do we have to sit here?" she demanded.

"As long as it takes," Sabinson answered, "and blow that goddamn smoke out the window. It makes me sick."

"I'm sorry. But I'm nervous. I only smoke when I'm nervous."

The audio man observed, "Miz Gomez, did you know that Mexicans smoke more than Americans?"

"You think so?"

"Yeah."

"Well," she retorted, "I'm a Mexican-American. Where does that put me?"

"Enough of that shit," Sabinson growled. "If the guy shows up, we're only going to have a few seconds to case the vehicle. Harry, you concentrate on the rear license plate of any truck that pulls up in front of us. Put the headlights on low so you can see better."

"We'll run down the battery."

Sabinson snapped, "Then start the engine, for cris'sake!"

Somewhat fearfully Estella asked, "What should I do?"

"Adjust the mirror on your side and sing out if you spot anything with only one headlight coming down the hill from behind," Sabinson instructed. "As they pass I'll try and see if I can get any kind of a fix on the driver."

A sound of soft snoring was heard from the rear of the van.

Sabinson turned around and spoke to the sleeping cameraman, who was stretched out on a blanket. "Morty," he hissed. "Wake up!"

The cameraman grunted. "Hmmm?"

"Pay attention! If we spot the guy we want to get some pictures of him driving away from the mailbox."

"I'm ready," Morty complained.

"You're *not* ready. Open the goddamn roof so that you can shoot through the top."

Morty countered, "Remember what that detective said: he doesn't want the guy to see the camera."

Exasperated, Sabinson answered, "We're *behind* him! How's he going to see you?"

"The back of a car isn't very interesting."

"The film editor and I decide what's interesting. You just take the goddamn pictures. Now, get organized!"

Estella tensed. "Something's coming with a single headlight. He's a couple of blocks back."

Sabinson picked up the walkie-talkie. "Mr. Jablonski, how do you read?"

"Loud and clear," Jablonski responded from his vantage point in the Honda. He was facing up the hill across the street, parked a few feet north of the line of mailboxes. "You got the single headlight?"

"Right." A few moments later a motorcycle roared by. "No dice," Sabinson said.

"The night is young," the detective observed.

Promptly at midnight the waitress removed her apron and hung it up on a peg on the back of the utility room door. Clem was slouched over a table in the back staring into space. "You gonna lock up?" she asked, anxious to leave.

"Ummm?"

"You staying?"

After a moment's thought, he nodded.

She hurried to the front door. "See you tomorrow." She stepped outside and started down toward Ventura Boulevard.

Clem locked the front door and flipped the "Open" sign in the window to "Closed." He turned off the lights and crossed to the utility room. Once inside, he switched on the ancient IBM PC. While waiting for it to boot up, he sat down at the small table on which it rested and slowly began to rub his hands together.

During the first ninety minutes of the stakeout by Jablonski and the Channel Ten news crew, eight small trucks that fitted the description of the one they sought, each with a single man in the cab, stopped while their drivers availed themselves of the mailboxes. Five of them posted letters directly in front of the main 91604 area post office, the others in the receptacles across the boulevard. A headlight on one of the vehicles had been dark. Two were driven by bald-headed men. None of them bore out-of-state license plates.

Jablonski yawned. If only this was a movie, he thought to himself, the time would be made to pass very quickly. First there'd be a shot of a digital clock on a dashboard showing the hour to be just after twelve-thirty, then an angle on a couple of detectives slouched down in the front seat of a black sedan, casing some nearby joint. Next a shot of a wristwatch showing that it was an hour later, followed by a brief sequence in which one of the detectives was busy eating a greasy hamburger out of a paper bag. Finally a bell would toll three in a church steeple. At that point the Bad Guy would show up and they'd nab him. It would take less than a minute of screen time to cover two and a half hours.

Sabinson busted in on Jablonski's ruminations. "I think I got him!"

The detective looked across the street at a small, dirty pickup truck that had stopped in front of the mailboxes. A ray from the streetlight bounced off what seemed to be the bald head of its driver as he leaned out of the passenger side to post a letter.

"How about his license plates?" Jablonski demanded.

"Not California. That's for damn sure. And there's not a hair on his head."

"Okay," Jablonski told the news producer, "let's roll."

As the truck started north on Laurel Canyon toward the intersection with Ventura Boulevard several blocks away, Jablonski made a U-turn and followed Channel Ten's van.

"You there?" Sabinson asked.

"Right on your tail."

The light was green and the truck barreled through it, speeding up as it moved along the deserted street. In order to keep up, the other two vehicles in the caravan accelerated.

"He may be headed for the freeway," Sabinson radioed. "Don't lag behind."

"If I do, it won't be by very much," the detective assured him. "Just keep me posted what exit he uses and where he finally stops. And don't approach him until I get there."

The truck turned onto the westbound Ventura Freeway. Because traffic was exceedingly light, it soon became obvious that the miniature motorcade would have no trouble staying together.

The truck continued westbound on the Ventura Freeway for twenty minutes when Sabinson announced, "This turkey is a long way from home."

Or, Jablonski thought to himself, maybe he's not going home. Maybe Mikki scared the hell out of him and he's headed for points west. "How far does this road go?"

Sabinson replied, "All the way up through central California."

Just as Jablonski was wondering whether their quarry was on his way out of town for good, the truck suddenly swerved onto a Reseda off-ramp and continued in a northerly direction on a maze of side streets.

"Slow down," Jablonski instructed, "I want to get in front of you so we won't be bunched up together. From the looks of this neighborhood, it won't be long now."

Moments later the truck made a sharp turn into a lane bordered by modest bungalows and swung into the driveway of a small, neatly kept house. The driver jumped out and let himself into the dwelling. Jablonski stopped half a block ahead of the van and motioned for it to pull over.

"Douse your lights," he instructed Sabinson, "and stay put."

The detective slid out from behind the wheel of his vehicle. Noting that there wasn't a sound or a movement anywhere in the vicinity, he tugged on his fedora and set out on his mission.

CHAPTER THIRTY-THREE

STAYING on the opposite side of the lane, Jablonski sauntered slowly past the bungalow. The thin rays from a streetlight on the corner, a quarter of a block away, fell on the horizontal boarding that covered the front of the house, outlining a row of strip windows. A flagstone walk led up to the front door, which was densely framed with greenery.

After determining that he was unobserved, the detective crossed the street and made his way back toward the pickup truck parked in the driveway. It sat between him and the house. He cautiously opened the door on the passenger side and and examined the interior. On the seat was a copy of the latest issue of *Playboy,* a pair of cheap sunglasses, and the wrappers from half a dozen Hershey Bars. He opened the glove compartment. Inside was a small cellophane bag that was half full of what appeared to be marijuana, some cigarette papers, matches, and a small black address book. He held the latter up to the light, thumbing through it. It contained names, addresses, and telephone numbers of men and women, all residing in various parts of the San Fernando Valley. Jablonski wondered if, in addition to everything else, the man he sought was a drug pusher.

As he was replacing the notebook, he heard agitated voices approaching. Suddenly the vocal mishmash was silenced by the rough commands of a man. Jablonski crouched down. Carefully, he peered around the back end of the truck. Parading toward him was the entire Channel Ten crew, hands raised high in the air.

"Jablonski?" Sabinson called out querulously. "We need you, Jablonski."

Following the quartet, carrying a double-barreled shotgun that was leveled at the news producer, was a tall, rather emaciated man of middle age, who was totally bald.

"Looks like your friend went off and left you," he announced somewhat ominously. "That is, if you really had someone else with you."

The bastard must have sneaked out the back door of his house, Jablonski determined. Putting his hands up, the detective stepped into view.

"What seems to be the problem, sir?" he asked.

"The problem is, these people followed me from the post office in Laurel Canyon clear out here. I'd like to know why they did that. I'd also like to know who the hell you are."

The door to the bungalow opened and a woman asked, "Are you alright, Harry? You want me to call the cops?"

"I'm okay."

"It is unnecessary to summon the authorities," Jablonski assured the man. "I'll make a deal with you. I'll show you my identification if you'll show me yours."

"What kind of a deal is that?"

"I need to know who you are before I can explain what we're all doing here."

The man considered the proposition for a moment. "You first."

Jablonski handed over his California investigator's license. The man perused the document, then reached into the back pocket of his trousers and produced a wallet. He tossed both articles on the ground in front of the detective.

"Move very slowly, Mr. Jablonski."

"I intend to." The driver's license identified the man as Harvey Brannigan and the address matched that of the bungalow. In addition, there were two credit cards and a piece of plastic bearing Brannigan's picture. He wore the uniform of a private guard. The adjoining legend stated that he was an employee of one of the branch banks in Studio City, not far from the post office on Laurel Canyon.

"Satisfied?" Brannigan asked the detective.

"Almost." During this exchange the people from Channel Ten stood frozen with their hands in the air. "Would you permit my friends to adopt a more comfortable position?" the detective asked.

"Not yet," Brannigan answered, retrieving his wallet. Using the shotgun as a pointer he gestured to the front of the truck. "All of you. Over there," he ordered. "Spread your legs and put your hands on the hood. You too, Mr. Jablonski." He turned to the woman in the doorway. "Pat down the lady, Billie."

"Harry, you sure you don't want me to call the cops?"

"I'll let you know." Holding the shotgun under his right arm, Brannigan frisked the four men.

When he had finished the detective said, "As you can see, we have no weapons."

Brannigan stepped back. "Get over here with me, Billie," he ordered. The woman hurried to his side. He told the Channel Ten group, "You can relax now," then singled out Jablonski. "I'm listening," he said. The weapon remained in firing position.

"As I'm sure these good folks tried to tell you when you bushwhacked them, they are a news team from Channel Ten. We were staking out the Laurel Canyon post office tonight in the hope that a bald-headed man in a small, slightly used pickup truck with out-of-state plates would show up and mail a letter."

"Then what?"

"As you witnessed, we planned to follow him and advise the police of his whereabouts."

"What'd he do?" the woman asked.

Jablonski answered, "Something pretty serious."

"I get it," Brannigan said, lowering the shotgun. "These reporters were angling for a scoop. They were gonna photograph the arrest and put it on the news."

"Exactly."

"Well, I'm not the guy you're looking for."

"I believe that's true," Jablonski said. "But, by way of confirmation, to whom was your letter addressed?"

"The goddamn phone company," the woman piped up. "If we didn't pay the bill by the close of business today, they were gonna shut us down."

"That should be easy enough to check." Jablonski turned to the news team. "Come along, it's past our bedtime."

"You people oughta be more careful," Brannigan called after them. "You could end up with an assful of buckshot."

"Jesus, that was scary!" Sabinson mumbled, as he hurried back to the van.

The cameraman opened up the back of the vehicle and got in. "Home and mother," he said slamming the door. The audio technician and Estella Gomez climbed into the front seat.

Jablonski checked his watch. "We've still got almost five hours before the morning mail is collected," he told Sabinson. "If we get lucky and come up with another candidate, don't stay glued to the guy's truck. Change lanes every so often, like I did."

The news producer looked mildly amazed. " 'Another candidate'? You're not suggesting we go back to the post office?"

"Hell yes, I am."

"Forget it," Sabinson responded. He joined his colleagues in the front seat of the van. "I'm pooped. I've had enough for one night."

"If you don't mind my saying so, that's shortsighted. My hunch is that we can still catch the guy."

Sabinson leaned out of the van window. "If you don't mind *my* saying so, I don't think your hunch is worth jack shit." He turned to the driver. "Let's go."

The van pulled away, leaving Jablonski standing alone on the deserted lane. He hurried to the Honda, jumped in, and, within minutes, was on the freeway heading back toward Los Angeles. As he crossed Ventura Boulevard heading up Laurel Canyon toward the 91604 area post office, he noticed a small pickup truck with one dead headlight pull away from the mailboxes on the opposite side of the street. As soon as was feasible, he reversed course. He caught up with the vehicle as it waited for the traffic signal to change at the intersection.

In the glare of his headlights Jablonski quickly determined that the truck was carrying Idaho plates. Before he committed himself to a chase, he wanted to see if the driver fit Mikki's description. While he was mulling over possible strategies on how he might best accomplish this, the light switched to green and the truck started north on Laurel Canyon. Jablonski recalled that there were parallel turn lanes leading onto the Ventura Freeway in both directions. If the driver followed this route, the detective knew there might be a chance to get a good look. During the long stretch up the empty boulevard, the truck moved over one lane, positioning itself on Jablonski's right. Nearing the freeway, it slid into a lane that provided ingress to the west. The traffic slowed for the red light at the intersection, and the detective crept up alongside. As the vehicles came to a stop, Jablonski snuck a look into the cab of the truck. The driver was totally bald.

The detective polished his rearview mirror with his coat sleeve and hunched over the wheel. The light changed and the traffic moved up onto the freeway. Immediately the driver of the truck slid over and nailed down the fast lane, moving along at a steady seventy miles per hour. Jablonski had to push the Honda to keep up with him. Being that this was the time of the night with the least traffic, he hoped that some bored highway patrol officer wasn't looking for something to do.

As the truck approached the intersection with the San Diego Freeway that led to the south, the driver cut across three traffic lanes and took the transition road marked "Santa Monica." Jablonski followed, being careful to remain a distance of two or three car lengths behind his quarry. After traversing the Sepulveda Pass, the two vehicles sped through Westwood. Several miles later Jablonski noticed a sign indicating that they were on the route that led to the Los Angeles International Airport. Briefly, he wondered if the man was planning to blow town as Miss Montgomery's husband had attempted to do several nights earlier. No matter, if that was the game, it would soon be up.

The truck took the Sepulveda exit and sped up a long hill. After a dozen blocks it turned left and continued down a badly lit road lined with inexpensive homes, all similar in design and color. After a mile, it turned right into a side street that was almost totally dark. Halfway down the block it pulled into a narrow driveway and parked short of a single-car garage. Even in the dimness it was obvious to Jablonski that the neighborhood was almost a dead ringer for the one he had visited earlier that evening in the Valley.

Straining his eyes, he watched as the man hopped out of the vehicle, unlocked the front door, and disappeared inside the house. Jablonski continued along the block. At the first intersection he made a U-turn and positioned his car so that he could keep an eye on both doors of the unpretentious dwelling. After a while a pale, flickering light could be seen through the window opening onto the front porch. Moments later, smoke wafted upwards from the small chimney on the side of the house.

Jablonski removed the flashlight from the compartment in the door of the Honda and walked back to the corner. He shone the light on the street identifiers atop the signpost and made a mental note of his whereabouts. Then, cautiously, he moved along the darkened sidewalk until he was directly in front of the house. Glancing around the area, he determined that if anyone else was out and about, he was as invisible to them as they were to him. He tiptoed up the short walk and, staying back four or five feet from the small picture window, painstakingly edged himself into position so that he could see into the living room. It was empty.

A few minutes later the bald-headed man, now naked, emerged from the back of the house and crossed to a television set. His beer belly and his near-pendulous breasts vibrated with each step he took. He squatted down in front of a VCR and pushed a button.

Because the TV set stood in profile to Jablonski's position, it was impossible for the detective to see the screen. After an appropriate pause, during which the tape presumably rewound itself, the man again pushed a button. Faintly, through the window, Jablonski heard the signature music of the Channel Ten news followed by Will Waterbury's reading of the lead story.

Without warning, the bald man turned and looked toward the window. Jablonski ducked away and scooted behind a nearby bush. Abruptly the shade was pulled down. After what he deemed to be a suitable period of waiting, he approached the parked vehicle. Having left home without a pad or a pencil, it took him the better part of a minute before he was sure that he had correctly memorized the numbers on the truck's license plate. In the hope of locating the vehicle's registration slip, he checked the glove compartment. It was locked. He considered trying to open it with his burglar's tools, but he didn't relish the possibility of being discovered in the process.

He retraced his steps and took refuge in the Honda. He slid the car phone out of its holder and dialed the Valley Precinct. Moments later Nancy came on the line.

"It's Jack," he told her. "Write this down." Quickly he recited the numbers he had memorized.

"Okay, I wrote it down. What is it?"

"The license on an old pickup truck with Idaho plates and one burnt-out headlight. Will you run it by their DMV and see what you come up with?"

"First thing in the morning," she promised.

Quickly Jablonski related the events of the evening. He followed this by an explanation of what he planned to do from this point on. "All clear?" he asked when he finished.

"As a bell," Nancy replied. "Sounds like you're hot. But we need a lot more before we can get a warrant to arrest this guy."

"You don't need a *lot* more," Jablonski corrected her. "You need *some* more, which, as I have just pointed out, I intend to get for you."

"My hero."

"Wait'll you see the size of this ape. A direct, personal confrontation without benefit of backup might have been disastrous."

Nancy asked, "When do you figure I'll hear from you again?"

"Probably sometime late tomorrow afternoon. Where'll you be?"

"Home. I don't have to leave for the station until just before midnight."

"Very well then. I will sign off and see if it's possible to get some shuteye in the front seat of a Honda."

"Goodnight, Jablonski."

"Goodnight, Nancy."

When Jablonski woke up, it was still dark. Sometime during the last few hours he had managed to get his right foot trapped under the brake pedal. It required considerable shifting and squirming to free himself. He opened the door and swung his legs out. As he straightened up, the sciatic nerve in his left calf registered a shock of pain along its entire length that was so severe it caused his knee to buckle.

He grasped at the car door to avoid losing his balance. Gingerly he stretched, trying to work out the cramp. When he was satisfied that he had some freedom of movement, he ran in place for a minute, then did six deep knee bends.

He got back in the Honda and dialed his secretary at home. After five rings, a sleepy-voiced Shirley answered.

"Yes?"

"Morning. It's Jack."

"Jack?"

"Your boss."

"Where are you?"

"In my car."

"What time is it?"

"Five after six."

"What's the matter?"

"If you'll eighty-six the inquisition, I'll explain." In the background Jablonski could hear Saul begin to cry. "Sorry I woke everyone up."

In a voice lightly tinged with sarcasm Shirley said, "We usually hit the deck around seven. What's an hour's sleep one way or the other, especially after being up half the night with the baby?"

"Is he sick?"

"He's teething. Stand by a second, Jack. Rob, give Saul a bottle." After some indistinguishable comments from her husband, she was ready to resume the conversation. "So, talk."

Jablonski informed Shirley of his whereabouts and what he was up to. "I need you to relieve me for a couple of hours while I get a change of clothes and something to eat."

Alarmed, Shirley asked, "But what if the guy takes off after you've left?"

"Do you have a phone in your car?"

"No. But Rob does."

"Borrow his. If you need me, you can call me either in my car or at home. My guess is that our boy works nights someplace in the valley. He'll probably sleep until ten or eleven and I'll be back here by then."

"But what if he *does* decide to leave?" Shirley insisted.

"You'll follow him and let me know where he goes."

"I never followed anybody before."

Exasperated, Jablonski said, "You never had a baby before, you never moved to California before, you never worked for a private detective before. Anyone who could meet such imposing challenges should certainly have no trouble following a pickup truck."

Shirley kept pressing. "What if I lose him?"

"The world will not end," Jablonski said. "At some point he will return to his house, where I will be waiting."

Reluctantly, his secretary agreed to help. "I've got to get dressed and fight the morning traffic. It'll take me at least an hour to get there."

"Fine."

Shirley finally arrived shortly after eight o'clock. "There was an accident on the freeway," she explained. "A big rig jackknifed at Wilshire Boulevard."

"You're finally here. That's all that's important. Just sit tight," Jablonski instructed her. "And don't do anything conspicuous."

"Someone sitting alone in a car for two or three hours isn't conspicuous?"

Jablonski ignored her question and walked to the Honda. When he got home, he fed Snoopy and took a shower. After changing into a pair of old slacks, he called Mikki and gave her a status report.

"You mean our news team just gave up and drove away?" she asked, incredulous. "Arnold will be furious when I tell him what happened."

"We're getting close, Mikki."

"Thank God. To be honest, I really haven't had a moment's peace, knowing the guy was running around loose. What's next?"

"Later today I hope to find out where the son of a bitch works. To get the cops off their duffs, I need a few more pieces."

Mikki asked, "If you come up with something, would you be willing to let us send a mobile unit to cover the action?"

"Is the twenty-five-thousand dollar reward still in effect?"

"Sure."

"Tell your boys to keep the motor running."

CHAPTER THIRTY-FOUR

When Jablonski returned shortly after ten o'clock, Shirley looked like she'd been let out of jail. "Why didn't you tell me how boring it is to sit around casing somebody's house?" she demanded.

"Because you were too busy bitching and moaning about how inadequate you were to handle the job. I take it you haven't seen him so far."

"That's right."

"Very well, then. You may hie yourself back to Brentwood and resume your normal post."

"When will you be back?"

"There's no way of knowing."

"One thing's been bothering me. What do you do if you have to go to the bathroom when you're on a stakeout?"

"You improvise. Now scoot."

Shortly before noon Jablonski's car phone jangled. It was Nancy. "I just heard from one of the detectives at the station," she said.

"Tell me."

"The truck is registered in the name of Florence Barren, eight-six-four-five Woodhall Street in Boise. As we speak, the authorities in Idaho are checking up on the lady."

"Let me know when you hear something."

"Of course. Right now I'm going to try and catch a few hours sleep. I haven't closed my eyes since I got home."

About two o'clock the bald man appeared in his backyard and

started doing chin-ups. Jablonski stopped counting at forty-five. After that, with the detective in tow, he went to the supermarket, where he picked up two six-packs of beer, some cold cuts, a bag of potato chips, and half a dozen chocolate chip cookies. From there he stopped in at a video store and bought several blank tapes. Finally he spent an hour in a shabby-looking establishment that advertised "Massages- $10 and up."

Shortly before four P.M. the man dropped off his purchases at the bungalow and made his way toward the San Diego Freeway. Due to the buildup of rush hour traffic, the vehicle flow northward toward the San Fernando Valley was erratic, moving between five and twenty-five miles an hour. As he followed the truck, Jablonski wondered how anyone in his right mind could elect to spend part of each working day engaged in such a punishing endeavor. When the truck finally turned off at the Coldwater Canyon exit of the Ventura Freeway, the detective rubbed his stinging eyes. The exhaust fumes of a thousand cars, many of which seemed to be manned by borderline maniacs, combined with the grinding monotony of extended patches of gridlock, had reduced him to a zombie-like state.

Half a dozen blocks east of Coldwater Canyon, the truck pulled into a small parking lot behind a mini-mall on Ventura Boulevard. It was now nearly five P.M. Jablonski watched his quarry enter the back door of an establishment called Dangerous Dan's. After putting the Honda in a nearby parking place, he walked around to the front. Clustered in a U-shape, running about a quarter of a block, was the usual collection of businesses associated with a mini-mall such as this: a computer supply store, a taco joint, a small pharmacy, a toy shop, and a one-hour photo developing place. Dangerous Dan's, located dead center in the U, specialized in hamburgers, and was almost fully occupied. The majority of customers were blue-collar types, with a handful of high school kids filling out the mix. The bald man, now dressed in white pants and shirt and wearing a tall chef's hat, was busy at the grill.

Jablonski found a seat at the counter. It soon became apparent that the sole waitress for this section was both inept and overworked. While waiting to get her attention, he filled the time by observing the big man prepare the various orders. Slowly it dawned upon Jablonski that he had accidentally stumbled upon a unique opportunity.

When the waitress finally came around, the detective asked for a hamburger medium and a Coke. He watched as she tore off the sheet from her pad and placed it in a circular device at the end of the counter used to establish priority among the incoming orders. After approximately five minutes, Jablonski's turn came. The chef scooped up a burger with a spatula and plopped it down on a bun that lay browning on the griddle. He added a slice of onion and the top half of the sandwich. Then he picked up a plate and slid the concoction onto it. This accomplished, he rang a bell to summon the waitress.

After the young woman had set the order down in front of Jablonski, he leaned over and examined the outside rim of the plate. It was with considerable satisfaction that he discovered the greasy thumbprint left by the chef. He consumed the food slowly, trying desperately to think of a way to remove the plate from the premises without anyone becoming aware of his actions. There were too many people around for him to pick up the article and shove it under his jacket or attempt to camouflage it in a napkin. As he sat pondering his dilemma, he noticed a nick in the dish adjacent to the thumbprint. Nonchalantly, he reached for a clean paper napkin. In the process of pulling it free of its holder, he managed to knock the plate to the tiled floor, causing it to break into half a dozen pieces. He jumped off his stool and, ignoring the waitress's offers of assistance, began scooping up the debris and placing it, piece by piece, on the counter. Spotting the telltale fragment, he palmed it and let it slide into his pants pocket.

"Don't worry about it, sir," the girl told him. "Happens all the time."

"Clumsy of me," Jablonski replied. He threw a ten-dollar bill on the counter. "Keep the change."

She looked at him like he was the Sultan of Brunei. "Oh, thank you, sir! I'll never forget you."

The detective took a last look at the bald-headed chef (who had ignored the whole episode) and hurried back to the Honda. He dialed Nancy's home number.

"Yes?"

"Hi. It's Jack. I think I hit the jackpot." Jablonski explained what had transpired in Dangerous Dan's. "Can you meet me at your office and maybe dig up a technician, so we can find out if there's a matchup between the thumbprint on the plate and one or two of the notes Mikki received?"

"I can sure as hell try. When'll you be there?"

"Five, ten minutes."

"I have to bathe and get dressed. I'll call ahead and get the wheels turning. See Sergeant Danny Ray."

Jablonski asked, "Anything from Idaho yet on the lady who owns the truck?"

"Yes, but it's not very helpful. She died about a month ago."

"Shit!"

"Those were my sentiments. You certain the suspect will be there for the balance of the evening?"

"Positive," Jablonski asserted. "He apparently works five to midnight. There's a television set over the counter. That's undoubtedly where he watched our girl."

"Where do you suppose he went to write the notes to her? Would a one-arm hamburger joint have a computer?"

"I don't know. That'll have to be checked out."

Shortly after seven o'clock the LAPD technician phoned the Valley Division and informed Nancy that the thumbprint on the plate from Dangerous Dan's matched thumbprints on the second and the fifth notes received by Mikki O'Reilly.

"I guess that does it," Jablonski said gleefully. "What time do you plan to drop a net on the bastard?"

"Just as soon as I check with my betters."

"Can I borrow your phone? I want to give Mikki the good news."

"Help yourself."

When Jablonski told Mikki what was about to take place, she became almost incoherent. "Jesus, Jack, that's great! What'd you say his name was?"

"I didn't say because I don't know."

Mikki proceeded to overwhelm Jablonski with questions. It wasn't until her curiosity about the details of the past hours was sated that she asked, "Have you told Arnold Tolkin yet? He'll want to send the news van to cover the guy's capture."

"I haven't, but I will."

"Are you going in with the cops?"

Jablonski looked over at Nancy. "I don't think Sergeant Baxter needs any help."

Nancy smiled and nodded.

"I have an idea," Mikki said. "You're only ten minutes away. Why don't you come up to my place so we can celebrate? Hilda's making onion soup for starters, followed by a seafood casserole."

"If you insist."

After he had hung up, the detective asked Nancy to call him at Mikki's as soon as the bald headed man was safely behind bars. "I promised to notify the Channel Ten news director. Do you have a ballpark guess about what time you and the boys might be arriving at the hamburger joint?"

"Once I get the okay, which shouldn't take long, we'll roll. Within a half hour, I'd guess. But you didn't hear it from me."

Jablonski nodded sagely. "Of course not. If we're lucky tonight, maybe we'll see your pretty face on the ten o'clock news."

As the cook cleared away the main course, Mikki said, "It's funny, but I almost feel sad now that you've broken the case. I don't have some unknown sickie to hate anymore."

"You are a forgiving soul," Jablonski remarked, brushing aside some crumbs. "A trait to be envied."

"What's the point of carrying negative feelings around? They just louse up your life. From now on, I'm thinking positive. The doctors are going to fix me up and everything will be just fine. So there."

"Good girl."

The cook placed a piece of homemade angel food cake in front of Jablonski.

"Jack, I forgot to tell you: we're in escrow on a new house."

"Wonderful! Where is it?"

"In Pacific Palisades."

"Beautiful area."

"And expensive." Mikki listened for a moment. "I don't hear you eating."

"I'm going to pass on dessert," Jablonski announced. "I've decided not to become a blimp again."

"What brought on that decision?"

"I'm not sure. Vanity, or maybe insecurity."

Mikki giggled. "Do you want to tell me her name?"

"Whose name?"

"The lady who's responsible for shaping you up."

"No one's shaping me up. I just thought it was time to get control of myself."

"That's one for the books. Most men your age only lose weight when they're trying to impress someone."

Off in the distance the telephone began ringing. Mikki jumped up. "Maybe that's Nancy. Help me into the den."

Jablonski answered on the sixth ring. "Yes?"

The policewoman sounded breathless. "Jack, get Mikki on another extension. I think both of you should hear what I have to say."

"I'll do better than that," Jablonski replied. "I'll put you on the speakerphone." He pushed a button and dropped the instrument back in its cradle. "We're listening."

"The guy's name is Clem Barren and, as you already know, he's the night chef at Dangerous Dan's. When we checked over the place, we found a beat-up old computer and a letter quality printer in a small utility room in the back of the joint. The lab is checking to see whether the sample sheet we took off it matches up. To the naked eye, it does."

"Did Mr. Barren go quietly?" Jablonski asked.

"As a mouse. He also admits that he wrote the notes."

"Fabulous!" Mikki exclaimed.

"Not so fabulous. He insists he was in Boise, Idaho, taking care of his sick mother from the middle of September 'til the middle of November when the lady died."

Mikki interposed, "Are you saying he wasn't in town the night I was attacked?"

"That's what he claims," Nancy answered.

Jablonski asked, "Did the Boise police have any idea how long it would take to check out Barren's alibi?"

"There isn't much they can do tonight. They hope to get back to us by noon tomorrow. Unless, of course, they hit a bunch of dead ends."

Suddenly Mikki said, "Does Channel Ten know about this latest development?"

"Nobody knows," Nancy replied. "We only found out about it a few minutes ago."

"What time is it?"

Jablonski checked his watch. "Five after ten."

Mikki exploded. "Sweet Jesus! If what this Barren guy says is true, our news story is all screwed up. Nancy, we'll call you right back." Mikki depressed the cutoff button on the phone and gave Jablonski the station's number. "Hurry up!" When it began to ring, he handed the phone to Mikki and leaned down to the television set and switched it on. While Mikki was trying to get through to the executive producer in the control room to tell him to kill the Clem Barren story, Jablonski watched the late news show as it unfolded. Just about the time Mikki began explaining the purpose of her call to the man in charge of the telecast, Will Waterbury introduced the videotape of the Barren capture made earlier in the evening. Estella Gomez, the on-the-spot reporter, was standing on the sidewalk in front of Dangerous Dan's.

"For God's sake, Bob, cut Estella off!" Mikki yelled into the phone. "Don't ask questions. Just do it! A minute ago the cops turned up some new information. If you broadcast the story in its present form, we'll look like idiots!" There was some unintelligible response. Mikki turned to the detective. "What's happening, Jack?"

"I think you're too late," Jablonski replied.

Estella was finishing up with the particulars that led to Clem Barren's capture. In the background officers could be seen leading him to a squad car.

"Now," the reporter was saying, *"let's talk with Sergeant Nancy Baxter of the Valley Division, who has been on this case from the beginning."*

Before Nancy could open her mouth, a flustered Will Waterbury appeared on the screen. *"Ah . . . due to some technical problems, we won't be able to bring you the Mikki O'Reilly story at this time."* He thumbed through some papers in front of him before continuing. Jablonski snapped off the set.

Quickly Mikki filled in the newscast's executive producer on the latest developments. "Write it up for Will. What a break for us, huh?" She listened for a moment. "You want a quote from me? You can say that, if the suspect's alibi is confirmed, I'm more determined than ever to see that my attacker is brought to justice." She listened again. "If you think that's too bland, make up one of your own." She slammed down the phone.

During her exchange with the man at the station, Jablonski had seated himself in the chair facing the desk.

"Where are you, Jack?" Mikki demanded.

"Right across from you."

She slid into the swivel chair behind the desk and put her head in her hands. It was a long time before she spoke. "If it isn't Clem Barren, then who is it?"

Jablonski shook his head. "Who indeed?"

Shortly before noon the following day, the Boise police confirmed that Clem Barren had spent mid-September to mid-November in their city, caring for his dying mother. After running his name through their computers, they also discovered that, while he was a resident of Boise in the late 1980s, he had engaged in several note writing campaigns involving local television celebrities. In each of the cases he was let off with a warning.

"What now, Jack?" Mikki asked after Jablonski phoned her about Barren's release from jail. She sounded tired and scared.

"We try harder."

"I've been thinking about it all night. What *are* we going to do . . . ?"

"Just keep remembering what you said about positive thinking. We'll catch the son of a bitch." Jablonski wanted to believe that. "Did Clem's final letter arrive this morning?"

"The mail hasn't come yet." After a pause Mikki said wistfully, "Maybe that fortune telling lady who helped find your dog could give us a hand."

"I wish. As I understand old Marla May's *modus operandi,* she needs the date and place of birth of a subject to get her motor started. As of this minute, we don't know the first thing about the guy who damaged you." Jablonski paused. "Or even if it was a guy."

"Are you suggesting some *woman* had it in for me?" Mikki asked, astonished at the idea.

"At the moment I wouldn't even disregard an alien from outer space."

She laughed. "I don't know why I think that's funny."

"You think it's funny because the light just went out at the end of the tunnel. In the dark, laughing is better than crying." Jablonski heard Mikki blow her nose. "Hang tight, kid. Look at it this way: if we hadn't uncovered the identity of the notewriter and established his innocence, the cops, all of us, would have gone on thinking he was the one we wanted. Now that we know it's somebody else, we can get on with the job."

"I hadn't thought of it that way. That makes me feel a lot better. Remember, I want to hear every development."

"When I crack this nut, you'll be number two to get the news."

"Who'll be first?"

"Nancy Baxter. I owe her."

"I guess, at the moment, she's kind of unhappy."

"At roll call this morning her captain suggested that all private eyes, particularly yours truly, should be flogged into unconsciousness on the steps of their club and be left to rot in the sun. And that was *before* the confirmation from Boise came in." Jablonski heard someone call out to Mikki.

"Just a second, Jack. Auntie Belle brought in the mail." There were a few seconds of offstage dialogue between the two women before Mikki came back on the line. "Clem's last note is here."

"Read it."

"It says, 'I'm heartbroken. If you think I'd ever do a single thing to hurt you, you aren't worthy of my love. Goodbye.' "

"I'll have Shirley send a messenger. I'd like to add the epistle to my collection."

"Sure." There was a pause. "Please catch whoever it is, Jack," Mikki said softly. "Please."

CHAPTER THIRTY-FIVE

"WHAT are you staring at?" Shirley inquired as she walked into Jablonski's private office.

Without glancing up, he responded, "Did the courier get here yet?"

"Yep." She handed him an envelope.

Lined up neatly on the desk in front of the detective were photocopies of all the notes that Clem Barren had written to Mikki. He added the latest one to the collection.

Shirley asked, "Can I peek?"

"Be my guest."

His secretary came around the desk and leaned over her boss's shoulder. "You ought to have those things memorized by now."

"Oh, I do," Jablonski acknowledged. He pointed to the missive that was hand-delivered to the TV station the night of the attack on Mikki. "From the start, I wondered about the significance of the apostrophes."

"What apostrophes?"

"There are two apostrophes in this one. In all the others this particular punctuation mark has been omitted."

Shirley scanned the threatening letter. *"Soon I must help you understand what is right. It is important. Maybe I'll put my mark on you. Then you'll be mine forever."* "You mean the 'I'll' and 'you'll'?"

"Exactly."

She directed her gaze to the remaining notes. "My God, Jack, you're right! There are no punctuation marks in any of the contractions." She pointed at the latest one. *"Im heartbroken. If you think Id ever do a single thing to hurt you, you arent worthy of my love. Goodbye."* Her eyes widened. "The 'I'm,' the 'I'd' and the 'aren't' are wrong. What do you think it means?"

Jablonski shrugged. "Whoever wrote the hand-delivered epistle is better educated than our recent suspect."

"That could cover half the people in California."

"Perhaps, except for one thing. It wasn't mailed. It turned up in the guard shack on the calamitous evening. I find the juxtaposition of the two facts provocative."

"Too bad the officers never saw whoever dropped off the note."

"Ummm." Jablonski rubbed his chin. "Funny."

"What?"

"When Petey Bosworth interviewed me for his school paper, he asked me what I thought was the most important quality a detective could possess . . ."

"I remember the article. You said it was a highly developed power of observation, or words to that effect." Shirley knit her brows. "Does that have something to do with the guards at the TV station?"

"Possibly. If a *stranger* had paid them a visit the day of the attack, one of them would have probably remembered that. But if it was someone they saw day in and day out, a staff member for example, that fact might not have registered." Jablonski got up and strolled over to the window. "Logic dictates that Mikki's attacker wrote and then hand-delivered the note for some reason presently unknown to us. Why was he in such a hurry to communicate with her, to put her off balance, to set her up?" Jablonski thought for a long moment, then swung back into the room. "See if Sergeant Baxter will take my call."

Shirley returned to her desk in the outer office and dialed the Valley Division.

Nancy opened with a broadside. "Jablonski, I can't imagine what you could say that would help piece together my shattered ego."

"And a good afternoon to you," the detective said magnanimously.

"Sweetness and light ain't gonna do it. That I can promise."

"What if I told you I'm onto something potentially auspicious in Mikki's case?"

"I bet you also have a bridge in Brooklyn I could get cheap."

"I'm dead serious," Jablonski countered. "Remember Yogi Berra's immortal words, 'It ain't over 'til it's over.' "

Nancy snorted. "I'm listening."

"If I dig up some computer printouts, could you get the boys downtown to compare them to the notes that were written to Mikki?"

There was a pause. "Sorry, Jablonski. Suddenly I'm gun-shy."

"For God's sake, Nancy, all I'm asking is that you run a few pieces of paper through the lab!"

"Why?"

"I'd rather tell you that when I see you. At the moment all I've got is an idea. I still have to dig up the evidence."

"Jablonski, if you screw me on this one, they'll hang me out to dry."

"Not to worry. With a wee bit o' luck you could turn out to be the Queen of the May."

Nancy sighed. "I'm back working days and I'm here until seven-thirty. You want to bring the stuff to the office?"

"How about a nice dinner?" Jablonski asked. "Give me time to do what I have to."

"Meet me at the Italian joint."

"You are a darling."

"Apparently."

Jablonski hung up and buzzed Shirley. "See if Mikki's available," he directed. Moments later she was on the line.

"Hi, Jack!" she piped.

"How you doin'?"

"Okay, I guess, but thinking positive isn't always so easy."

"If it was, everybody'd do it. I need a favor."

"Sure."

"Am I correct in assuming that there are a bunch of computers and printers at your TV station?"

"A couple dozen at least."

"How many in the news department?"

"Four or five. What are you after?"

"I need a sample off each one of those."

Jablonski could hear her intake of breath. "You think somebody at Channel Ten is mixed up in this mess?"

The detective chose his words carefully. "That is a possibility I am about to explore."

"You mean like Arnold Tolkin or Will Waterbury?"

"Or Max Sabinson, the segment producer, or Bettina Rawls, the lady you replaced on the ten o'clock news."

"But didn't you . . . ?"

"All those people got a fast once-over the first time around. But now, it would seem, a more careful examination is indicated. Can you give me a hand?"

Mikki thought for a moment. "There's a kid at the station named Jerry who's in charge of maintaining the computer equipment. He's always had the hots for me. He'd probably do anything I asked."

"Good. Two more things. Have him label each page so we can identify which printer is which, and tell him to keep his mouth shut."

"Assuming I'm successful, you want the stuff delivered to your office?"

"Have the young man call Shirley. She'll drive down and get it."

"Okay. And Jack?"

"Yeah?"

"I think you're spinning your wheels. There's nobody in the news gang who'd want to hurt me." She paused. "Except maybe Max Sabinson." There was an anguished sigh. "Jesus!"

"Steady up, Mikki. We've got work to do."

Nancy was waiting in a booth in the back of the Italian restaurant when Jablonski came hurrying in. "Goddamn traffic," he mumbled, thrusting a manila envelope at her.

She looked at her watch. "Ten minutes is within allowable limits."

Mr. Mastantonio, the owner of the place, was passing by. "Don't listen to her, mister. She just got here."

Nancy shrugged. "So much for *largesse*."

Jablonski unfolded his checkered napkin and placed it on his lap, then beckoned to the waiter. "I'm having a double Cutty on the rocks," he informed Nancy. "What is your pleasure?"

"A glass of Pinot Grigio." She shook the contents of the envelope onto the table. There were four pages. "I take it this is the stuff you phoned me about."

"Indeed. It came from the news department at Channel Ten."

The same limerick had been typed on each of the computer printouts.

> There once was a rock star named Rice,
> An addict to all kinds of vice.
> Old men and boys
> And mechanical toys,
> And on Mondays he meddled with mice.

Nancy allowed as how she'd read worse.

Jablonski mentioned the discrepancy between the letter delivered to the station the night Mikki was assaulted and all the others. "I want to know if one of the printers that produced this doggerel was used on the correctly punctuated note. If the guys at the lab can't come up with a match, we'll get samples from every printer in the TV station. I'm convinced that there's a very good chance our quarry is lurking somewhere within the confines of Channel Ten. And, most likely, is living in fear that soon he or she will be unmasked."

"Can't be a she," Nancy pointed out, "unless you want to go outside the charmed circle."

"Elucidate."

"Remember Bettina Rawls, the lady who Mikki replaced on the ten o'clock news?" Jablonski nodded. "The final report on her whereabouts at the time of the attack finally turned up on my desk last week. The night in question Miz Rawls was involved in a tryst with one Herbert Deeters. At the Magnolia Motel in West Covina, I believe. The desk clerk positively identified them both." Nancy rearranged the silverware in front of her. "It sure would help if we had a motive."

"It would indeed." He indicated the printouts. "I hate to be pushy, but when . . . ?"

"A lab technician is standing by downtown to analyze this stuff. I thought I'd drop it off after dinner."

After the waiter had set down the drinks, Jablonski raised his glass. "To your forthcoming vindication."

They clinked glasses.

* * *

The following afternoon, as Jablonski returned from lunch, Shirley announced, "Nancy on one."

The detective picked up the phone. "That was fast."

"Bull's-eye, Jack! The printer on the desk of the assignment editor at Channel Ten News was the one used on the correctly punctuated note."

"Hooray!"

Suddenly Nancy sounded apologetic. "There's something else."

"Uh oh."

"As soon as my captain hears about what the lab turned up, he'll want to get into the act."

Jablonski said, "Plenty of room for everyone. But tell him he better step lively."

After dinner, Jablonski sat down in his living room and coaxed Snoopy up onto his lap. The two of them sat staring into the fluttering embers of the fire. No doubt about it, Jablonski decided, the assailant had to be someone known to Mikki, someone who had been a visitor to her home. And, in order to attempt to shift the blame for her disfigurement to some anonymous malcontent, he had to have previous knowledge of the contents of the notes that Mikki had received.

Jablonski rolled the three most likely suspects around in his mind. With the facts presently in his possession, the segment producer, Max Sabinson, was the only one who seemed to have a reason to harm Mikki O'Reilly. Unfortunately, it didn't seem like a very good reason. As far as Jablonski knew, the police hadn't bothered to dig very deeply into Sabinson's background. The quickest and easiest way to eliminate the man from consideration would be to recheck his alibi.

At the time of the attack the producer said he was flying up to the Sea Ranch, a coastal development northwest of San Francisco. Who went with him? When did he leave? When did he arrive?

Will Waterbury, the anchorman, had a witness. His wife, Edna, vouched for the fact that her husband had returned home from the newscast as usual, about eleven-thirty, and had immediately gone to bed. Unless his sixty-year-old mate was lying on his behalf, it would seem that Waterbury was out of the ballgame. But, following the episode with Clem Barren, Jablonski had determined not to make any more assumptions.

Arnold Tolkin, Channel Ten's news director, reported that he had stayed late at the station finishing up some report or other that the station management had requested. The guard at the main gate reported that Tolkin had signed out at three twenty-two A.M. But surely, Jablonski reasoned, there were other ways that the executive could have exited the establishment unnoticed. Using this hypothesis, the news director could have done the deed, returned, then later departed in the normal fashion.

With each of the men, the elusive *why* had to be nailed down. Even if their alibis weren't ironclad, what compelling reason might any one of them have for blinding and disfiguring Mikki O'Reilly? What might she have known about one of them? What could she have done to provoke such a violent attack?

Snoopy followed Jablonski into the kitchen, where she gratefully devoured her evening cookie. After that, the two of them retired to the bedroom. Tomorrow morning, the detective decided, he would begin by looking up the charming Mr. Sabinson.

CHAPTER THIRTY-SIX

First thing after breakfast Jablonski phoned Arnold Tolkin and asked the news director if he was busy for lunch.

"I'm not. On one condition."

"Which is?"

"If you're still on Mikki's case, please give us a chance to redeem ourselves. I chewed Sabinson's butt good for leaving you high and dry the night of the Clem Barren stakeout."

"No hard feelings. Having a double-barreled shotgun pointed at you can be a major discouragement. And, yes, I am still on the case."

"Le Dome at one o'clock?" Tolkin asked.

"Sounds fancy."

"It is, but Channel Ten is paying." The news director gave Jablonski the address. "Is this business or pleasure?" he inquired tentatively.

"Probably a little of both. One more thing. At the moment, if you were Max Sabinson, where would you be?"

"Let me check the schedule board." There was a momentary pause. "Max worked late last night and isn't due in until five this afternoon. My guess is he's sound asleep in somebody's bed."

"As opposed to his *own* bed?"

"It's an open secret around the station, Mr. Jablonski."

"Jack."

"Jack. A while back Max was diagnosed as having pancreatic cancer. They gave him six months."

"I see." Jablonski thought about that for a moment. "And, as a result, Mr. Sabinson is indulging in sexual overkill as a compensation against future losses?"

"Or, to put it more simply, he's fucking his brains out."

"A dangerous pastime these days."

"For his partners, possibly."

Jablonski asked, "What's Sabinson's home address?"

Tolkin gave the detective directions to an apartment complex in Marina del Ray. "What are you looking for, Jack?"

"I'll tell you at lunch."

If one isn't a permanent resident, the odds of finding a parking place in Marina del Ray, the pseudo-Bohemian community located on and near the ocean several miles southwest of Santa Monica, are approximately the same as having a 747 make a successful landing on your roof. In despair, after half an hour of fruitless searching, Jablonski left his car to the ministrations of a worker in a nearby tune-up parlor and walked a half mile to the wing in which Sabinson resided. The units were packed together, some at ground level, others up a half-story. The more expensive ones fronted on a canal. Even at ten o'clock in the morning, the boat traffic was moderately heavy in both directions. Small rowboats outfitted with outboard engines darted around sizeable yachts and sailboats of all types and descriptions.

After observing this peaceful scene through a walkway leading to the channel, Jablonski set out to isolate apartment 16B. Because of the corrosion caused by the salt air, many of the numbers blended into the dark brown color of the door frames on which they were mounted. As a consequence, they were nearly impossible to read. More than once Jablonski had to go halfway up a set of steps before he could decipher the markings. Finally, at the far end of the first structure, he found what he was looking for.

Tacked under Sabinson's doorbell was a note that read: "Do not disturb before noon." Jablonski pushed the button. In response, there was absolute silence from within. He repeated his action several more times, then began knocking. Moments later he heard a young woman giggling. Pleased to find the unfortunate Romeo in residence, albeit with concubine, Jablonski waited to be admitted. Before this happened, there was a montage of sound: locks clicking, chains hitting against the interior panel, and the knob being jerked back and forth half a dozen times. Finally the door slid open about twelve inches.

A tousle-headed platinum blonde, not a day over eighteen, with sleepy eyes, and a lower lip guaranteed to cause a reaction in any male not totally blind, leaned down and, in a Marilyn Monroe voice, inquired, "Yes, what is it?"

"I'm looking for Max Sabinson."

The girl stood up straight and, from a height of six feet, peered down at Jablonski. "Max is otherwise engaged." She started to close the door.

Jablonski stuck his foot in the crack. "It's important."

"Right at the moment I'd doubt that Max would think so."

"Inform him Jack Jablonski is here."

"Who?"

"Jablonski. And mention that the cops'll be along pretty soon and maybe he'd like to talk to me first."

The teenager looked down at the detective's foot. "If you don't mind."

Jablonski backed up a step and the girl closed the door. Within a minute Sabinson appeared, barefooted and tugging at the sash on a silk bathrobe. "What's this about cops, for cris'sake? I got a hot pair of twins inside."

It was difficult for Jablonski to believe that the creature who had opened the door could be duplicated. "Twins?"

"Yeah. And they work by the hour. Come back around noon."

"That's not possible. I'll only need ten or fifteen minutes."

Sabinson looked around, then motioned the detective inside. "We'll go out on the balcony."

As Jablonski passed the open door to the bedroom, he couldn't help but look inside. Lying nude on a king-size bed that was covered with what appeared to be black satin sheets, were two identical creatures seductive enough to entice the most devoted celibate into a life of sexual excess. They were passing the time of day by playing with each other.

"Don't go away," Sabinson called over his shoulder to the girls. "I'm not finished."

"There's no rush, honey," one of them replied. "We're just getting warmed up."

Briefly Jablonski wondered how much the duo got for their time and trouble.

"Out here," the newsman directed, pulling aside a sliding door that opened onto a small balcony overlooking the canal. He selected a wicker chair and flopped into it. "Tell me about the cops. What the hell do they want with me?"

Before seating himself, Jablonski scooped out a place on a small sofa covered with overstuffed pillows and glanced down at a beautiful mahogany Chris-Craft that was gliding by. "Same thing I do. Since the elimination of Clem Barren as a suspect, the general feeling now is that someone at your TV station was responsible for what happened to Mikki."

"Did the cunt tell you that?"

"Are you referring to Miss O'Reilly?"

Sabinson's voice oozed sarcasm. "In case you didn't know, your client is a self-centered, opportunistic, bossy little broad."

Jablonski shook his head. "The other day it was obvious there was no love lost between you two, but I didn't realize the depth of your disgust."

"You saw what she was like. She gives me a stomachache everytime I have to work with her."

Jablonski stared down at the boats in the canal for a long time before he spoke. "My next question is indelicate and I apologize for it."

"If it's about my health, what you heard is true. The docs tell me I'll check out before summer."

Jablonski looked toward the bedroom. "In the meantime, you seem to be managing pretty well."

"I already wrote the words for my marker. 'Here lies Max Sabinson, who went down fighting.' Get it: 'went *down*'?" The newsman laughed bitterly.

"Memorable." Jablonski leaned forward in his seat. "Mind if we review your alibi?"

"Sure. I flew up to Sea Ranch the night Mikki got nailed. Left about ten. Arrived just before one-thirty in the morning. Drove to my house. Stayed two days and came home. Period."

"Ought to be easy enough to confirm your movements with the airlines."

Sabinson shook his head. "I flew my own plane. A Cessna one eighty-two. Took off from Hawthorne, where I tie down."

"Okay. Let me revise my supposition. Ought to be easy enough to check with the Hawthorne control tower."

"They don't keep records of takeoffs and landings unless you file an instrument flight plan."

"Which you didn't."

Sabinson nodded. "Gorgeous night. Little windy. I've been making that trip for a long time. Could do it in my sleep."

Briefly, Jablonski wondered why there wasn't some rule against a person with terminal cancer flying himself around in an airplane. "Anybody see you leave here?"

"How the hell would I know?"

"You take anybody along?"

"Nope."

"Meet anybody up at Sea Ranch when you arrived?"

"Christ, I told you, I got there about one-thirty in the morning."

"I'm not familiar with the area. Which airport did you land at?"

"Sea Ranch has its own strip up on the top of a hill. Short. About three thousand feet. Pilot-controlled lighting. Piece of cake. Unless there's bad weather. Then you have to land at Santa Rosa where they have an instrument approach and drive over."

Jablonski thought for a minute. "I would assume Sea Ranch is fairly large."

"It is. I bought a house near the ocean about five years ago. Best investment I ever made."

"How'd you get from the airstrip to your residence?"

"I keep an old clunker parked up there. Lots of pilots do. No car rental service available."

Jablonski sat back. "Not much of an alibi, is it?"

"No, it isn't. And who gives a flying fuck? If I messed up Mikki, which I didn't, I'd be six feet under before the goddamn case ever came to trial." Sabinson stood up. "Anything else?"

"That ought to do it," Jablonski replied.

"When do you think the cops will arrive?"

"Hard to say. But you can be sure it will be in the next day or two."

Sabinson led Jablonski past the open bedroom door, where the twins were wrapped around one another busily exploring the inner meaning of life. Sabinson stopped and watched them. "Can you let yourself out?" he asked the detective.

"Indeed." As Jablonski started for the front entrance, Sabinson loosened the sash on his robe and disappeared from view. Moments later a wave of giggling was heard.

As the detective was walking back to reclaim the Honda, he realized that nothing Sabinson had told him eliminated the man as a suspect. He could have attacked Mikki, then driven to the Hawthorne airport and departed at two-thirty or three in the morning. Which would put him in Sea Ranch at six or six-thirty.

Hating a hostile female isn't a very good motive for a murderous attack. Although, Jablonski had to admit, it was better than some of the others he'd heard about during his career. He wondered if there was anything Sabinson had chosen to omit. Probably.

In a newspaper column Jablonski had read, it was decreed that the Regency Hotel in New York City was the home of the power breakfast, while Le Dome, on Sunset Boulevard, was specified as one of the local spots to have a power lunch. Being unsophisticated when it came to the interpretation of such arcane lingo of show business, Jablonski assumed that the adjective *power,* as it related to food, either meant more and better vitamins or an overwhelming caloric content. In either case, having developed an unrelenting series of hunger pangs during his encounter with Max Sabinson, he looked forward with considerable anticipation to what he hoped would be an interesting culinary experience.

The *maître d'* at the front door was dressed in a silk shirt, with the sleeves rolled up. He wore no tie. His pants ballooned out at the sides, appearing to be at least two sizes too large for him.

"How may I help you?" the man inquired.

The detective said, "I'm looking for Mr. Tolkin."

"Wonderful!" he gushed. "You must be Jack. Arnold is waiting for you."

Jack? Arnold? Briefly Jablonski wondered whatever happened to headwaiters who wore tuxedos at noon and had indeterminate European accents.

"Caroline," the *maître d'* called out. A gorgeous, trim brunette in her mid-twenties flowed over. "Show this gentleman to Arnold's table."

"Follow me," the young woman directed.

Following her was a pleasure. It wasn't quite a miniskirt she was wearing, but it was close enough. And her legs, sheathed in the sheerest black silk, were custom-made. Jablonski hoped that his host was seated some distance away.

Because the restaurant was packed, the two of them had to pick their way through clumps of waiters and arriving and departing guests. Arnold Tolkin was waiting in a quiet room with gold wallpaper, located in the rear of the restaurant. It was elegantly decorated and held only four tables.

"I picked this spot so we could talk," Tolkin said, rising and extending his hand. "I hope you approve."

Jablonski replied, "Looks perfect to me."

The news executive looked over at the young woman. "Caroline, tell Pierre we are pleased as punch."

"Okay, Arnold," she said, turning and undulating off toward the front of the restaurant.

After he was seated, Jablonski said, "I have two questions. First, doesn't anyone in Los Angeles have a last name?"

Tolkin laughed. "Of *course* they do. But don't you think it's much more *fun* to use the more familiar form of address?"

"Up to a point. Last week a kid who came to read the gas meter called me Jack. I had a little trouble with that."

"What's number two?"

"Pardon?"

"Your second question."

"Do you realize that you can walk the streets of New York or Chicago or Washington, D.C., for days at a time and seldom see a female face or form that would invite a second look?"

"I think that's a bit of an exaggeration."

"Possibly. What I want to know is: how come every other girl out here looks like a goddamn refugee from a centerfold?"

"Moom pitchers," Arnold answered. "They come from farms, from metropolises, from trailer parks and mountain cabins, with expectations high and hopes burning bright in their usually ample breasts. They seek recognition, stardom, their name in lights, the adoration of the masses. But, alas, it is infrequently that one of them even comes close to her goal."

From the way Tolkin was prattling, Jablonski decided the newsman must be strung out tight.

"And what happens to the rejects? you ask. They become hookers, hostesses, airline stews, waitresses, models, cops, clerks and, if they're somehow able to abandon their fantasies and get themselves trained, occasionally office workers. The rare one who's lucky lands a heavy-breathing executive and lives happily ever after in Bel Air or Beverly Hills." Tolkin smiled. "Shall we order and abandon the small talk?"

"I'd say it's time."

After a tall, young waiter, with a mass of curly brown hair and a pair of shoulders that were twelve inches wider than the rest of him, had taken their drink order, Tolkin winked at the detective and said, "I saw him first."

Jablonski let that one pass. He replied, "In the matter of Mikki O'Reilly."

Tolkin nodded. "I figured."

"Would you like to run down what you were doing the night she was attacked?"

"I don't mind. But I've already told the police all there is to tell."

"That you worked until about three-thirty in the morning in your office and then went home."

"That's the truth."

"Things have changed, Arnold. Now that there is no longer a prime suspect running around loose, we must explore other avenues." The waiter set down a Bloody Mary in front of Tolkin. Jablonski had ordered a Diet Coke. "Presently we've shifted the investigation to embrace certain people at Channel Ten."

"You spoke in the plural. Or is that the royal 'we'?"

Jablonski cleared his throat. "I've been working very closely with Sergeant Baxter of the LAPD."

"Nancy. A lovely woman. She's the one who took my statement. Have you come up with something new?"

"The police recently discovered that the note, the one that was hand delivered to the station the night of the attack on Mikki, was typed on a printer that sits on the desk of your assignment editor."

"Jesus! A couple dozen people, maybe more, could have used that machine."

"Once we determine why this particular letter was conveniently planted on the desk in the guard shack within a few hours of its composition, we will have our man."

"Do you know for a fact that the time of writing and delivery were more or less continuous?"

"Not for a fact. But, with everything that's come to light lately, it's a reasonable assumption. Someone at Channel Ten must have felt he needed to move quickly. Otherwise, why wouldn't he have mailed the note?"

Tolkin took a long pull from his drink, then wiped his lips. "And you're curious whether I might have had any reason to do Mikki harm?"

"In my view, what you gave the police is a non-alibi. You sat in your office working away. No one saw you. You made no outside telephone calls. You originated no faxes. For all anyone could tell, you could have taken a couple of hours and gone to a movie."

"Or sneaked up to Mikki's house and poured acid on her?"

Before Tolkin could continue, the waiter intervened. "Would you gentlemen care to order?"

"I think we would," Tolkin replied somewhat grimly.

Jablonski chose the chickenburger with a side of the house's special coleslaw, and the executive settled for a salad.

"Now where were we?" Tolkin asked.

You know goddamn well where we were, Jablonski thought to himself.

"Oh, yes. You're wondering if there could be some hidden reason why I might have wanted to disfigure our golden girl." Tolkin looked away. After an almost embarrassingly long period of silence, he spoke. "Mikki didn't tell you about us?"

The detective shook his head. "The lady said nothing."

"We are on sensitive ground here, Jack. I hate to include anyone else in on the secret, but if I don't come clean, so to speak, and somehow you later dig up what I'm about to reveal, I could come out looking like a suspect. Which, I assure you, I'm not." The newsman looked away.

"Please, go on."

Tolkin sighed heavily. "Foolishly, about a year ago, in the lull before the nightly news went on the air, I was busy doing a young man in my office."

"I beg your pardon?"

The executive squirmed in his seat. "With an outsider, such as yourself, it is difficult to be more precise."

"Bullshit, Arnold. I'm a big boy."

"There is a handsome youth of Latin extraction who delivers from the local deli. If the tip is generous enough, he is happy to participate in some fun and games. Is that clear enough?"

"It is."

"I thought he had locked the office door and he thought I had. While we were fused together on the sofa, Mikki O'Reilly knocked and entered, catching us in what is popularly described as a compromising position."

"So what? I thought in Hollywood anything goes."

"That is a myth. For example, the owner of Channel Ten is an eighty-year-old millionaire who never got past the Immaculate Conception. Were he to discover my sexual preference, I would not only be out on the street, but his not inconsiderable influence would no doubt be applied to keeping me in a permanent state of unemployment in the news business."

"You're saying if Mikki squealed . . ."

"I could end up selling shoes. Or worse."

Jablonski fiddled with the salt and pepper shakers before continuing. "In plain language, as a result of her intrusion, Mikki holds a certain amount of power over you as far as her future is concerned."

"She does. But never once, in any way, has she attempted to influence my running of the department. Never *once*."

"Her rise up through the ranks was due entirely to her performance on the evening news."

"Yes. When she was the weather girl and first began to wear all those sexy costumes, it wasn't more than a dozen weeks before the ratings edged upwards. That's a fact. You can look at the record."

"Sometime later, if I recall correctly, you moved her out of the studio and made her a segment reporter."

Tolkin nodded. "Which upset the audience. Letters and phone calls came in by the hundreds. Segment reporters appear only occasionally. They wanted to see Mikki every night."

"So you promoted her to sub-anchor with Waterbury."

"After several months."

Jablonski surmised, "And the ratings rose again."

"Almost immediately. Believe me, Mikki didn't have to blackmail anybody. She's got a corner on charisma. After about six months I had an inspiration. I figured if there was some way to put the focus more on *her,* maybe we could squeeze out another half point in the Arbitron ratings. I decided to move Will Waterbury out and make him a roving commentator on all our news shows."

"And substitute Mikki as sole anchor at ten o'clock."

"Right."

Jablonski looked puzzled. "Strange that she never mentioned this to me."

"I never told her. I figured I had to start with Waterbury. When I suggested the change to him, he said he wanted to think about it. I lay back for a while and did nothing. A wise decision, as things turned out."

The waiter brought the food. Without waiting for Tolkin to be served, Jablonski cut into the chickenburger and took a big bite. "Forgive me for forging ahead, but the aroma is not to be denied."

The executive picked at his salad. "I can't think of a way to make my alibi verifiable. I guess it comes down to whether or not you believe me."

Jablonski wanted to talk to Mikki before he bought into Tolkin's scenario. "You are very persuasive, Arnold."

They ate in silence for a moment. "You talked to Max Sabinson?" Tolkin asked.

"This morning."

"I assume you will also be meeting with Will."

"His wife is his alibi. I'd be more interested in seeing what she has to say," Jablonski replied. "Can I get a home address from you?"

"Sure." Tolkin shook his head. "A sad case."

"Mrs. Waterbury?"

"Yeah. Lush City."

"That's a shame. Do you think she'll be functional if I drop by after lunch?"

"Hard to say. Probably. She's not a spectacular drunk. She just keeps nipping during most of her waking hours."

After Tolkin had paid the check and the two of them were standing on Sunset Boulevard waiting for their cars to be delivered, the executive said, "Don't forget, Jack, if you break the case, I want to know about it fast. It'd be a big story for us."

"Sure, Arnold."

"And I trust you to keep my secret."

"To the grave and beyond," Jablonski assured him.

Presumably because he was better known and regularly tipped the attendant five dollars, Tolkin got his car first. As his host swung out into the fast-moving traffic, Jablonski pondered on the merits of the power lunch. As far as he could determine, the most powerful thing about it was its price.

Will Waterbury and his wife Edna lived on a tree-lined street in the Hancock Park area of Los Angeles. Their impressive two-story residence had a balcony that ran halfway across the front and overlooked a patio on which a set of rattan porch furniture rested. A furled yellow umbrella stood rigidly in the middle of a circular table, and boxes of flowers, built into the railing that surrounded the area, were welcome splashes of color against the pale gray walls of the house. A rolling shutter was mounted over the downstairs French windows. A single car garage, an oddity in an elegant Southern California neighborhood, was adjacent to the main structure. Inside it sat a Rolls Corniche.

Before driving over from the restaurant, Jablonski had considered calling Mrs. Waterbury to announce his intentions, but determined that he might accomplish more if his visit was a surprise. As he climbed the steps leading to the front door, he saw the face of a woman peering out at him from behind a heavy damask drape. He nodded and smiled. Immediately, she vanished. Before he had a chance to ring the bell, she opened the door.

"Are you here about the pilot light?" she demanded.

"The pilot light?"

"Yes. The heater in the family room won't go on."

"No, I'm afraid not."

Mrs. Waterbury showed the ravages of time. Her face was deeply tanned. Wrinkles flowed like tributaries across her forehead and down her cheeks. She was carelessly dressed in a pleated gray skirt and a pale blue cashmere sweater that had a grease spot near its bottom edge. The red smudges on her front teeth bore witness to the manner in which her lipstick had been applied.

"Then who are you?" she demanded. Her breath was sour and smelled of bourbon.

Jablonski introduced himself and requested an interview.

"What for?"

Patiently he explained about his relationship to Mikki O'Reilly and that he wanted to discuss the fateful night of the attack on the young woman.

"What is there to discuss? My husband had nothing to do with what happened."

"That may be true, but I really would appreciate it if you would indulge me for a few minutes."

Mrs. Waterbury looked the detective up and down. "I don't like strangers in my house. *Especially* after Mikki's experience."

Jablonski indicated the patio chairs. "Why don't we sit out here?"

Mrs. Waterbury considered the idea. "All right. I'll be back in a minute."

When she returned she was carrying an old-fashioned glass filled with liquor in which two ice cubes floated. At the very least, Jablonski figured, it was a triple. He helped the woman into a chair and sat down facing her.

"Talk softly," Mrs. Waterbury instructed the detective. "My husband is having his nap upstairs. He always has a nap before going off to work."

The detective noted the open door leading onto the second floor balcony. "I shall remain unobtrusive at all times, I promise."

Mrs. Waterbury took a sip from her drink, then coughed discreetly.

Jablonski continued, "The night of the unfortunate event involving Miss O'Reilly, I understand your husband returned home about an hour after the conclusion of the news broadcast."

"That's correct. Shortly after midnight."

"I see. You know that because you waited up for him."

"I *never* wait up. I'm always asleep by ten-thirty."

More likely passed out, Jablonski thought. "That's a conundrum. How could you know the time of his arrival on the night in question if you were asleep?"

"He always gives me a kiss before he gets into bed."

"And then you check the clock. Is that it?"

"Sometimes I do. Usually not." She took another big sip. "On that particular night the bedside clock was flashing."

"Flashing?"

"The Santa Ana winds were blowing very hard. Whenever that happens the power goes out and the electric clocks flash. While Will was in the bathroom, I reset the one by the bed."

"How did you know what to set it to?"

Mrs. Waterbury shook her head in disgust. "You're a persistent bastard, aren't you?" Bastard came out "bashtard." "I looked at my wristwatch. I keep it on the bedside table."

"And it was indicating just after twelve midnight?"

"That's right." She knocked back the rest of her drink. "How is Mikki anyway?"

"She's a plucky young woman."

Suddenly tears came into Mrs. Waterbury's eyes. "Terrible for someone so young to get brutalized like that."

"Terrible." Jablonski decided it was time to make tracks. "You have been very helpful."

The lady blinked several times. "What'd I say?"

"Please give Mr. Waterbury my best." Jablonski got up, made a small bow, and retreated to his car.

CHAPTER THIRTY-SEVEN

AFTER finishing the dinner he had picked up at a fancy French takeout place on Montana, Jablonski remained seated at the kitchen table poring over several lists of facts that he had compiled on sheets of yellow, legal-sized paper. Snoopy lay at his feet chewing on a tennis ball.

He arranged three of the pages in a line in front of him and cleared his throat. "What we have here, Snoop, is: one, a news producer dying of cancer who hated Mikki's guts; two, an executive who participated in an unorthodox activity that Mikki accidentally witnessed; and three, an aging anchorman who might be re-assigned because of Mikki's growing appeal to the audience."

The detective sat back in his chair and closed his eyes. On the face of it, none of the men seemed motivated strongly enough to punish Mikki so cruelly. To further muddy the waters was the fact that each of them had a relatively fuzzy alibi. Sabinson's and Tolkin's were circumstantial, and Waterbury's wife was hardly a person one would normally count upon to give an accurate account of anything.

In the hope of uncovering something he had missed, Jablonski rethought the case.

On November 8 last, a note addressed to Mikki O'Reilly was discovered lying on the desk in the guard shack located at the mouth of Channel Ten's parking lot. How it got there nobody knows. One of the private cops at the station brought it to Mikki just before airtime. Following the news broadcast, she discovered her car had a flat tire and walked over to the guard shack to call the AAA. Will Waterbury, discovering her plight, gave her a ride home. The anchorman waited at the house while the local patrol checked the premises. At his urging, Mikki took a sleeping pill, turned on the alarm, then retired. Waterbury let himself out the back gate, which was not connected to the alarm system. He punched the button on the inside doorknob, locking the portal behind him, and went home, arriving shortly after midnight.

Several hours later neighbors heard cries, presumably made by Mikki, but neglected to respond. Early the next morning she was found unconscious at the foot of the front steps to her house. Her dog had been poisoned, and the alarm and telephone wires were severed. No extraneous fingerprints were discovered, a fact which seemed to indicate that the assailant had worn gloves. Period.

Over and over, Jablonski ran his eyes up and down the columns of facts that he had assembled. His failure to identify a single item that might lead him to a solution of the crime was maddening. Either somebody was lying or he was making assumptions that what *seemed* to be correct *was* correct. He'd done that once before on this case and he was determined not to do it again. He squeezed his eyes shut and concentrated so hard that the heat emanating from his body threatened to raise the ambient temperature.

But he could conjure up nothing of consequence.

The next morning, feeling more frustrated than ever, he telephoned Nancy. After summarizing the three interviews he had conducted the previous day, he asked, "Did you guys do any better than I did?"

"We're starting this afternoon."

"Why the foot dragging?"

"My boss wants to be sure we have all our ducks in a row before we make a move. He's phobic about getting involved in another screw-up on the O'Reilly case. In large part thanks to you, I might add."

"Why do you find it necessary to keep bringing that up?"

"Fair is fair. The *captain* keeps bringing it up. *I* keep bringing it up."

Jablonski poured himself a second cup of coffee. "If you discover something useful, you've got my number."

"I *wish* I had your number, Jablonski," she said wistfully. The line went dead.

The detective returned to his lists. Although he still had lingering doubts whether any of the men was motivated strongly enough to perform such a heinous act, the other option, that the deed had been committed by some heretofore unthought-of person, seemed even more unlikely. After another fruitless hour of retracing oft-traveled paths, he decided to select the candidate who had the most to gain by visiting such harsh treatment upon his client and concentrate exclusively on him.

If Sabinson had messed up Mikki, the only thing that would accrue to him was perverted pleasure. Does a dying man need that kind of solace?

As Mikki's appeal to the viewers grew, Tolkin's reputation as the news director could only be enhanced. He had everything to gain by keeping Mikki healthy.

By using this approach, Waterbury became the number one suspect. Now all I have to do, Jablonski told himself, is to try and punch a hole in the anchorman's alibi.

The detective fixed a bologna sandwich on pumpernickel that he washed down with a beer, then headed for the office. As he was driving east on San Vicente Boulevard, he became aware that a jam-up of cars occupied the intersection at Barrington. The near-gridlock had caused long lines of angry motorists to extend in all four directions. The mix-up was underscored by the wild soprano squealing of the horns on the Japanese cars and the deeper honking of the American models.

As he edged closer, he identified the cause of the trouble: instead of producing the normal red, orange and green sequence, the traffic signals were malfunctioning, continuously flashing a single red light. In California this means that a motorist must come to a full stop, then wait until it is safe before proceeding. The various concepts of what was safe were what compounded the confusion. Unfortunately the police hadn't as yet arrived at the scene to restore order and, as a result, the deeper animalistic urges of the trapped participants were getting more and more out of control.

As Jablonski started to make a left turn up Barrington, a 1969 Impala cut him off. The detective rolled down the window and shouted at the pimply-faced youth at the wheel of the other car, "Age before beauty, shrimp! Back up!"

"Fuck you, Elmer!" the kid bellowed, getting out of his car. "You want to make me?"

In addition to trapping Jablonski in the middle of the intersection, the abandoned Impala caused the creeping lines of cars converging on it to come to a dead halt.

The youth stood his ground, hands on his hips, and glared at Jablonski. "Get your ass out here!" the youth snarled.

Jablonski locked the door, rolled up his window and crossed his arms. Within moments, the cacophony became so overwhelming that the young man was blown back into his car by the sheer force of it. Then, after giving Jablonski the finger, the kid edged the Impala back far enough to allow the detective's car to break free. As he turned up Barrington, Jablonski tipped his fedora to the boy and pulled into his parking spot in the gas station.

Strolling over to his office, Jablonski considered the number of things that people depend upon to get them through the day: telephones, water, gas, electricity. He looked around at the mess being caused by the flashing traffic lights and shook his head.

Then he remembered the clock in the Waterburys' bedroom.

"Good afternoon, Jack," Shirley chirped as he opened the office door.

"Maybe it is and maybe it isn't."

"What's that supposed to mean?"

"So far the day has only been fair, but maybe I just thought of a way to improve things." He plopped his hat on the rack and shed his jacket. "See if you can locate somebody at the Department of Water and Power who can tell you whether or not there was a power outage in the Hancock Park area the night of last November eighth."

"How long a power outage?"

"It doesn't matter. For my purposes a second would be long enough."

Shirley thought for a moment. "That was the night Mikki was attacked."

"So it was. Get cracking."

While Shirley worked her way through the bureaucracy of the City of Los Angeles, Jablonski stared out at the cars as they crawled along Barrington. He mused on the fact that an electric clock that plugs into a socket starts to flash whenever the flow of electricity to it is interrupted, even momentarily; and such clocks don't automatically resume with the correct time when the power comes back on. They must be readjusted by hand.

Since it was flashing, the one on the table in the Waterburys' bedroom had to be of the type that uses 110 volt AC. When Edna Waterbury mentioned that she had to reset it, Jablonski hadn't given her remark a second thought. But, a few minutes ago, a more ominous possibility occurred to him: what if there *hadn't* been a power outage the night of the attack on Mikki? What if Will Waterbury had caused the bedside lamp to begin flashing *simply by unplugging it for a moment?*

What a perfect way to set up an alibi! Because of her addiction to strong drink, Mrs. Waterbury was usually dead to the world by ten-thirty. Although she said her husband normally returned home by midnight, she didn't always look at the clock. Consequently, on many nights, she couldn't know with any certainty what time it was. If, the night of the attack on Mikki, Will had returned *two or three hours later than usual,* picked up his wife's wristwatch from the bedside table and turned it back to eleven-thirty, then momentarily unplugged the electric clock, she would never be the wiser. The rest would have been easy: wake her up for a goodnight kiss, then suggest she check her wristwatch and reset the flashing clock while he was in the bathroom brushing his teeth. Later, when she had gone back to sleep, he would have adjusted both the wristwatch and the electric clock to the correct time.

Shirley stuck her head in the door. "No dice."

"Hmmm?"

"No power outage in Hancock Park on November eighth."

"Not even for an instant?"

"That's what the man said. Sorry."

Jablonski jumped up and clapped his hands together. "We're rolling! Get me Arnold Tolkin at Channel Ten. It's urgent."

"What's urgent?"

"Later!" Jablonski bellowed. "Start dialing."

While Shirley was completing the call, the detective nervously paced back and forth behind his desk. When he heard two buzzes, he dove for the intercom. "Yep?"

"Line one. His secretary at the station is patching you through to Tolkin's car. He's on his way back from lunch."

Jablonski punched the appropriate button. "Arnold?"

The crackling of static greeted him. A man's voice could be dimly heard, "Hello?"

"Arnold, can you hear me?"

"Barely, Jack. But you better talk fast. The reception in this part of town is horrible."

"Can you remember what day you broached the possibility to Waterbury of giving up his anchor post and becoming a roving commentator?"

"Hell no, I can't."

Jablonski drummed on the desk for a moment. *"Where* did you tell him? In your office?"

"No, it wasn't in the office. I figured I'd loosen him up at lunch." There was static for a moment. ". . . went to Le Dome, I remember that."

"But you don't recall the exact date?"

"I'll check my calendar and call you when I get to my desk."

"First thing. It's important."

Tolkin asked, "Is this the big story I've been waiting for?"

"If what I'm thinking turns out to be right, it's a *very* big story. However, I don't think it's one you've been waiting for."

"Sounds mysteri . . ." Static drowned out the rest.

"Hello, Arnold?" Jablonski jiggled the cutoff mechanism. "Hello?" He slammed the phone down into its cradle.

His secretary, who had wandered in during the conversation, seated herself in a chair in front of Jablonski's desk. "What was that all about?"

The detective reminded Shirley of his interview with Edna Waterbury the previous afternoon. "That call you just made to the Department of Water and Power seems to confirm a notion that occurred to me on the way in here today."

Shirley sat up on the edge of her chair. "Which is?"

Briefly he outlined his suspicions concerning the clock in the Waterburys' bedroom. "Now if it turns out that Arnold Tolkin's lunch with Will Waterbury took place *on the day of the attack, or maybe the day before,* we're on the way to nailing the bastard."

Shirley looked doubtful. "You honestly think getting moved out of the anchor chair is enough motivation for Waterbury to splash acid into Mikki's face?"

"It's a question of power, I'd say. How much does his position mean to him? What happened to Walter Cronkite after Dan Rather moved in? Or John Chancellor when Tom Brokaw took over?"

"Neither of them splashed acid on their replacements."

"Fortunately for all concerned. But switching from anchorman to commentator isn't a lateral move, even for giants. Cronkite and Chancellor more or less disappeared from view the minute they were moved into new jobs. The same fate would inevitably await our man."

Shirley's eyes glazed over. "So Mr. Waterbury decided to knock Mikki out of the running."

The phone rang.

Jablonski said, "If this is Arnold Tolkin and he tells me what I *think* he's going to tell me . . ." The detective snatched up the instrument. "Jablonski."

"Jack, Arnold. I had lunch with Waterbury on November seventh."

"Thanks for the quick service."

Tolkin asked, "What's this all about?"

"I have to collect a few more pieces before I can tell you."

"Meaning I'm no longer a suspect?"

"That's right."

"When . . . ?"

"Hard to say. I'll keep in touch." He replaced the phone in its cradle and looked over at his secretary. "It tracks. The day before the attack on Mikki, Tolkin informs Waterbury he's thinking of making him into a roving commentator. This goes over with Will like a lead balloon. Being aware of Mikki's ambitions, and afraid of losing his power base and prestige, Waterbury moves fast and formulates a plan to dispose of the lady *before she can get an inkling of what's in the works and add her not inconsiderable clout to the equation.* At the same time, he creates an alibi for himself." The detective leaned back and put his hands behind his head. "I wish that what we had wasn't so goddamn circumstantial."

"What's next?" Shirley asked.

"Figuring out how Waterbury planted the note in the guard shack the night of the attack. Without that piece of the puzzle, the son of a bitch will never be held responsible."

Shirley thought for a minute. "Seems like he's the only one who could tell you about that."

"Maybe not." Jablonski checked his watch. "It's almost three o'clock. I'm going over to the TV station and sniff around."

"Should I tell Mikki anything if she calls?"

"Not a peep. If you do, she might want to alert Tolkin, a move that could screw everything up."

The outer door opened and closed. "Halloo?" a voice called out.

Jablonski arose and stretched while Shirley hurried out to deal with the intruder. "Marla May!" the detective heard his secretary exclaim. "I haven't seen you for a day or two. Where have you been?"

"Out of town. I make a house call in San Diego several times a year. An old gentleman who's unable to get around." The psychic appeared in the doorway. "You are extremely inconsiderate, Mr. Jablonski. I wanted you to know that."

The detective hurried around the desk. "I'm very sorry, Mrs. Willowbrook. Very sorry, indeed. Of what am I guilty?"

"You, sir, last Saturday night, walked out on me while I was still in a trance. I didn't come out of it until noon Sunday. Over twelve hours in a rocking chair, motionless, was extremely hard on my bones. It took the chiropractor three adjustments to straighten things out."

"I am deeply sorry, Mrs. Willowbrook. I wasn't sure how to go about awakening you. Perhaps you would allow me to make restitution."

At that suggestion, the old woman showed signs of thawing. "That is very kind. The treatments were a hundred and twenty dollars even."

Jablonski looked over at his secretary. "Please draw our neighbor a check."

"Right away," Shirley answered.

The detective continued, "And please let me assure you that anytime, *anytime,* I can be of service, you need only to call."

"Likewise, Mr. Jablonski. Likewise."

* * *

Not having previously secured a pass to park in the Channel Ten lot, Jablonski felt himself fortunate to find a spot on the first cross street north of the TV station. It was nearing five P.M. when he approached the guard shack. He hoped and prayed he'd discover that one of the men who had been on the four to midnight shift the night of the attack was working today.

A man of about seventy, white-haired, pot-bellied, dressed in a wrinkled blue uniform, slid back the window and leaned out. "Help you?"

As Jablonski started to answer, one of the helicopters utilized by the station to cover news stories and bring the videotape back for editing and insertion into the various broadcasts roared overhead and disappeared behind the administration building.

"How do you stand that racket?" the detective shouted over the din.

"Me? I just turn down my hearing aid when they go by." The guard waited until the noise had diminished, then made an adjustment to the earpiece he was wearing. "Help you?" he repeated.

Jablonski produced his most doleful expression. "Maybe you can and maybe you can't."

From somewhere inside the shack a voice asked, "Got a problem, Dan?"

"Dunno," the old man said. "Waitin' to hear."

A strongly built officer, thirty-something, with dark hair hanging down over his collar, wearing a uniform identical to that of his ancient associate (but neatly pressed), ambled over. Jablonski looked from one man to the other, then spoke confidentially.

"I imagine you both know Mikki O'Reilly."

The white-haired man said, "Checked her in and out ever' night since she came to work over a year ago."

"What about her?" the younger man asked.

"You know what about her," the detective answered. He produced his PI identification. "Mikki's in bad shape."

"You workin' for her?" the ancient one named Dan asked. The detective nodded. "Damn shame what happened. Mikki's a wonderful person. Always had a cheery hello. Gave me a real nice Christmas present last year."

"Whenever she came around, I always wished I was single," the younger one added. "Hell, in her case, if she'd given me half a chance, I would have made an exception." The telephone rang and he stepped away to answer it.

Jablonski beckoned the old man closer. "We got a problem."

"We do?"

"Remember a while back when Mikki was attacked? November eighth?"

"Never forget it."

"Someone on duty in this shack found a note addressed to her."

"Me."

So far so good, Jablonski thought. He feigned surprise. "You?"

Dan pointed to the desk in the background. "Was stuck in the corner of the blotter. Funny thing, though. When I first came on duty at four o'clock, it wasn't there."

"How do you know?"

"I always have my dinner right at the desk when I come on."

"And when you sat down to open your lunch box, there was no letter."

"That's it."

"You sure?"

"Positive."

"You didn't have any visitors at any time during your shift that afternoon or evening?"

"We don't let visitors in here." The old man pulled out a package of Camels and offered one to Jablonski.

"No thanks. I swore off."

"I swore off too. Twenty, thirty times. Then, every time, I swore back on. Man my age, what the hell's he got to worry about?" Dan produced a kitchen match from his pants pocket, scratched it across the windowsill, lit up, and sucked in the smoke. He held his breath. After a few seconds he exhaled explosively. "Goddamn, that's good. Get a rush on an empty stomach that makes your scalp tingle."

Jablonski steered the conversation back to his client. "You were saying nobody, *nobody,* dropped in here last November eighth while you were on duty?"

The old man cocked his head. "What you looking for? I already told the police everything the day after the assault."

Jablonski smiled. "Occasionally people leave things out."

A Plymouth van pulled up behind the detective. "Step aside," Dan ordered. "Help you?" he inquired of the driver.

The man replied, "Got a package for Bettina Rawls."

The guard handed him a clipboard. "Sign on line seventeen." After taking back the board, he raised the barrier that blocked entry to the lot and pointed off to his left. "News building over there."

As the car drove off, Jablonski moved back into position. "Mind if I call you Dan?"

"Hell, no. Go ahead. Everybody else does."

"Except me," the young guard interposed as he rejoined the two. "I call him Smokey, on account he's exhaling in here all the time. Gonna give me lung cancer."

"Were you on duty the night Mikki was injured?" Jablonski asked the junior member.

"Not the *night*. I had the shift just before, from eight that morning until four."

The detective lowered his voice. "I'd like to let you both in on a secret." The two men moved in surreptitiously. "If you could think back to November eighth and come up with an explanation for how that note got into this shack, you could bust the case wide open. Get yourselves some of the reward money, too."

"We could?" Dan asked, open-mouthed.

"There's twenty-five thousand bucks sitting in a drawer in the boss's office. Does that spark up your brain cells any?"

The officers looked at each other, then the younger one shook his head. "Nobody delivered anything while I was on duty. That's all I know. You can check the log for that day."

"And for that evening too," Dan declared.

"The note didn't come from outer space," Jablonski insisted. "How about staff members? Any of them stop by?"

At that moment the detective heard the toot of a horn behind him. He glanced over his shoulder as the older guard activated the mechanism that raised the arm of the barrier.

"Evening, Mr. Waterbury," Dan called out.

The anchorman's Rolls Corniche rolled into the parking lot.

"Evening, Dan," Waterbury responded.

The car swung left and continued down to a spot near the door to the administration building where it parked.

"Some car, wouldn't you say?" the younger guard commented. "Cost plenty. But then I guess Mr. Waterbury's *got* plenty."

"Indeed," Jablonski agreed.

During this exchange the old man was watching the anchorman exit his car and walk over toward the office structure. After a moment he turned back to Jablonski.

"Would Mr. Waterbury count?" he asked.

"I beg your pardon?"

"As a visitor, I mean. I just remembered that one night two, three weeks ago he stopped in here. Wanted to make a phone call."

Jablonski tensed up. "Was it November eighth?"

The old guard shrugged. "No way to say exactly."

"Try."

He shook his head helplessly. "Sorry."

"Can you remember if it was before or after Mikki got hurt?"

Upon hearing the detective's question, Dan snapped his fingers. "It was before. *Right* before. Actually it was the same night. November eighth. It all comes back to me because *after* the show Mikki found out she had a flat tire and Mr. Waterbury took her home."

Jablonski breathed a silent sigh of relief. "Could you let me in there with you?" he asked. "I'd like to run down the whole sequence." The younger officer opened the door and Jablonski stepped inside and took a seat at the desk. "You said Mr. Waterbury wanted to use your phone. I noticed an aerial on his Rolls. Did he happen to say why he didn't use the phone in his car?"

"Told me it was busted."

Jablonski recalled Mikki mentioning that, during the ride home on the night in question, she had phoned the local patrol and asked them to be at her house when she arrived. It would be a cinch to confirm this by checking the phone company's records.

"Tell me, Dan, do you remember what was so urgent that Mr. Waterbury couldn't wait until he got to his office?"

"Said he forgot his reading glasses and that he couldn't do a lick of work without them. Started dialing his wife. Wanted her to bring them right over here. That's when I noticed the glasses was pushed back on his head, buried in his hair. When I showed him, Mr. Waterbury laughed, got in his car and that was that."

"Why are you so interested in Mr. Waterbury?" the younger officer asked the detective.

Jablonski tried hard to conceal his excitement. "I'm interested in everybody and everything that might help me find the guy who put Mikki out of commission. Can I use your phone?"

"Local call would be alright," Dan said.

While Jablonski dialed Nancy Baxter, several cars arrived simultaneously, demanding the attention of both of the officers.

Once the sergeant was on the line, Jablonski spoke in low, urgent tones. "I'm over at Channel Ten. In the guard shack."

"What are you . . . ?"

"I can't go into detail now."

Nancy said, "Incidentally, I just got back from Waterbury's house less than an hour ago. There's no way to nail *him*."

"Yes there is." Jablonski looked up at the guards, who were busy giving directions to some visitors. "Earlier, I had a couple of major insights. Those, plus what I just found out here, positively indicate that old Will, the son of a bitch, is our guy."

"Good for you. But let me ask you something: why do I feel wary of the word *indicate,* even when it's preceded by the adverb *positively?*"

"I'm going in now and nail the gentleman. I suggest you round up a couple of your boys and come over and pick him up."

"Speaking officially, I think it would be better if you'd keep your distance until we get there."

"Speaking unofficially, I can't wait to get my hands on the rat bastard."

"You came up with a witness?"

"No."

"His wife blow his alibi?"

"Not to my knowledge."

"Waterbury has a girlfriend on the side and he confessed to her."

"Wrong again."

"Then what you're sitting on is circumstantial, as in 'positively indicates.' "

"If you want to split hairs."

"What you had with Clem Barren was circumstantial. And need I remind you again what happened?"

Jablonski demanded, "Are you coming over here or not?"

"Anytime a citizen calls, we respond. But you'll forgive me if I don't use the siren."

CHAPTER THIRTY-EIGHT

HURRIEDLY, Jablonski made his way through the corridors of the news building until he reached Will Waterbury's office. The outside door stood open and he could see the tight-lipped matron who served as the anchorman's secretary removing a document from one of the drawers in a bank of filing cabinets. He stepped inside. When she didn't immediately look around, Jablonski cleared his throat.

"Remember me?"

"Yes. Yes, I do. You came in a week or more ago."

"That's right. Jablonski. I'm here for a word with your boss."

This statement caused the woman to slam shut the file drawer and retreat to her desk, where she ran her finger down the list of the day's appointments.

"I don't see your name here."

"You might say this is sort of an emergency."

"Mr. Waterbury's on the phone just now. Have a seat. I'll buzz him when he's finished."

Briefly Jablonski considered busting in on the anchorman, but thought better of it. "Will he be long?"

"There's no way of knowing." She pointed to an old leather sofa. "Please."

After almost ten minutes had gone by, Jablonski saw the light on the secretary's telephone blink out. Because of her fascination with the current issue of *People*, the woman failed to note this.

Jablonski arose. "I think Mr. Waterbury's free now."

The secretary looked up from the magazine. "So he is. What was your name again?"

"Jablonski. Jack Jablonski."

She punched the intercom.

Waterbury's voice boomed out into the room, "Yes?"

"Mr. Jablonski is here. Wants to see you. Says it's an emergency."

"Come in, Mr. Jablonski," the anchorman directed. "I've been expecting you."

The old bastard is cool, the detective thought to himself. Presently, however, he will be a lot warmer. Jablonski entered the inner sanctum.

"Expecting me, Mr. Waterbury?"

"You visited my wife yesterday and just now I saw you at the guard shack. It was inevitable that you would turn up here." He threw some papers into the out basket. "The police spent an hour this afternoon at my house. After a rigorous cross-examination of Mrs. Waterbury and myself, they gave me a clean slate."

"Is that so?" Jablonski leaned over and put his hands on the anchorman's desk. "Recently I came into possession of some facts that the authorities don't have."

Waterbury sat back in his chair and crossed his arms. "That's nonsense, Jablonski. You have no *facts,* as you put it. Do you realize that if you persist in your endeavors you could end up ruining my career?"

The detective smiled. "That's one of my objectives."

"I'm dead serious," the newsman said gravely. "Even though I'm guilty of no wrongdoing, if I am even *perceived* to be a liar, or worse, the public will turn on me in a second and I'll be out on my ear. You must cease this pointless pursuit at once."

Jablonski lowered himself into the rickety chair in front of the desk. "It's over, Mr. Waterbury. I have busted your alibi."

"Mrs. Waterbury is my alibi and I can assure you she will not be swayed. By you or anyone else."

Jablonski stared at the anchorman. When the silence became almost unbearable, the detective allowed the corner of his mouth to turn up just the slightest bit. "When you arrived home after attacking Mikki, you unplugged the clock in your bedroom for a moment. This caused it to flash repeatedly. I think you know the rest."

Waterbury turned pale. "I can't imagine what you're talking about."

"Yes, you can. You have a very good imagination, which, it seems, you have used with considerable brilliance up to now."

The anchorman's shoulders sagged and he made a choking sound. "I don't suppose there's some arrangement we could work out that would cause you to go away."

"You are correct."

Waterbury sighed heavily. "Then I guess we'll have to take a ride."

"Not like in those old gangster movies, I hope." Jablonski waved off the idea. "No, I don't think so. I have other plans."

"You will have to change them." The anchorman reached into the top right-hand drawer of his desk and produced a snub-nosed .38. "I honestly believed this day would never come." He pointed the weapon at Jablonski. "Up. Hands on the wall and spread your legs."

"What if I start hollering?"

"That is a very dangerous option," Waterbury said quietly. "Now, if you please, move."

Jablonski hauled himself to a standing position and reluctantly followed directions.

Quickly Waterbury patted him down. "Happily, no pistol."

"Firearms make me nervous," the detective responded through gritted teeth. He wished to hell that Nancy would hurry up and arrive.

Waterbury slipped his gun hand into the pocket of his jacket. "We'll go out the back door of my office and walk down the steps to the parking area." He produced a set of keys and tossed them to Jablonski. "You will drive my Rolls."

"Where are we going?"

"I'll give you directions once we're enroute. Right now all I'll tell you is this: since Clem Barren's innocence was uncovered, I have devoted myself to developing an emergency escape route." He motioned to Jablonski, indicating that it was time to go.

The darkness covering the parking lot helped accent the flashing lights on the two squad cars stopped near the guard gate.

"Foiled, Mr. Waterbury," Jablonski said gleefully, indicating his saviors. "I suggest you hand over your pistol and come quietly."

For a moment Waterbury looked confused. Suddenly he snapped, "Back inside!"

Quickly, with the anchorman jabbing the gun into Jablonski's side every other step, the twosome moved down the deserted corridor and exited through a door in the opposite wall of the building. Standing on the helipad was a Bell Ranger.

"Move!" Waterbury ordered.

A young man in a leather jacket was busily cleaning the helicopter's bubble. "Hi, boss," he greeted Waterbury. "You look like you're in a hurry."

"A big hurry, Bob. Wind this thing up and let's go!"

"Got a big one on the hook?"

"Real big," Waterbury responded.

"Where's the cameraman?" the pilot asked.

"We don't need one. This is just for a looksee."

"Okay. Hop in."

Waterbury indicated that Jablonski should precede him. After they were both seated on the bench behind the pilot's chair, the youth climbed aboard and closed the door. He flipped a few switches and the low rumble of the rotor winding up was heard.

"Put on your headphones, guys," the young man directed, "or you won't be able to hear yourselves think."

Waterbury again nudged Jablonski with the .38 while indicating that the detective should keep his mouth shut.

After the three had donned the big leather cups, each set with an attached voice-activated microphone, the pilot grasped the collective with his left hand and increased the pitch angle of the rotor blades while simultaneously edging back on the cyclic, a stick mounted between his legs. As the whine of the rotor climbed higher and higher, the chopper lifted off into the clear evening sky.

"Where to, boss?" the pilot inquired.

"There's a pad next to the fire station up on Coldwater Canyon near where you start down into the Valley. You familiar with it?"

"More or less. It's pretty desolate up there. Do you know if it's marked?"

"It is."

"May take me a little while to locate it."

"As quickly as possible, Bob, if you please." Waterbury pulled the gun out of his pocket and held it loosely on his lap.

Spotting it, the pilot said, "What's that for?"

"So that neither you nor our guest will make any mistakes."

"What the hell's going on here, Mr. Waterbury?" the young man demanded.

"You don't need to know that. Just do as you are told."

Jablonski flashed back on the time last year when he was trapped in a two-seat Cessna 150 over the ocean with a pilot he had knocked unconscious. Things were somewhat better at the moment. However, if he made a wrong move, the potential for an accident was high.

He began reviewing the possible ways he might wrest the weapon from Waterbury. Unfortunately, every one of them posed the same danger: if the gun went off during a struggle and the bullet hit the pilot or the fuel tank, they all would be goners.

But, what the hell, he decided, I just can't sit here.

As nonchalantly as he could, the detective slid his arm up along the back of the bench. "You're very creative, Mr. Waterbury. You should have been a mystery writer."

The anchorman smiled. "I was. Back in fifties television. In New York. Put your hand back in your lap."

This guy doesn't divert worth a shit, Jablonski thought ruefully.

"*Martin Kane, Private Eye*," and "*Suspense*," come to mind. But scriptwriting work was too sporadic. I gave it up and became an announcer."

The pilot's eyes bugged out as he listened to the unfolding dialogue.

Jablonski said, "You sure made up a pretty good scenario when you decided to go after Mikki."

Waterbury leaned over and tapped the young man on the shoulder with the gun. "Bob, I know L.A. from the air better than most. Don't take any detours."

"Believe me," the pilot answered.

Jablonski continued, "I'd like to get the rights to your yarn. Make a hell of a TV movie. 'Older newscaster petrified of being pushed out of the limelight by gorgeous young upstart. Uses series of letters from an obsessed fan as his cover. Writes one of his own on computer in the news room and plants it in the guard shack under the pretense of calling his wife about his reading glasses. Lets air of out one of the girl's tires, rendering her car inoperable. Offers her ride home. Suggests she take sleeping pill. Exits through back gate that isn't hooked up to alarm system, deliberately leaving it unlocked. Waits outside for an hour or so until girl is dead to the world. Comes back and poisons dog. Cuts phone and alarm. Splashes acid. Runs out, this time snapping the catch that locks the gate from inside. Goes home. Pulls the plug momentarily on the electric clock in his bedroom.' " Jablonski took a breath. "Did I get it right?"

"Close enough," Waterbury responded bitterly. "Now let me tell you another scenario. Since it is nearly pitch black outside, once I leave you, I will literally disappear into the more or less uninhabited area I have selected. I shall then hop into a vehicle, untraceable, of course, that I have carefully secreted nearby."

The crafty bastard, Jablonski thought to himself. What next?

As if in answer to the detective's unspoken question, Waterbury said, "Locked in the trunk of the car are two suitcases. One holds a tropical wardrobe, the other five hundred thousand in cash. No one will ever find me."

With a mind as devious as this bastard's, that is probably true, the detective admitted to himself.

Suddenly Waterbury sounded bittersweet. "I'm not looking forward to a happy life, but at least I will be free." He shook his head. "Why couldn't Arnold Tolkin have left well enough alone?"

Before Jablonski could reply, the young pilot pointed down to his right.

"Is that what you're looking for, Mr. Waterbury?"

The anchorman took a moment to orient himself. "Very good, Bob. Very good, indeed. Let's descend."

"How do you know we won't radio the police the minute you're out of here?" Jablonski asked.

"I expect you will. What will you advise them to look for?"

"For one thing, a sixty-five-year-old TV personality getting on an airplane."

Waterbury laughed. "Surely you don't think I plan to *fly* out of Los Angeles, even with my new passport."

Jablonski bit his lower lip. The bastard might get away with it.

"Bob," the anchorman said, "as soon as I'm on the ground, depart the area quickly and pray that I'm not tempted to put a slug or two into the engine when you're fifty feet up."

"The minute you're outside, I'm history."

Gracefully, the young man set the chopper down on the helipad. Waterbury jumped out and waved the craft away. As the pilot began to feed in takeoff power, the anchorman was suddenly nailed by a hot, white beam from a spotlight. Jablonski looked around.

Hovering a hundred feet above and to the right of the Bell Ranger was a police helicopter. As the anchorman tried to run for cover, the finger of light remained glued to him.

"Stay put!" Jablonski yelled to the pilot. "Waterbury's luck just ran out."

"Jesus!" the youth said, cutting the power.

"And don't forget a single goddamn word the man said."

"Don't worry."

As the rotors wound down, the detective hopped out of the craft. Moments later three squad cars, sirens howling and lights flashing wildly, converged on the area. The two officers in the lead vehicle jumped out and made a beeline for Waterbury, who was standing, paralyzed, in a gully at the edge of the winding road. In moments he had been handcuffed, read his rights, and led off.

Jablonski stood patiently until the police got around to him.

"You Jablonski?" a burly patrolman asked.

"I am."

"You'll have to come down to the station and make a statement. The pilot, too."

"Is it safe to leave this thing parked here?" the youth asked, indicating the helicopter.

"We'll leave a man with it until you get back."

While the detective was wondering how the police had appeared so miraculously, Nancy Baxter pulled up in a black-and-white.

"Nancy! How did . . . ?"

"When we arrived at Channel Ten, who we went right up to Waterbury's office. His secretary said you were inside with him. Which, of course, you weren't. Through the back window I spotted the two of you getting into the helicopter and figured you weren't going for a joyride. I called Central Dispatch. Fortunately, they had a chopper in the area and were able to latch onto you."

"God bless Guglielmo Marconi!"

Nancy grabbed Jablonski by the sleeve. "Tell me what you've got isn't entirely circumstantial."

The detective turned to the helicopter pilot. "Bob," he said, indicating the policewoman, "meet Nancy. This young man is our star witness. During the flight over here, I told old Will how I thought he went about disabling Mikki. Foolishly, for him, he confirmed my conclusions."

"That's right, ma'am. Took a minute for me to understand what the two of them were talking about but, once I got the gist, it was plain as day that Mr. Waterbury is the one who hurt Miss O'Reilly."

"For God's sake, Jablonski, let me in on what happened!"

Quickly the detective divulged the line of reasoning he had pursued that led to Waterbury's admission of guilt.

When he'd finished, Nancy admitted, "I'm impressed. A flashing traffic light near your office and you broke the case. What a lucky coincidence!"

"In the words of Marla May Willowbrook, 'There is no such thing as a coincidence.'"

"What then?"

"Hunches. Instincts. Premonitions. Keenness. The tools of the superior deductive mind."

"Your immodesty is only exceeded by your charm, Jablonski."

"You are too kind, Nancy. But remember, without your quick grasp of the situation back at the helipad, my contribution would have gone for naught. As the result of the media attention that will be engendered once the facts of the Waterbury-O'Reilly case come to light, you will, no doubt, be promoted to lieutenant. I, on the other hand, will merely be flooded with dozens of inquiries involving the minor miseries of the confused and angry citizens of our town who are unable to handle their own affairs."

"I feel for you." She slipped her arm into his. "Wanna ride down to the station with me?"

"A pleasure."

"Cheer up, Jablonski. Perhaps hidden somewhere in the welter of calls for help to which you'll be subjected, a twisted, vicious, depraved serial killer will be lurking."

"God, I hope so."

They approached the squad car.

"After you, Nancy," the detective said, opening the door.

"Thank you, Jack."

He got in after her. "Do you realize that's the first time you ever called me Jack?"

"I thought I'd try being a little less aggressive for a change. When's your wife due back from the east?"

AFTERWORD

A few days later, Jablonski picked Daphne up at the airport. During the drive home he inquired whether she was too tired out from the trip to make a home-cooked meal. "If you are, we can always grab a bite in the neighborhood."

"I'm not a bit tired, Jack. I slept almost all the way."

They stopped at a supermarket several blocks from their house and purchased the supplies necessary for the concoction of a meat loaf, Jablonski's all-time favorite dish.

After giving Snoopy the requisite amount of petting and scratching behind the ears, Daphne unpacked her bags and headed for the back of the house to begin dinner preparations. Sometime later, when the urge for a Cutty Sark on the rocks became overwhelming, Jablonski joined his wife in the kitchen. She was pouring A-1 Sauce over her creation prior to putting it in the oven.

"Jack, do you have any idea what I'd say if I was one of the three bears?"

"The image is too bizarre to merit a response."

"I'd say, 'Who's been cooking in my kitchen?'"

Being totally unprepared for this verbal ambush, Jablonski emitted a sound somewhere between a Wha? and a Hmmm?.

"One doesn't have to be a detective to know that hands other than mine have been busy out here. The salt and pepper shakers are up with the canned goods; the vegetable steamer is on the wrong shelf; my mother's porcelain dinner service has been piled on top of our everyday dishes. Shall I go on?"

"It isn't necessary."

"Well?"

"Well, what?"

"Since you are unable to prepare anything more complicated than a cheese omelet, a third party must have been abroad in my domain, and I think I'm within my constitutional rights to inquire as to the person's identity."

"You want the truth?"

"Whole and unblemished if, under the circumstances, you can manage that."

"No matter how much it may hurt?"

"Now stop that, Jack! Who was the Mystery Chef?"

Jablonski feigned resignation. "Her name is Nancy Baxter. She was the detective assigned to the Mikki O'Reilly case."

"And by what process did an L.A. cop get from the station house into my house?"

"She wants my body."

"And she had to cook dinner for you in order to get it?"

"That was her plan."

"Why didn't she ask you to *her* house?"

"Her kid was having a party."

"You'll have to do better than that, Jack."

"Believe me, that's as good as it gets."

Daphne slammed the oven door and turned on the gas. "What'd you do *after* dinner?"

"We rescued an unconscious schoolteacher from a dumpster full of garbage in the Brentwood Mart."

"You what?"

"You asked for the truth, Daph. And truth is, as you know, stranger than fiction."

Finally Daphne smiled. "Even more to the point, I should think, is the fact that you're too good a detective to leave incriminating clues lying around the kitchen."

"There's yet another possibility."

"What?"

"Maybe I left things that way to make you jealous."

Daphne took Jablonski's face in her hands. "Okay, I'm jealous. Satisfied?" She gave him a peck on the nose.

Jablonski poured two fingers of scotch in his glass. "I'm curious. What would you have done if I'd gone to bed with Miz Baxter?"

Daphne tore off several pieces from a nearby roll of paper towels and wiped her hands. "There is arsenic in the meat loaf."

The news of Will Waterbury's assault on Mikki O'Reilly generated a groundswell of sympathy for the young woman. Just before Valentine's Day she underwent a successful operation for corneal implants. Shortly thereafter, her plastic surgeon, a leading light in Beverly Hills medical circles, completed the last in a series of skin grafts, procedures that made the young woman look almost as good as new.

Each step in her recovery was duly reported on Channel Ten's newscasts, so that, when Mikki was finally able to report for work, her return to television was as eagerly awaited as was Jane Pauley's, following the latter's dismissal from the *Today* show.

The Nielsen rating the night Mikki resumed her career, now as sole anchor, was higher than any ever recorded in the history of a local Los Angeles newscast.

Largely due to the public clamor, Will Waterbury was held without bail. After an inordinate amount of legal jockeying, his trial for felony assault and battery was finally scheduled to take place the following June. During the ensuing time he filled his days making notes for a book he plans to write, tentatively titled *My Checkered Career,* for which he received a hundred-thousand-dollar advance from a notorious New York publisher. Serial rights went for a substantial amount to the *National Enquirer.*

Arnold Tolkin, Channel Ten's news director, had his contract renewed at a much higher fee and extended for another three years. He now has his own table at Le Dome.

* * *

Max Sabinson's pancreatic cancer went into remission. As a result, he has become extremely religious, devoting all of his spare time to helping wayward youths.

After much effort, Shirley Bernstein-Mandlebaum convinced her part-time babysitter, Piedad, to move in permanently, so that Saul would have continuous care while she and her husband were absent from the house. As a consequence of this action, the toddler now largely ignores his parents except for the days that Piedad has off. During these periods Saul exhibits an advanced and seemingly uncontrollable case of anti-social behavior.

Recently, for the first time in their marriage, the psychiatrist screamed at his wife.

Following the death of his mate of fifty-odd years, a grieving husband consulted Marla May Willowbrook. While in a trance, during the first session, the psychic told the client that the deceased wife had met someone "on the other side" and had expressed a wish that he go forth into life and enjoy himself. Not long after that, Marla May and the client began dating.

Romance also flowered at the opposite end of the age scale. Shortly after Miss Montgomery's return to Petey Bosworth's school, the youth became enamored of Darlene Valerie Hoskins, a thirteen-year-old with silky blonde hair that hangs down to her waist. Currently Petey performs periodic stakeouts of the girl's house to be sure she isn't cheating on him.

Miss Montgomery's husband was convicted of first-degree assault and is now serving a five to seven year sentence. To date, his wife has not filed for a divorce.

* * *

After becoming the butt of too many jokes at work, Clem Barren departed for Sacramento and moved into a mobile home park. When he's not frying up Big Macs, he spends his time shopping around the TV dial, hoping to find someone who loves him.

Following Will Waterbury's conviction, shortly after Labor Day, Jablonski collected the twenty-five thousand dollar reward posted by Channel Ten's management. He wrote a check for a thousand dollars to old Dan, the guard in the station's parking lot, for his part in helping to finger the anchorman.

Snoopy gave birth to a litter of six puppies, the result of an inadvertent encounter with a dachshund the night she escaped under the fence. Her offspring turned out to be so adorable that the Jablonskis were unable to supply the demand engendered by the new arrivals.
    Snoopy has since been neutered.